NELDA SEES GREEN

NELDA SEES GREEN

Murder takes a cruise

To my good friends
Mark & Janie Crocker
Love
Helen F. Sheffield

April 2008

Helen F. Sheffield

Library of Congress Control Number:		2007903225
ISBN:	Hardcover	978-1-4257-7697-8
	Softcover	978-1-4257-7661-9

To order additional copies of this book, contact:
Xlibris Corporation
1-888-795-4274
www.Xlibris.com
Orders@Xlibris.com
38672

I dedicate this book to my mother, Eva West Amrhein,
who was champion of the underdog. She managed to
spread her love and time to family members,
friends and strangers, in her short life-span of fifty-four years

ACKNOWLEDGEMENTS

I would like to thank the following people, and departments for their help in writing this book: Brazos Writers Critique Group; My daughters, Deborah Sheffield and Carol Sheffield Lapin; Good friend, Marselaine Clarke; Pharmacist, Ronald Petty; Warren Fowler of the Bryan Texas Fire Department; Brazos County's Sheriff's Department of Texas.

PROLOGUE

A welcome quietness settled over Witherspoon Academy in early June. School was out for a while causing teachers to breathe a sigh of relief. Five of the instructors had plans for a cruise. Three of these had plans for murder.

Teachers: Winnie Speer, Doris Hodge and Celeste Fogelman sat in a booth at Sanders Bar and Grill. No smiles were exchanged between them when they sat down, only grim determination and a lot of anxiety showed on their faces.

Now that Winnie was faced with the reality of the crime they planned, her dark eyelashes became wet with tears and her thin lips quivered. She spoke with a little moan as her small hands shredded a paper napkin. "I don't know if I can see it through. Justine is a human being too."

Doris, shifting her plump body in the booth, shook her round head until her neat bun of auburn hair threatened to topple. "Justine is a blood sucking blackmailer and you know it."

Celeste, had the qualities of a team leader. She reached over and covered Winnie's hands. "There is no other way. If she tells what she knows, we'll lose our jobs and no other school will ever hire us. If we let her, she'll continue blackmailing us forever. Besides, she's going to kill herself."

Doris' blue eyes registered surprise. "What do you mean?"

"I mean Justine is allergic to peanuts. She'll die if she gets a good bait of them."

Drying her eyes on the shredded napkin, Winnie nodded. "But she carries an EpiPen loaded with epinephrine. That's her security blanket."

Beautiful, blonde Celeste smiled. "Someone will take her EpiPen."

"Now, which one of us would be guilty of that?" Doris asked.

Celeste pulled three white envelopes from her purse and shuffled them around on the table. If you draw the envelope with a green dot inside, you will be responsible for removing her EpiPen. No one will know who drew the green dot."

Winnie looked scared. "And who will see that she eats peanuts?"

"The chef on the boat of course," said Celeste. "Justine has a birthday when we're at sea. We'll have a party."

Each member of the trio slowly picked up an envelope, placed them in their purses and stared at each other. Celeste stood up laughing. It's a joke you dummies. Justine isn't worth going to jail over."

Doris hit her fist on the table. "That's a pretty gruesome joke, Celeste, sorry I fell for it. But I'm glad we're finally going to do something about this blackmailing. Let's all confront Justine at the end of this trip. She'll have no choice. If she doesn't stop, we'll go to the police."

"Suits the heck out of me; you're in, Winnie?" Celeste asked.

"I suppose. But you know I have to work with her."

"Yeah, that's tough. Now let's all go home and pack."

"Adios," whispered Winnie.

*   *   *

Justine Scales was ten miles away in her cottage located on the Academy grounds, when the conspiracy took place between her hapless associates. She was packing for the cruise and thought she knew why she'd been invited to go with them. They would cozy up to her so she would lower their payments. Of course she'd have to turn them down. They should have to pay for their erring ways.

She laughed; who said Librarians had no fun? It delighted her to remember how she came up with the soiled goods on each one.

Librarians from other schools can be such good friends and love to talk. So lo and behold, by holding back what she knew about certain parties, she now had three feathers lining her nest. It was like becoming a queen.

Justine threw her square body on the bed, tucked a pillow under her royal head and thought of all the fun she'd have with her three lowly subjects. And of course a queen needed a consort. She smiled at the thought of Daniel Hall being on the cruise with them. Soon visions of gently rolling green waters in the Western Caribbean lulled her to sleep.

CHAPTER ONE

Sugar Is Dead

Tears flowed down Nelda Simmons' face as she hung up the phone. The thought of her best friend's old Labrador retriever dying made her heart heavy. Sally Pennington had brought him home when he was just a small bundle of brown fur thirteen years ago. There were so many memories she had to share with Sally about Sugar when her friend stopped grieving. Now was not the time.

Nelda faced another crisis. Sally refused to go on the Caribbean cruise they had booked together. All Nelda's pleading about how it would be good for her to get away from home didn't convince Sally. She asked Nelda to find a replacement for her. Not an easy task at this late date. Naturally, Nelda thought of her niece, Sue Grimes. There was no one she had a better time with than her young niece. But could Sue take a week off from work with such short notice? There was only one way to find out.

She called the clinic where Sue worked as a nurse. Marcie Toliver, the clinic receptionist, greeted her old friend warmly.

"Nelda, it's good to hear from you. How have you been?"

Nelda shook her head and smiled. There was only one thing wrong with knowing everybody in town, you felt obligated to visit a few minutes, even when you were in a hurry.

"I'm doing great, Marcie, but I need to talk to Sue right away."

"I'm sorry, but Sue took the day off. She said she had a headache."

"Thanks, Marcie. I'll go over and check on her."

Nelda automatically opened the broom closet and found her purse and car keys hanging on a hook. She walked out the back door locking it behind her, boarded the station wagon and took off. Even though her mind was not on what she was doing, years of repetition guided her through the process without a hitch.

What a predicament, thought Nelda. I've been planning this cruise for a year, and now I may have no one to share it with. This brought to mine her late husband, Jim, but if the truth be known, he wouldn't have gone with her either. As sheriff for many years, he was more content trying to solve a mysterious crime than going on vacation. Of course Nelda hadn't complained, because she loved solving mysteries too. She had been her husband's unpaid deputy for many years.

A few minutes later she drove up in front of Sue's apartment. There were no visible signs of anyone being at home, however Sue's old car was in the driveway. Nelda got out, walked the few steps to the front door and knocked softly. After waiting a few minutes with no response, Nelda knocked louder. There was absolute silence inside; suppose the poor girl was so sick she couldn't come to the door, thought Nelda. The mother instinct took over and Nelda dug in her purse for the key to Sue's apartment.

Exasperated with searching for the key in her crowded purse, she dumped everything out, and found the house key Sue had given her. Her hand shook as she turned the key and opened the door, making Nelda realize how nervous she was.

"Sue! Sue!" she called out, "It's Nelda. Are you there?" She stepped inside and closed the door.

A tall, slim blonde appeared in the hallway beyond. She was clutching a terry cloth robe together with one hand, while wiping tears from her eyes with the other. "Oh, Aunt Nelda, I thought you were Walter, and I don't want to talk with him now."

"Are you ill? Marcie said you came home with a headache."

"Well, really! Did she call you about that? Everybody treats me like a child." With that remark, she sat down on the couch in her tiny living room and sobbed.

Nelda sat down next to her and patted her on the back. "She didn't call me. I went to the clinic to tell you about a change in my vacation plans. So, out with it. Are you and Walter quarreling about something?"

"Yes we are. He wants to postpone the wedding until next year. I could just as well postpone it for the rest of my life." With that, she continued crying.

"Okay, now I know that you didn't quit loving each other, so why does he want to put it off? It must be for a very good reason." Nelda put her hand under Sue's chin and lifted her head gently, as she waited for an answer.

"He says he needs to pay off more of his debt on the clinic before we marry. It's like he's been listening to Dr. Laura's program on the radio. A woman shouldn't marry a man who's heavily in debt! You know that wouldn't be a problem with me. I could help him pay off his debt."

"Well, I'm sure he feels like he couldn't give you the attention you need if he married now. Walter has always been a stickler for doing the right thing. Even, when I taught him as a student in high school, he wanted to do everything perfectly. Now, he wants to concentrate on his business, so he'll have more time for you later. He loves you as much or more than he did when he was just a doctor working for someone else."

"Maybe so. I know there's no one else. He doesn't have time to cheat on me."

Nelda smiled. There was a glimmer of silver lining in this love spat. "I tell you what. You need a break from Walter. How about coming with me on a cruise to the Western Caribbean? I'll give you your birthday present early."

Sue sat up straight; Nelda had her niece's full attention now. "But, I thought you had this all planned with Sally."

"Well, we did have it planned, but something really sad has come up."

"Is something wrong with Sally?"

"No, Sally is fine, but she had to put Sugar to sleep. That dog was her best friend." Nelda's eyes teared up just thinking about how Sally must feel.

"I'm so sorry, Aunt Nelda. With Sally never marrying, I guess that dog was the nearest thing she had to a child. I remember when we went to Galveston. He ate a raw fish washed up on the beach, and you had to sleep in your car so you could take care of him outside." Sue smiled remembering how she and Walter had driven up and found Nelda sacked out in her car.

"I remember lots of things about Sugar, especially the time Sally and I were almost killed going to pick him up after he ran away. But let's not dwell on the negative. There were lots of good memories about him too, and there will come a day when Sally and I will relieve those. Now, you need to think about my offer. Would you like to go on a cruise? That medical temporary service will find a replacement for you."

Sue got up, tightened her robe belt and almost smiled. "Why not? This will get me away from Walter so I can think straight. Another good thing about it, Walter will not have to pay my replacement as much as he is paying me. That ought to make him happy."

"Well, start the ball rolling. I'm going home to call the cruise line and change Sally's name to yours. We have three days to get ready."

Sue planted a kiss on her aunt's cheek. Nelda wondered about the mood changes in young people. They didn't seem to brood as long as her older friends.

*   *   *

The next few days were spent in a flurry of purchases and returns, then finally the filling of two large suitcases by Nelda and Sue. Could they possibly use all the clothes they were taking with them? Nelda shook her head as they headed south toward their debarkation pier in Galveston, Texas.

Sue was dressed in one of her new outfits. She made a pretty picture in a sundress fashioned from a bright blue floral print. Nelda didn't see any benefit to wearing new clothes just to travel and board the ship. She dressed in comfortable navy blue shorts and a white shirt with a navy collar.

Nelda and Sue didn't have any trouble finding something to talk about as they traveled. Sue seemed energized after making up with Walter. Her voice was animated as she told Nelda how she handled the situation.

"I just walked right up to Walter and told him how hurt I was that he had canceled our wedding plans. Then I said, 'If we don't get married next year the engagement is off.'"

"And his reply was?"

"He'd never lose me. We'll be married next year regardless of his financial state."

"That's good, because if everybody married when they were financially able, we wouldn't have very many weddings. When Jim and I exchanged vows, we had a second hand car and two low paying jobs. It didn't make any difference to us if we didn't have the money for a movie or eating out. We were happy."

"I suppose one more year of being single won't hurt." Sue continued. In the mean time, I'm happy you invited me to take the cruise. I don't suppose we'll have time to look around Galveston, before we board the ship?"

"No, but we'll have time enough to eat lunch at Fisherman's Wharf. We'll eat on the pier, park our car in the lot provided by the cruise line, and then take a shuttle back to the pier. Maybe we'll tour 'The Strand' when we get back. Lots of history in Galveston."

"I know," said Sue. Did you read that special in our local paper about the 1900 hurricane that killed all those people in Galveston, and practically demolished the town?"

"I did and had forgotten what a devastating storm it was. The storm changed Galveston forever. They were then the nation's fourth-richest city."

Sue looked out the window at the sky. "Hurricanes are so destructive. Do you think New Orleans will ever be the same after Katrina?"

"They're trying hard to rebuild. Maybe the city will even be better."

"You don't think another is due to hit Galveston do you?"

"Who knows," said Nelda, running a hand through her short, brown hair.

"At least they have a seawall now. Of course it won't protect a good portion of the island. But life goes on, so let's not conjure up any trouble."

"You sure you don't want to go to New Orleans and consult with that soothsayer we talked with last year?" Sue looked at her aunt with a mischievous grin.

"Please, I can still hear her warning me about seeing the color blue. What hue do you think she would choose for me to be afraid of this time?" Nelda looked up at the blue sky.

"Well, they say in the cruise brochure that the Western Caribbean has green waters."

"Sue, let's drop the subject. The fortune tellers warning turned out to be more a reality than I would have ever dreamed. Bad things did happen when I saw the color blue."

They traveled some distance in comfortable silence, and then Sue sang out, "I see gulls up ahead. Are we still on interstate 45?"

"We'll be on this highway all the way to the island. You're looking at birds over the west bay. No blue-green waters around here."

"No," answered Sue, and not a storm cloud anywhere."

Nelda rolled on down the highway with expectations of sitting on a pier with a delicious seafood lunch. It was a great way to whet her appetite for the week to come.

CHAPTER TWO

Bad Karma

Eating in Galveston was always a treat for Nelda, and especially in a restaurant that allowed you to look out over the bay. Sue and Nelda were seated at an outdoor table, watching the birds with fascination. Several seagulls made lazy circles in the cloudless sky, as the braver ones landed on the wharf to beg for food. Opened multicolored umbrellas were over the tables for several good reasons, and not all of them had to do with the weather. An old waiter, with skin like a prune, impatiently shooed the birds away as a young Latino cleaned up the bird droppings with a pail of water and a mop.

"I wish people would quit feeding those damn birds," Nelda heard the waiter grumble.

She shook her head and smiled. "One person's pleasure is another person's misery," she said to Sue.

"I don't suppose you're just talking about the birds, Aunt Nelda."

"Just being philosophical," she said.

A young couple came in hanging on to each other as though they thought their partner might vanish if they didn't hold fast. Finally, the lovebirds chose a table, sat down and moved their chairs close together as they studied the menu. Sue stared at them, and then quickly looked away with a forlorn look on her face.

Nelda knew Sue was thinking about Walter, and the delayed honeymoon. Before she had a chance to console her, a large sea gull swooped down to steal a piece of French bread from a messy table that was left unattended by a group of teenagers. As the bird rose in the air with its steal, it was accosted by a smaller gull that plucked the bread out of the larger one's beak. An aerial battle took place over their heads. Sue's moment of sadness passed as she and her aunt laughed at the birds' antics.

The waiter had just brought Nelda's and Sue's lunch when a group of five, carrying hand luggage, walked on the deck. One of the girls with chunky heels stumbled on a rough plank, falling against the food laden table. The impact caused Nelda's shrimp dinner to slide off the table onto the floor. The girl gained her balance then leaned against a post rubbing her ankle.

A petite brunette rushed over to console her. "You all right?" she asked in a shrill, little voice.

"I'm okay, Winnie. Thank you."

"My Lord, what a mess," one of the women said looking at the shrimp scattered on the rough planks. "What in the hell is wrong with you, Doris?" She turned toward Nelda and said, "I'll ask the waiter to bring you another order." She put her hands on broad hips and stared through thick lenses at her auburn headed companion, who was responsible for the spill.

A tall, well proportioned blonde spoke out. "That's enough, Justine. She didn't do it on purpose. You've been on Doris' back all day."

"That's right, Celeste, and I suppose you'll find transportation for her back to the cruise parking lot, so she can get her passport out of the pocket of her car?"

"Okay ladies," said the only male in the bunch, "let's all sit down, order our food, and then work out Doris' problem later." He smiled showing beautiful white teeth.

Nelda and Sue were mesmerized by the soap opera being played out in front of them. When the group sat down, Sue spoke in a whisper. "I know that girl who bumped into our table. She's a school nurse. I've attended several meetings with her. Doris is really a nice, intelligent person."

"Well, I just think it's terrible for that tacky woman to humiliate her," Nelda replied. "Undoubtedly they are taking the same cruise we are. Why don't we offer to take your friend to the parking lot to get her passport? We'll park our car, and ride the shuttle bus back."

"Great idea, Aunt Nelda."

While they waited for Nelda's second dinner to arrive, Sue went over to where Doris was seated. "Hello, Doris, do you remember me?"

Doris was biting her bottom lip, deep in thought. She looked up in surprise. "Sue! Sue Grimes, how nice to see you."

The other four at the table stopped talking, and looked up expectantly at the slim, pretty blonde talking to Doris. After a brief hesitation, Doris rose and introduced Sue to the others.

"These are my faculty friends from the Witherspoon Academy: Celeste Fogelman, Winnie Speer and Daniel Hall." She paused for a moment and then continued, in a cool tone, "also Justine Scales."

"Pleased to meet all of you, and that's my Aunt Nelda Simmons, over there." She pointed toward Nelda, who had heard and watched the whole proceeding. Nelda smiled and waved to the group.

"Could we talk for a minute, Doris?" Asked Sue.

"Sure." Doris followed Sue to where Nelda was seated.

"Sit down with us. Nelda and I couldn't help but overhear your dilemma with the passport. Are you sailing on the Liberation this afternoon?"

"Yes, boarding time is 1:00 p.m. I've already parked my car and we've checked our luggage. I feel like an idiot."

"Well stop it," ordered Nelda. "We're going on that cruise too, that's why we're eating early. How about going with us when we park our car? Then, we can ride the shuttle bus to the dock."

"Thanks, I appreciate that a lot."

After they finished eating, Doris joined Sue and Nelda as they left the restaurant.

* * *

On their way back from parking the car, Doris confided in Sue and Nelda.

"We wanted to take a vacation before summer school started. This was our only chance to get away."

"I understand that," said Sue. "We work the whole year, except for a week's vacation."

"Justine is our head librarian and she's tough to be around. However, I'll have to give her credit for being a top notch librarian. The kids respect her. She stays late to help them with their projects. We invited her because she has no friends. Just thought this trip would make her more human. Now I have my doubts . . . Her attack on me was so ugly."

"Yes it was," agreed Nelda. I'm glad the others came to your rescue. What positions do the others hold at the academy?"

"Well, I guess Sue told you I'm the school nurse; Celeste coaches several sports; Winnie, poor dear, is assistant librarian. I'll never understand how she can stand it. Daniel is the liaison between the departments. He's only been with us a short time."

"A very handsome, young man," Nelda stated smiling at Doris.

"And guess who's taken a shine to him?"

"Who?" Sue asked.

"Justine. She guards him like a jealous girlfriend, and he's young enough to be her son.

CHAPTER THREE

The Inspection

When they arrived at the loading dock, the employees from Witherspoon's Academy were waiting for them and seemed delighted to see Doris. Even Justine managed a smile.

"That's nice of all your friends to wait here for you, Doris." Sue said.

"I suppose so," said the school nurse, "but I also have their loading passes. It was my job to make reservations for everybody."

"Touché," responded Nelda with a big smile. "Don't let anyone get you down from now on. You're on vacation, so enjoy this cruise."

"Believe me, I will, but I'm not sure Winnie will enjoy it."

"Why?" Sue asked, as they approached the Witherspoon group.

"Winnie is rooming with Justine."

Sue grimaced as Nelda shook her head in sympathy for Winnie. Then, the subject was shelved as they joined the long line waiting to enter the cruise ship, *Liberation*.

Daniel Hall dropped back to welcome them. "Glad you made it back when you did. It looks like there are a lot of folks ahead of us."

Doris thanked Daniel for his concern then turned to Nelda and Sue. "Guess I better join the group or get strung up. Thanks again for the lift. Let's get together, once we're on board."

"Sure, we'll look forward to it. See you a little later," Sue responded, while Nelda nodded her approval.

*   *   *

Inside the embarkation center were winding chutes leading to desks where uniformed employees checked passports and hand luggage. "This ship can hold almost two thousand guests," Nelda whispered to Sue. There must be two hundred people ahead of us. I feel like mooing as we move through these roped off passages. It reminds me of round-up time on the Ponderosa."

"Calm down, Aunt Nelda, only the young and foolish are supposed to be short on patience."

"Glad I have something in common with the younger set," Nelda responded.

Forty minutes later, Nelda and Sue made it to their respective check-in desks. They were given keys to their stateroom on the Empress deck, E54 a room with a view.

Their cabin was on the seventh deck, highest deck with passengers, except for private suites located on the Verandah deck.

Nelda looked toward the boat entrance in time to see Daniel led away by one of the officers on duty. Even though she hardly knew the young man, she felt uneasy about his detention. Was there no place she could go and just have fun and not worry about somebody else? Why was Daniel selected for further search?

"Did you see what happened to that guy from the academy, Aunt Nelda?"

"Yes, I don't suppose he was foolish enough to have a gun or knife on him in his luggage. Of course there might be something wrong with his passport. I just hope they don't hassle him too much."

"Well, with the danger of terrorists they can't be too careful. I'm still wondering how all those people ended up sick on the cruise ships in previous years. Wouldn't that be awful if it happened to us?"

"Let's not think about that, Sue. I'm really looking forward to this trip if we ever get through inspections and get settled on the boat."

*   *   *

They had no trouble finding the Empress deck where their stateroom was located. Their bags were sitting out in the hall waiting to be unpacked. Nelda was glad when they finally used their key to open the door of E54. Their stateroom was larger than she anticipated. A good sized dresser and two beds fit comfortably around the walls of the room. In a corner over a table, Nelda spotted a 29" TV bolted high up on the wall. Sue stuck her head out of the bathroom, announcing that the facilities in that room were compact, but nice.

They carried their bags inside the room and were pleasantly surprised to find two Bon Voyage gifts on the dresser. There were red roses to Sue from Walter, and a bottle of Zinfandel wine to Nelda from her sheriff friend, Joe Coates.

Sue read the note attached to her roses and sighed. "That's sweet of Walter to send roses. I know his conscience is bothering him because we're not here on our honeymoon, but I think I like your gift better."

"I never expected this wine from Joe. He shouldn't have."

"Oh yes he should. You solved his last crime for him, and besides that he's sweet on you. What did he say in his message to you?"

"He told me to stay out of trouble," Nelda smiled. No need for him to worry. Right now all she wanted to do was put her things away, so she could flop on the bed. Just a few minutes rest would revive her from a sleepless night and all that waiting in line. Of course she certainly didn't want to spend too much time in her cabin. According to the cruise line brochure, the ship was like a small community with oodles of places to go and have fun.

"Sue, let's unpack and rest a few minutes. Then we'll see what this ship has to offer."

"Not on your life. Just get your tush off that bed. We've got to see where all the action is going to take place."

"Well you can explore all you want, but for the next hour I'll be right here. Come get me after that."

"Okay." Sue frowned resignedly. "I'll just pinpoint everything for us. I'll even locate the most important place, the dining room."

Sue piled her things on the other bed before brushing her blonde hair, adding lipstick and tucking her shirt in her shorts. Nelda breathed a sigh of relief as Sue pulled the door open and slammed it behind her.

Nelda pulled her shoes off and stretched out on the bed. She closed her eyes, but sleep wouldn't come, because she was busy replaying the scene in the seafood restaurant.

She thought there was something peculiar about the Witherspoon Academy employees. Doris had talked profusely about all of them. From her descriptions, and Nelda's own intuition, they just didn't mesh. According to Doris, they had nothing in common except that they all were employed at the academy. If that was true, why were they taking this trip together?

No one seemed to like Justine, the head librarian, whose disposition was almost as bad as her hair cut and ill fitting clothes. Who invited her?

Celeste Fogelman, Woman's Athletic Director, was certainly a contrast to Justine, with a figure and face reminiscent of a young Ava Gardner. Her clothes looked expensive too. How did she fit into this group?

And what about Winnie, that whiney assistant librarian, she's going to be stuck in the same state-room with Justine for five whole days. Why would she torture herself? Nelda remembered Doris calling Winnie a wimp. Maybe so, but her over-all demeanor and big brown eyes made you want to mother her. Did Justine force her to come on the trip?

Doris claimed she'd never been on a cruise before, and that was the reason Celeste invited her. That sounds reasonable, at least more so than Daniel coming on the cruise to be with Justine. Just maybe Daniel was attracted to Celeste. That would certainly give him an excuse for tagging along. Oh well, she'd sort it out in good time. Nelda turned her face toward the large ocean view window above Sue's bed, drinking in the bright blue sky dotted with circling sea gulls, and soft cumulus clouds. After a few moments, her eyes closed in sleep.

* * *

Someone knocking on the door woke Nelda up. She hurriedly slipped on her shoes and answered the door. Sue was standing there with Daniel.

"I forgot my door pass, Aunt Nelda, and guess whose stateroom is right across the hall from us?"

Nelda pushed her hair out of her face, and looked up at Daniel who stood there smiling with the whitest teeth Nelda had ever seen outside of a tooth whitener commercial. "We're glad to see you on board. I was concerned when that officer took you away."

"My shoes were the bad guys. The inspector detected metal in my heels. I guess they thought I was trying to sneak a bomb on board."

"Glad you got that cleared up. Do the others in your party have rooms next to you?"

"No, they're further down the hall. We're all supposed to meet in the Piano Bar at 5:30. It's right outside the dining room assigned to this floor. Why don't you and Sue join us?"

"Sue is my social secretary, so if she said okay, I'd be delighted."

"Great, we'll see you then." Daniel turned and walked away.

Sue pushed Nelda into the room, shut the door and motioned for her to be seated. "I found the Nautical Spa and Gymnasium. I signed up for a body massage, and you need to do that before everybody else does."

"Everybody?" Nelda lifted her eyebrows.

"Well maybe not everybody, but they only have a certain number of slots they can fill. I even saw Celeste signing Justine up for one."

"Really, I think I'll pass that treat up," Nelda said smiling. "Celeste probably thinks a massage will calm Justine down, make her more human."

"I guess, but it's supposed to be a birthday present to Justine from the academy group. They'll celebrate her birthday at dinner tomorrow night."

Nelda stood and gazed out the window. "Hey, I think we're moving out to sea, the seagulls are gone and the water looks clearer."

"Just think," Sue said with a happy tone. "We have all night and all day tomorrow to explore this ship before we arrive in Cozumel."

Humming some bars from John Denver's "Sunshine on My Shoulders," Nelda studied a brochure about activities on board, while Sue put her things away. "Okay, Sue, for right now let's check out the library and stick our noses in the casino. We have a couple of hours before dinner is served, and remember we have to dress up to eat in the dining room, no shorts."

"What a bummer. But maybe it's good for us. At least I'll get to show off one of those new dresses I bought."

"Good let's get going." Nelda raced Sue to the bathroom and won. In a few minutes, she came out in a white pants suit.

"You look smashing, Aunt Nelda, almost as pretty as I'm going to look in my blue sundress."

"According to Mohandas Gandhi, Sue, true beauty consists in purity of heart."

Smiling, Nelda's niece shook her head, knowing she could never outdo her aunt.

*   *   *

On the ship directory, the ship had nine decks, each designated by a particular color. Nelda and Sue climbed one floor to the Admirals deck, where the dining rooms, library, beauty salon, shopping mall and game room were located. They visited the library which contained computers, models of the first built cruise ships, books, and games.

"Look, Aunt Nelda, we can take a picture here and send it with a message to anyone we want to."

"At what price," asked Nelda?

"Well, if you've got to ask, you can't afford it, you old tight wad. We should have called to thank the guys for our bon voyage gifts while we were in port. It's nine dollars a minute out here to use the telephone."

"You have to remember, Sue, there are no relay towers out here in the ocean for our cell phones. If you want to call, the signals are sent from the ship." Nelda was gazing out the window enjoying the view of white caps on the water. There was something so soothing about a rolling ocean, unless you were on a party boat deep sea fishing. She shook her head remembering that bad experience.

"Are you through here, Aunt Nelda? Let's go see if we can find the piano bar. A glass of wine before dinner would be nice. We can visit the casino later."

"I suppose so. There's nothing in here I need now. I've brought a mystery in case I need something to read."

"You won't have time to read. Now let's see, the piano bar is beyond the elevators. We're almost there," Sue said, keeping in step with Nelda.

Walking into the piano bar, they found the Academy group ahead of them. They were perched on stools surrounding a grand piano where a black man, dressed in a tuxedo, was belting out Cole Porter's song, "Blue Moon." Nelda was delighted that the man was playing a song she recognized.

Nelda and Sue stood in the back of the room until the song was finished before approaching their newly acquired friends. Daniel slid off his stool when he saw them and invited the duo to join the others.

"I think I'd rather sit in that big booth over there." Nelda pointed to the corner of the room. "There is room for all of us and we'll be able to talk."

To Nelda, these people represented a jigsaw puzzle. Her curiosity was aroused. She had to find out how they fit together. Being able to observe them in one place, would certainly give her some clues.

Sue followed Nelda to the large booth followed by Daniel, Doris, and Celeste. Justine and Winnie waited for the next song to end before moving. Nelda noticed that Justine had dressed in a candy striped tent like dress without a belt, and Winnie wore a brown suit with big shiny white buttons. The other three with their bright colors reminded Nelda of the American flag. Daniel had on a bright red shirt with white pants, Celeste sported a tight fitting blue dress that showed off her figure, and Doris wore a white dress that reminded you of her profession as a nurse.

The waiter came over to the booth to take their orders. Nelda and Sue ordered glasses of white wine and Daniel ordered another beer. All the others were still sipping on their previous orders. The waiter returned in a few minutes with their drinks and several bowls of chips and nuts.

"Well, how about it. Are you ready to have some fun?" questioned Sue.

"You bet," answered Celeste. "I don't know about the rest, but after dinner, Doris and I are going to check out the clubs and do some dancing. How about coming along?"

"Not tonight, answered Nelda, Sue and I want to play Bingo and then attend the Mexican Folkloric Show."

"A folk show sounds boring," commented Justine, arranging her folds of garment in her lap. "Winnie and I have decided on the Karaoke dancing. Kind of shake down the lobsters we're ordering tonight."

A lot more than the lobsters will be shaking, Nelda thought. She looked over at Sue, who was smiling as though she read Nelda's thoughts.

"I think I'll just float from one event to another," chimed in Daniel, showing his pearly whites. "But we do have a big event coming up tomorrow. It's Justine's birthday."

"We heard," said Sue reaching for a bowl of nuts, "and what a way to celebrate."

"We'll sing to you tomorrow," offered Nelda.

The conversation was interrupted by Winnie snatching a bowl of nuts away from Justine. The contents of the bowl spilled out on the table causing the librarian to curse at her assistant.

"What are you trying to pull, Winnie?" She picked up some nuts and threw them at her.

Winnie wiped her face as tears ran down her cheeks. "Do you want to kill yourself, Justine? Then, go ahead and eat the peanuts."

Sue and Nelda looked perplexed, while the others exchanged fugitive looks.

CHAPTER FOUR

Show Time

Winnie fled from the booth without going into the dining room for dinner. Fortunately, Nelda and Sue were not assigned to the Academy group's table and they were able to enjoy their meal. Doris came over while they were having dessert.

"Sue, you and Nelda please forgive Winnie's behavior at the piano club. You see Justine is terribly allergic to peanuts, and could have an anaphylactic shock from any small quantity that enters her body. This triggers severe respiratory problems."

"We thought that was the case," Sue responded. "Does she carry an EpiPen?"

"She has one in her suitcase, but doesn't ever take it with her."

Nelda shook her head. "Now, I know why Winnie grabbed the bowl of mixed nuts away from her."

"Maybe our librarian has a death wish." Doris bit her bottom lip and looked down. "Anyway, Justine is taking food back to her room for Winnie. She realizes Winnie was just looking out for her and she overreacted."

Sue patted Doris on the shoulder. "Thanks for coming over, Doris. Nelda and I feel that Justine is like a loaded gun with a quick trigger. It doesn't take much for her to go off."

"That's true. We're hoping this trip will settle her down, so she can relax and have some fun. Tomorrow we're going to meet in the piano room again before dinner. We're going to toast Justine with some champagne for her birthday, and present our gifts. Please join us. It will seem more like a party."

Nelda and Sue looked at each other, before agreeing. They waved goodbye as Doris walked back to her table.

Nelda rolled her eyes. "I'm getting a little tired of the tension we've encountered because of Justine. Let's try to keep our distance from that group after tomorrow tonight."

"I'm with you, Aunt Nelda. Someone has to speak up in that group and set her straight."

*   *   *

The next morning Nelda awoke at 8:00 a.m. She couldn't believe it was so late. At home, she was always up by 6:00 a.m. having coffee on her big back porch. The Folk Show was good, but staying up until midnight made for a very long day. Of course, Sue could sleep until noon and then be good for another twelve hours.

Nelda was dying for a cup of coffee. Probably she would be too late for the dining room and would have to find the restaurant on the Wheelhouse Deck. Making as little noise as possible, she took a shower, dressed and was on her way out when Sue woke up.

"Good morning, Aunt Nelda," she said half opening her eyes. "Don't tell me you're off to breakfast, and you were going without me?"

Sue looked so young and vulnerable with her long, blonde hair partially covering her face. Nelda could still see the little girl in her, and thought maybe Walter was wise to put off their wedding for now. Let Sue have the single life for a little longer. Could Sue handle the responsibility that comes with a home and children? Walter wouldn't be much help now, as devoted as he was to his work.

"Give you ten minutes, girl. I've got to have my coffee." Nelda was amazed at how fast Sue could dress, once her niece set her mind to it.

"Well, how do you like my new yellow top, Aunt Nelda? Do you think I stand out enough?"

"I don't think we'll have any trouble locating you if you fall overboard. Your red shorts and sandals are nice too. Of course, they'll never find me with my old blue blouse and white shorts."

"That's true," teased Sue, "but I'll miss you."

*   *   *

The Wheelhouse Bar and Grill was three floors up from the Empress Deck. Sue and Nelda opted to walk, because they needed the exercise. There weren't many people up and about. Both smiled at all the "Do Not Disturb Signs" hung on the doors.

After entering the grill, they found the service line with choices to satisfy most breakfast lovers. Nelda chose coffee, toast, scrambled eggs and fruit, while Sue had a bowl of shredded wheat and a cup of hot chocolate. Smart girl, Nelda thought. She was so thankful that Sue hadn't picked up a canned soda. Seeing young people drinking carbonated drinks early in the morning made her shudder. If she didn't know those drinks contained several teaspoons of sugar, maybe she wouldn't care. Of course she thought the diet ones were equally as bad, if not worse. A person needed a good breakfast to start the day, and for her that included two cups of coffee.

Nelda put her cup down after enjoying her breakfast with java that was fresh and hot. "I suppose by the time we finish here the gift shop will be open. Why don't we pick up that birthday gift for Justine? And there are a few other people to consider."

"Such as?"

"For starters, Sally, poor Sally, all she'll do while we're gone is sit around and moan over her dead dog. It would have been good therapy for her to come on this trip."

"It was her choice," Sue reminded her. "Don't forget Joe, he's back home guarding your house. He deserves something nice, especially after that bottle of wine he sent."

"Well, of course." As Nelda stood up to leave, she spotted Celeste coming toward them. The tall, picturesque blonde exuded good health.

"Hello girls! Happy to see some breakfast eaters. I think the rest of our gang is still in the sack. Glad I caught up with you. We've decided to have the surprise party for Justine at the dinner table. You know champagne, cake and everything. Please join us for tonight. Some of the people assigned to our table have teenagers and would rather eat their dinner in here. What do you say? You could take their place."

"Why not?" answered Sue, getting the nod from Nelda. "I don't suppose the waiters will mind. Of course, we have the cutest one from San Salvador whose name is Adolfo. We'll go back to him after tonight."

"Great, got to hurry."

"Wait a second," Sue said. "Have you any thoughts as to what we could give Justine for a gift?"

"Humm, since our gift is a massage, give her some of that great smelling massage oil from the gift shop."

"Doesn't the masseuse furnish her own?" Nelda asked.

"Sure, but sometimes it smells medicinal, like *Icy Hot*. See you tonight"

Nelda didn't see anything wrong with the way Icy Hot smelled. In fact, it reminded her of Vicks Rub. She grew up using that for everything from mosquito bites to a stuffy nose. Oh well, there was no accounting for the way people thought. Of course she wouldn't use Icy Hot for cologne, but for a massage it would be glorious.

They watched Celeste rush off to greet a deeply tanned man with an athletic build. After embracing, the couple joined the breakfast line.

"Well so much for staying away from the academy gang, Aunt Nelda."

"True, but I've got to say that Celeste doesn't waste time making friends," commented Nelda.

"Weeeee," whistled Sue, "and what a friend."

*   *   *

The shopping mall was located two decks below the Wheelhouse Bar and Grill where they had eaten breakfast. It was open and ready for business. Stopping at the entrance, they surveyed the contents of the store. There were rows of shorts, shirts, jackets and other clothes, with and without logos of the cruise ship. The shelf lined with hats fascinated Nelda. She guessed at Joe's size, and selected a white one with a picture of palm trees and blue water on the front of it. How, she wondered, would a landlubber cotton to that?

For Sally, she chose a mug with a picture of the cruise ship on it, and a small ceramic picture frame. Before giving it to Sally, she'd put a picture of herself and Sue in the frame. Sally considered them family.

Sue held up a white shirt with a seagull on the pocket. "Walter will look handsome in this."

"Walter will look handsome in anything," Nelda declared. "Now let's see about the massage oils they have here."

In a glassed in case, Nelda and Sue discovered bottles of oil with different scents. Nelda fell in love with the one that smelled like gardenias, but Sue thought the aroma too intense. She preferred a lightly scented one called Ocean Breeze. It had the clean smell of juniper berries and a beautiful green color.

"That's nice too, Sue, we'll purchase your choice." Nelda looked at the price. "My goodness, the price of oil is going up. That small bottle is twenty dollars. It's no wonder they have it in a case."

Sue, who was always broke, didn't seem perturbed about the price of anything. If she had the money she'd spend it and if she didn't, she'd just turn away.

"I'll buy the massage oil and you pay for Walter's shirt. I'm leaving all my money to you anyway. I might as well spend as much as I can."

Sue laughed out loud. Nelda was always threatening to die poor. "Thanks, Aunt Nelda, that's exactly why I have to marry a rich man."

"Sue," said Nelda in her preaching mode, "money is fine, but you need to marry for love and to someone with an iron clad commitment to marriage, like Walter."

"Thank you, Parson Simmons."

*   *   *

When they arrived back at their room and opened the door, there was a little surprise waiting for them on Nelda's bed. After cleaning the room to perfection, the cabin steward had twisted a towel into the shape of a duck. It was lying on the bed with Nelda's sun visor on its head; how clever the steward was. Sue and Nelda agreed this guy would receive his gratuity at the end of the trip, if he kept this up.

"We need to decide what to do today," Sue said as she filed on a broken fingernail.

"There are several things that sound like fun."

"Such as?"

Sue picked up the activity schedule and read from it, "Ice carving, line dancing, bingo, guest talent show and a lot more. Then tonight there is a big Broadway show."

While thinking about the choices, Nelda rubbed her stiff neck and wished she had brought her polyurethane foam pillow from home. The cabin mattress was comfortable, but the pillow was terrible. Guess she'd just have to live with it. "I vote for ice carving and bingo today and the show tonight, but I'll compromise if you want to do something else."

"Good choices! I'm with you, Aunt Nelda."

*   *   *

By four o'clock in the afternoon, Sue and Nelda arrived back at their room tired and hot. "I tell you, Aunt Nelda, by the time that guy got through sculpturing the ice Indian, I was hot enough to jump in the tub with the ice shavings. I'm going to take a cold shower and rest before dinner."

"It did get hot," Nelda agreed, but the sculptor was fun to watch. He was a wizard with that chisel and hammer. After we clean up, let's have some wine to fortify ourselves before meeting with the Witherspoon group."

"It'll take more than that little bottle of wine from Joe to do that, but it's a start."

After showering, Nelda and Sue wore white, terry cloth robes provided by the cruise line. The women sipped wine and watched the classic movie "Lawrence of Arabia with Peter O'Toole."

"That movie is so cool, Aunt Nelda."

"It's wonderful. Makes you want to check out more of those old goodies. But we've got to get moving, because this is captain's night at dinner. Everyone is supposed to really dress up."

"And let's not forget Justine's gift," Sue said. "Dang it, I forgot to get a birthday card. I'll just use a magic marker and write on the label."

"Tacky, tacky," Nelda's replied.

*   *   *

As Nelda and Sue entered the dining room, they spotted the birthday party already seated in the same general area as their own table. They explained to their waiter why they were moving to another table and then joined the party.

Witherspoon Academy employees were looking good in their evening clothes: Winnie wore a white, frilly dress with very little makeup, while Justine sported a navy blue one with a wide belt that had a slimming effect. Her hair was curled and swept back from her round face. Celeste was stunning in a white linen sheath that left nothing to the imagination about her good figure. In addition, Mexican jewelry with onyx stones adorned her wrist and neck. Doris never seemed to shed the nursing persona. Her pink two-piece suit mimicked the uniform worn in some pediatric clinics. And Daniel was very handsome in a blue jacket with white trousers.

Seeing this group together was like going to a masquerade party, Nelda mused. Their clothes projected how they wanted other people to perceive them. The message that Winnie sent out was sweet and innocent; Justine would love for people to think she was thin and in charge. Celeste longed to be the sexiest person in the room. Doris was a nurturer in real life and dress. And Daniel exuded good looks and charm for a possible liaison with a pretty lady. Nelda laughed at herself. What image did she and Sue present to the public? She had on a discrete, black cocktail dress and Sue wore a girlish, plaid sun dress with spaghetti straps. All right she thought, enough philosophizing and on with the party.

"It's about time you got here," said Celeste smiling. "We've been waiting until you arrived to open the champagne."

"Well open away. The gangs all here," Nelda proclaimed.

Sue placed the birthday package they had brought in the center of the table with all the other gifts. "Happy birthday to you, Justine."

For once since Nelda had met Justine, she looked happy and relaxed. Maybe this was a good idea. Nelda echoed Sue's greeting.

The party was noisy and the toasts were plentiful. After dinner, everyone joined in the conga line. Then the birthday cake with lighted candles was presented with a flourish by the waiter. Justine closed her eyes for a few seconds as though making a wish, before blowing out the candles. Nelda wished she could have been privy to that wish. Maybe, it would help her to understand what made Justine click.

After opening her gifts, Justine held up the appointment for a massage and the massage oil. "These are fabulous gifts. I can hardly wait for that rubdown, especially after being in that conga line."

Everyone smiled, because they could hear the drums again. They all stood up to join the line. Nelda could see that periodically some members of the party stopped to rest and have another sip of champagne.

Finally, they were all back at the table. Sue said, "I think we will enjoy the Broadway show tonight. I've seen some of the girls in the lineup and they are gorgeous."

"I saw them too. In fact I have a date with one of them after the show," Daniel said and then grinned.

Justine turned red in the face. "You have a date with one of those harlots?"

"You don't know anything about the show girls," Celeste said, with a frown.

"You butt out, pretty girl," Justine shouted.

Daniel rose from the table. "Justine, let me make this perfectly clear. You are not my keeper." With that remark he charged out of the dining room.

Sue and Nelda thought it a good time to leave too. They thanked everyone for inviting them then walked away.

"Well, Aunt Nelda, Justine has finally alienated everyone in their group."

"A strong term, Sue, but it matches the situation so well.

CHAPTER FIVE

Rub Out

It was late when Nelda and Sue returned to their cabin after the Broadway Show. Nelda quickly changed into her gown and crawled into bed hoping she'd have no trouble sleeping. Her neck was stiff from sleeping on the not-so-soft pillow.

"Goodnight," she called to Sue, who was in the bathroom. Then, she turned with her face to the wall, but sleep eluded her. Finally, Nelda went through the exercises that sometimes relieved her nervous tension. She concentrated on relaxing each part of the body from head to toe. Unfortunately, she couldn't get past her head, because the scene of an angry Justine kept repeating itself in her memory like a damaged, video tape.

Why was this woman on the path to self-destruction? Was there anything she could do to help Justine get along with her companions? After what seemed hours to Nelda, she formulated a plan to help the librarian. She would talk to each member of the academy group about Justine's behavior. There must be a reason for her ill temper.

With a sigh, Nelda beat on her pillow, before lowering her head in the spot she'd hollowed out. Eventually sleep did come, accompanied by a very strange dream.

It seemed she was caught up in a life-like drama. The characters in this story included Sue, herself and the academy group. Each of the characters had thick auras around their heads. The auras were variegated in color. She noticed the one around Justine's head was outlined in red, black in the middle and sinking. Auras over most of the others were a mixture of blue, yellow and red in color, but Sue's Aura shone gold with aqua green at the bottom, the color of Caribbean water. While she gazed at Sue's aura, it started sinking and black slowly covered the green. Nelda awoke with a scream. No! No! It seemed so real; Sue's life energy was ebbing away.

"Aunt Nelda! Sue called. You're having a nightmare.

Nelda sat up in bed. "Yes, I suppose I was. It was so strange; all of you had auras around your heads."

"You mean like halos?"

"Well, sort of. I half expected to see one around your head this morning." Nelda tried to laugh, but worried thoughts wouldn't let her. "Sorry I woke you up."

"It's time to get up, anyway. I'm going to have a massage and facial at 8:30 this morning. What are you going to do?"

"Have coffee and toast, and then go to the gym."

"Ugh, I just remembered. Justine and I have an appointment for a massage at the same time."

"Well, try to be nice to her, Sue."

"You're kidding aren't you? Last night you were disgusted with her behavior, and now I'm supposed to be nice."

Nelda slowly pulled on a light blue warm-up suit. "I've had lots of time to consider the woman's disposition. She needs our help."

"And everybody else's help too, but I'll try to tolerate her for your sake."

*   *   *

Both women finished dressing and left the cabin, Nelda for the Wheelhouse Grill and Sue the Nautica Spa, all on the same deck. They planned to meet back at their cabin at 10:00 am.

Sue and Nelda climbed the stairs to the Wheelhouse Grill. There they parted, Nelda toward 'life saving coffee,' Sue for her beauty treatments. There was no envy in the older woman toward her niece for having a body massage, because Nelda thought it was a waste of money. After going through the food line, she settled in a booth where she could look out over the ocean. It was so peaceful with an Aspen blue, cloudless sky meeting the aquamarine Caribbean waters. Suddenly, someone touched her shoulder, she jumped.

"Good morning, Nelda," Doris stood by her with a tray full of food. "Could I join you for breakfast?"

"Of course, I was admiring the view. It's going to be a beautiful day."

"It's gorgeous, and I'm really looking forward to shopping in Cozumel. We should be there in thirty minutes according to the ship's newsletter."

Nelda studied the younger woman's demeanor as she drank her coffee. Doris seemed to have a cheerful outlook on life, and being a nurse, perhaps she was sympathetic toward people with problems. She decided to talk to her about helping Justine.

"Doris, why do you suppose Justine is always on edge? I have a feeling she's terribly unhappy."

The school nurse immediately took on a guarded look. She stared down at her food while twisting on a paper napkin, before raising her head in defiance. "Nobody can help her. She uses her background for being nasty to everyone."

"What's her background?"

"Well, she was the oldest in a large, poor family without a father. She was expected to help raise all her siblings. Claims she never had any fun growing up and God passed her by when he was handing out looks. Justine is bitter and thinks other people should make it up to her because of her pitiful upbringing."

"God must have given her intelligence. How else could she have finished college and gotten such a nice position at the academy."

"Oh, yeah," answered Doris. "She knows the library business. The only friends she has are other librarians in Texas high schools."

"Well, that's something positive, don't you think?

"Not really," the nurse replied. "They only see her at meetings. With us, she knows our soft spots and uses those to her advantage. We have to tolerate her."

Nelda realized she was not helping her cause, but it sure gave her a clearer picture of Justine. The problem of how to make the head librarian more likable would be more difficult to overcome than she anticipated.

*   *   *

Nelda showered after finishing the Walk-A-Mile exercise class. She was just drying off when she heard someone come into the room. Surely they weren't coming in to clean the room without knocking, or maybe she didn't hear them knock.

"Hello," she called through the bathroom door. "Who's there?"

"Aunt Nelda," screamed Sue. "Open up so I can talk to you."

Nelda quickly put on her robe and opened the door. "What's wrong? You're early Sue, I didn't expect . . ." Her voice trailed off as she saw Sue's pale face.

"Justine Scales is dead." Sue sat down sobbing.

"What do you mean dead? Did she fall over-board, have a heart attack or what?"

"I mean she had an anaphylactic reaction," Sue said, drying her eyes on the bed sheet.

"Where did she get the peanuts?"

"I don't know, Aunt Nelda. All I know is I heard a big commotion behind the curtain where Justine was having a massage. When I rushed in there, the masseuse was screaming for help. She said Justine was having a fit. I told her to call the ship's doctor. By the time he arrived, Justine was unconscious."

"Did you tell the doctor about her allergy?"

"Of course I did. He gave her a shot of epinephrine, but it didn't help. She's gone." Sue didn't shed more tears, just looked sad.

"Is it unusual for a person who has an allergic reaction to die that fast?"

"I'm not an expert, but in nurse's school we learned that you can't build up a tolerance for peanuts by eating them. If you know you're allergic to those nuts and eat them, you're dead."

"What's going to happen now?" Nelda sighed. "I guess the academy group will be called in for questioning. I wonder if she accidentally killed herself."

"Who can tell? You saw how she was pigging out on those mixed nuts the other evening when we were waiting for dinner. But most likely she deliberately ate peanuts, so her so-called friends would have a miserable vacation after she died."

"Sue! I can't believe you said that." Nelda shook her head in dismay. "It must have been an accident. Our only link to them is your friend, Doris, but we'll help anyway we can."

"You're right. I'm sorry I said such ugly things about her. It just seems so unfair for the others. Now, they're going to have to explain Justine's behavior instead of being free to go ashore and enjoy themselves."

"No one dies at a convenient time," stated Nelda. "Let me get dressed and we'll see what we can do. After that, I see no reason for us to just sit, we'll go shopping as planned."

"Good, maybe the others will have that attitude too, except for her assistant, Winnie. I really believe she had some sort of an attachment to Justine."

They both scurried to get dressed. Nelda was just slipping into her comfortable walking shoes when someone knocked on the door.

"Sue, you're dressed, get the door."

The younger woman opened the door to find Doris standing in the doorway with a tissue in her hand. Her eyes were red and the woman seemed completely distraught.

Doris walked in and slumped in a chair in front of the vanity. "I suppose you've both heard the news, since Sue was at the health spa with Justine?"

Sue walked over and put her arm around her friend. "I was there when she died. Did she deliberately eat peanuts, Doris? Was she really trying to kill herself?"

"I honestly don't know what happened. Winnie declared that Justine didn't have anything to eat before she left for her massage, just a cup of coffee that was made in their cabin."

Nelda walked over and sat on the bed near Doris. "I'm really sorry this happened. Sue and I were talking about what we could possibly do to help. We hope you can continue on with your vacation if you feel up to it."

"I suppose," Doris said fidgeting with the pleats in her white shorts, "there will be a hearing of some kind. There was a detective that came around to talk to us. The academy group is to meet in his office in two hours. That's all I know."

"Would you like for us to hang around until he talks to all of you?" Sue asked.

"No, it's okay. You hardly knew Justine. Hopefully, we'll be able to tell the detective everything he wants to know."

As Doris got up to leave, she trembled and seemed almost afraid to step out into the hallway. It was as though she expected to encounter trouble. She looked up and down the corridor before making her way back to her cabin.

"Well, what do you think about that?" Sue asked leaning against the closed door.

"I'll tell you what I think; she's not telling us all she knows. There is something not kosher in that group. I feel the tension when any of them are around, especially when they are all together. And one other fact, Doris is afraid."

"I know what we need to do, Aunt Nelda, let's get out of here before you start solving another mystery. I'd like to visit some of the gift shops in downtown Cozumel."

"Mostly to look I hope," muttered Nelda grabbing her handbag. She knew how impulsive her dear niece could be.

*   *   *

Before they had an opportunity to climb into a cab, a good looking pirate approached them. His costume was reminiscent of Long John Silver's, and his bearded face sported a black patch over one eye. He drew his rubber knife and laughingly threatened to have their hides if they did not have their picture taken with him. Sue and Nelda couldn't resist that invitation.

"It will be in the picture gallery tomorrow," he assured them as he turned to search for his next victim.

Smiling, they boarded a taxi that had seen better days. There was no air-conditioning and the seats were worn. Worst of all was the strong smell of tobacco smoke. Nelda wanted to roll her window down, but couldn't get the handle to turn. The only thing that seemed to be in good shape was the taxi driver's gift of gab and the rear view mirror.

"Hello, *Senoritas*, my name is Roberto." The small man with long black hair adjusted the rear view mirror, so he could see both of them. Welcome to Cozumel. You know that name comes from the Mayan word 'Cuzamil,' meaning land of the swallows. This island she is twenty eight miles long and eleven miles wide. We have everything on this island, even a jungle. Whatever you want to do, you can do: scuba dive, sailing and all water sports. But shopping is good too, many bargains. You are going to love it here."

Sue spoke up. "Your English is great, Roberto. Where did you learn the language?"

"In school and in the U.S.A. I worked there building highways for many years. Learning English helped me get this job." He spat out the window and Sue ducked. He then lit up a long thin cigarette.

Nelda held her tongue, she didn't mind him repeating facts that she had read in the ship's newsletter, but the foul smell from his cigarette snaking its way to the back seat was another matter. She could stand it for just so long.

"Roberto, how far are we from the street that has all the shops?"

"Maybe five minutes or so down this road."

"Stop, and let us out, we'll walk the rest of the way. It will be good for us."

"Whatever you say, *Senorita*. You have a good time, I know it."

And thanks for the compliment, she thought silently, *senorita* in deed, more like old teacher.

After paying the cab driver, Nelda and Sue walked briskly to the market where people laughed and talked while looking for bargains in the Three Shop Emporium. They entered the silver shop first.

"Oh, Aunt Nelda, look at this silver necklace. Have you ever seen such intricate work?" Sue lifted the shiny necklace toward her aunt.

"Yes, that would look lovely on you. And I think it would be a good time for me to buy Sally another gift, maybe this album with the little silver dog on the cover."

"I don't know, Aunt Nelda. She might want to forget about dogs for awhile, with her just losing Sugar."

"No, I don't think one should forget their loved ones. You just have to think about all the good times you had with them. This album could be filled with pictures of Sugar. Goodness knows she has enough photos of him to fill up several albums."

"I'm sure you know her best, Auntie." Sue moved closer to Nelda and spoke in a whisper. "That man in the white shirt, who just entered, is watching us closely."

"Yes he is. I can't believe he thinks we're shoplifting."

As Sue and Nelda stood at the glass counter looking at several pieces of jewelry designed from silver, the robust man in the white shirt approached them while pulling identification from his pocket. He spoke to them in a low, modulated voice.

"I am Detective Moor from the Cruise Ship Liberation. Are you Nelda Simmons and Sue Grimes?"

"Yes," answered Nelda. Why are you following us?"

"I'm investigating the death of Justine Scales. You both knew her, and Ms. Grimes was with her when she died."

"Yes," Sue admitted, "I was there getting a massage too. Her death was accidental wasn't it?"

"We're not sure. Both of you must return with me to the ship. There are some questions that must be answered."

Sue's face paled, while Nelda's took on a stubborn determination. "We'll be back in a little while Sue. Please don't let this upset you."

Both women followed Detective Moor out to his car after paying the cashier for the album and necklace. Nelda had a bad feeling about the cause of Justine's death. She also wondered if anybody else in the academy group had a black aura around their head.

CHAPTER SIX

Accident or Murder

Nelda and Sue, along with the vacationing Witherspoon Academy's group, gathered in the ship's library. The chief of ship's security, Detective David Moore, stood before them with his back to a shelf that displayed models of former cruise ships. He looked a little like Agatha Christie's Monsieur Poirot, with his little mustache, shiny black eyes and fixed smile. However, when Moore spoke, his words came out with a Southern drawl.

"Ladies and Gentleman, my name is David Moore and I'm head of security on this ship. A list of your names and occupations were given to me by my assistant Don Gomez." He pointed to a young man dressed in khaki pants and a bright Hawaiian shirt standing in the corner of the room. "Your friend, Daniel Hall, helped him in making the list. Let me see if I can identify everyone. Please raise your hand when I call your name."

While the detective called each name, Nelda studied the faces of the group. She had a good vantage point, because she and Sue were sitting in chairs by the computers. The others, Celeste, Doris, Winnie and Daniel were seated at a table by book cases filled with paperback and hard back books. She was amazed at the one emotion shown on each of their faces. Fear! You could see it in their wide eyes and rigid expressions as they exchanged guarded glances. The only one who showed any sorrow over Justine's death was Winnie. Her eyes were red from crying.

After the detective established their identities, he continued speaking. "I'm sorry about the death of your fellow traveler, Justine Scales. For your information, the ship's doctor, Isaac Lamb, thinks Justine Scales' death was due to an allergic reaction. I'll try to finish this meeting as soon as possible, but there are some questions I must ask each of you for my report.

Nelda wondered how Doctor Lamb could be so sure of what caused Justine's death. Surely there would be an examination other than his. She raised her hand. "Will there be an autopsy?"

"Oh yes indeed, Ms. Simpson. We need to know the exact cause of death, even though the doctor thinks an allergic reaction is the reason."

Winnie turned her watery, brown eyes toward the speaker. "Has her brother, Charles, been notified of her death?"

"Yes, he has. Moore flipped open his notebook. Let's see, you're Winnie Speer aren't you?"

"I am," whispered Winnie, "and I've been Justine's assistant in the Academy's library for the last five years."

"You also shared a cabin with her on this cruise?" Moore made a notation on his pad.

"Yes. I suppose I know Justine better than anyone here." Winnie wiped her wet face on a handkerchief then twisted it in her lap.

"Now, tell me what happened this morning. Try not to leave anything out. Even if you don't think it's important."

"Okay, I'll try to remember what all occurred this morning." She wiped her face one last time and focused her eyes on the detective. Her small, shrill voice could barely be heard over the noises made by passengers on their way to an elevator located right outside the library.

"We overslept this morning. Justine had an appointment for a massage at 8:00 a.m. As soon as she woke up, she rushed into the bathroom, got dressed and took her pills. After that she poured herself a cup of coffee, before racing out the door."

"Do you know what kind of pills she took?"

Winnie looked down thoughtfully before answering. "Of course I do. She was always lecturing me about alternative supplements.

She took Co Q10, multiple vitamins, antioxidants and a new pill she's added for her eyes. All of that plus two prescription drugs for high blood pressure and high cholesterol."

"Did she take them all at one time?"

"The pills for each day were in individual little cups. She just poured them out in her hand, and then downed them with water."

"When she left for the spa, did she have any food with her?"

"No, and I never saw her again." Her voice cracked as fresh tears flowed down her cheeks.

Moore waited a minute or two for Winnie to gain her composure then he asked, "Do you know of any foods or insect stings that your friend would be allergic to?"

"Peanuts are the only things I'm aware of. She told me that when she was a child, she ate peanuts and almost died. The doctor said she probably would die the next time she ingested them, unless she had an injection of epinephrine."

"One last question for now, what kind of mood was Miss Scales in when she left the room?

"Justine was not a happy person. Her mood was more like excited, because she was going to the spa for a free massage. That was her birthday present from all of us."

"I see. Thank you, Ms. Speer," Detective Moore murmured. "Now please go back to your cabin with my assistant and gather up Ms. Speers things, including those pills you talked about. It's important you do this right away. We'll be sending everything home to her brother. If I need any more information, I'll let you know."

Winnie got up to leave, but took her time gathering her things, before making for the exit. It was as though she didn't want to miss out on what the others would have to say.

After Winnie and Detective Gomez left, Moore turned his attention back to those still seated. "I'm trying to establish exactly where Justine might have gotten hold of peanuts to start her adverse reaction. According to Dr. Lamb, the allergic emergency would begin almost immediately after the ingestion of the nut. Anyone have any ideas?"

No one spoke for a few seconds. They just looked at each other to see who would break the silence. Finally, Doris spoke up, "none of us were with her all the time, not even Winnie. However, there was one incident that was pretty upsetting. We were sitting in the piano bar the first night we were here, and Justine was eating from a bowl of nuts. Winnie grabbed them away from her. Justine reacted very angrily by cursing at her."

"I see," Moore responded, smoothing down his small mustache. "Were there any peanuts in the bowl?"

"I didn't see any, but there could have been."

Nelda noticed that Doris glanced at the others, probably waiting for them to verify her story, but no one spoke. The only movement in the room was Moore writing in his notebook.

"Anybody remember eating peanuts from that bowl?"

They all responded with a negative nod. Nelda remembered it was too close to dinner to fill up on nuts. She didn't recall seeing anyone but Justine eating them.

The detective put away his pad. "Thanks for coming and try to have a normal day. I may need to get in touch with you later. We'll just see how the autopsy comes out." As everyone moved toward the library door, he tapped Nelda on the shoulder. "Ms. Simmons, could I have a word with you alone?"

Nelda was taken aback by his question. What could she possibly know that would help him? "I suppose so," she said. She then spoke to Sue, "I'll meet you in our cabin in a few minutes."

After they'd all cleared out, Detective Moore pulled out a chair for Nelda to sit down at the table. He sat across from her with a little smile on his face. "I've done a little checking into your background Ms. Simmons and I've found you've had a very interesting life."

I didn't know I was on the internet. What did you learn about me?"

"You've been quite busy solving mysteries in your part of Texas. I suppose it all started with that sheriff husband of yours."

"That's when my snooping started. Since then I've been lucky in solving some crimes. So who's been telling tales about me?" She knew if he got in touch with the sheriff's office in her county, it was Joe Coates who spilled the beans.

"Let's just say it was from a reliable source. Is there some mystery about Justine Scales' death, Ms. Simmons?"

"Please call me by my first name. But in answer to your question, I know of no mystery, because I hardly know these people. The school nurse, Doris Hodge, is a friend of my niece, Sue Grimes. They are both nurses and attended some medical meetings together. My first time to meet the academy group was in Galveston where we all ate lunch before boarding the ship."

"What was your impression of Scales? Was she suicidal?"

"I have no idea, Detective. She was an extremely unhappy person, causing misery to those around her. Very low self esteem too, if I had to guess. Now, I know you're worried about where she got the peanuts, if that's what killed her. This would probably make the cruise line's insurance company squirm if she ate the goobers in your restaurants or bars."

"You certainly tell it like it is, Nelda. To my knowledge, peanuts are not on the menu. Probably not in the bars either. It's my business to make sure her death was not homicidal or the fault of the cruise line."

"I suppose your next move is just to wait and see what the autopsy results are?"

"That's it. No use jumping to conclusions."

"I suppose that's wise. I doubt that anybody would jump ship at this point. Do you intend to interview us again?"

"Only, if we suspect foul play. You will keep your eyes and ears open for me won't you?"

"Of course, happens to be something I enjoy most."

*   *   *

On her way to meet Sue, Nelda worried about how scared the Academy people looked when Moore talked to them. Did the detective sense that too? Or was this just her imagination? No, it was fear in their eyes, she could swear to it, but she just didn't know the cause. She'd think about it some more after she had time to mull it over. Meantime, her niece deserved some fun.

Sue was in the bathroom packing a beach bag when Nelda got to their cabin.

"Better hurry, Aunt Nelda, I've booked us for the Party Boat and it leaves in thirty minutes."

"Oh yeah, how did you know I was a party girl?"

"It just shows in those bloomers you bought for a bathing suit."

Nelda laughed. Sue had made fun of her bathing suit when she bought it, but at least it left a lot to the imagination. With her wrinkled hide, it was better that way. "Well tell me about it. What's there to do on this party boat?"

"I'll tell you while you pack your bathing suit, but first tell me why the detective asked you to stay?"

"It seems he's found out that I'm nosey and love to solve mysteries. Now, how about me sharing that beach bag?"

"Sure, don't forget your suntan lotion. We'll be out in the sun once we reach the beach club, unless of course you want to snorkel."

"Snorkeling sounds like fun to me. I don't suppose there will be loud music, crazy dancing and wild young people on the boat," Nelda said, as she folded up a beach towel.

"You know I wouldn't be going otherwise. Here, let me stick my cell phone in that bag. It's time I tried calling Walter. Sue looked at the phone wistfully. Of course he'll probably be with a patient when I telephone. He certainly spends more time with strangers than with me."

"I don't want you to dwell on Walter's faults anymore on this trip. Just think about how sweet he is, and how lucky you are to be engaged to such a great guy."

"You're right, Aunt Nelda. I'm a selfish ungrateful little twit.

They both laughed as they rushed out to the dock. Nelda could hear the music on the party boat before they got to it. The melody had a hypnotic disco beat that would soon have most of the passengers dancing. Would she be able to endure the exhibition of all that cheerful energy? You bet! The third deck on the boat would be about the right distance for her to be. Sue was in agreement, so they dodged in and around the merry makers as they climbed the stairs to sunlight and the open sea.

"Isn't this great, Aunt Nelda? I'm so happy you brought me along on this trip.

"It's my pleasure and you know it." Nelda pointed to some empty benches near the back of the boat. Let's sit here where the wind can tousle our curls."

Her niece snickered, Nelda's hair was short and not going anywhere with all the hair spray she had on it. But the sea breeze would benefit both of them. They had just settled down when the academy's school nurse made her way to the third deck. She looked despondent, and her mind seemed miles away. Sue had to call her name several times before she acknowledged her greeting.

"Oh! I'm sorry, Sue, I was too deep in thought to even look around. I'm glad you and Nelda are on board. It was stifling and lonesome in my cabin; I just had to get away. I wish I'd never come on this cruise."

Sue scooted over and made room for Doris. "What are the others doing this afternoon?"

"Well, Celeste spends most of her time with her boyfriend. I think he's a coach from her old school, and Winnie is sitting in her cabin watching old movies."

"Do you know her very well?" Sue asked.

"I've spent more time with her than the other two. She helps me give flu shots to the faculty."

"What about Daniel? Did he leave the ship for a tour or shopping?

"I haven't seen Daniel. He's sort of a mystery man anyway, can't imagine why he came with us."

"Well, don't worry about anything," Nelda said. "Let's just live it up starting now."

"I can't do that, Nelda; I'm scared Justine's death may not have been an accident. I know you've had experience with that sort of thing."

"What makes you think it might have been a homicide, Doris? Tell me what you have on your mind and I'll try to help you."

Doris started crying without uttering a sound. Tears ran down her face leaving trails in her foundation makeup. She dried her face on a beach towel before continuing. "I know this is going to sound absolutely terrible, but please bear in mind I didn't kill Justine. I know someone is going to tell the detective about this incident, so that's why I'm telling you and Sue."

Sue moved closer so she could hear Doris over the music. "What incident, Doris? You're talking in circles."

Doris spoke with her head down. "One week before this cruise Winnie, Celeste and I met in a bar to celebrate the end of school, but it turned out to be more than that. Justine had been blackmailing us, so Celeste suggested that we draw slips of paper to see who would take her out."

Aunt and niece exchanged looks of dismay.

"Good Lord! What did that mean?" Nelda asked.

Tears filled Doris' eyes. "The person who drew the green dot was supposed to steal her EpiPen."

"Who got the slip with the green dot?" Sue questioned breathlessly."

"I . . . . did." sobbed Doris.

CHAPTER
SEVEN

Downed In the Sea

Nelda considered Doris' story unbelievable. Even though Justine was blackmailing them, how could three grown women sit in a cocktail lounge and plot to kill their associate? Surely, they could come up with a better solution. They were all educated, and there were other options, like seeking help from the law.

A feeling of dismay caused Sue's eyes to film over with tears. "I'm truly amazed at you, Doris. You went along with this scheme, and didn't say anything?"

"No, I never agreed to Celeste's plan. Besides, after we all looked in our envelopes, she told us it was a joke."

"You're kidding? What kind of warped sense of humor does she have?" Sue responded.

"Okay," Nelda said. "Let's get this whole thing in perspective. You and Winnie fell for Celeste's 'so called' joke."

"Yes! And I know I shouldn't have taken the envelope, much less open it."

"That goes without saying. Did the others know your envelope had the green dot?"

"No, none of us showed the others our slips of paper."

"Well, thank God for small favors," ventured Sue.

"What exactly did Celeste say when you and Winnie looked in your envelopes?"

"She laughed out loud and said, 'It's a joke, dummies, Justine is not worth killing or going to jail over.'"

That was exactly what Nelda thought, but what horrible things had these three academy employees done to justify paying blackmail? Would Doris be willing to share that information? Looking at the chastened, auburn-haired lump of a girl sitting next to her, she decided it was worth a try.

"Why was Justine blackmailing you?" Nelda looked directly into Doris' tear drenched eyes.

"I know it's going to sound so trivial, but you have to understand that public schools and most private academies have very strict guidelines for hiring teachers. Sometimes unsavory records follow educators from one school to another. In my case, a friend's daughter brought marijuana cigarettes to school. One of the kids saw her and told me. I knew there was going to be a search for drugs that day at school. So I took them away from her and flushed them down the commode."

Sue shook her head, wiped the moisture from her brow and adjusted her sun glasses. "So, how did the school officials know you did it?"

"The silly fool told on me. She got expelled and they didn't renew my contract."

Nelda moved to a seat in the shade. "Speaking as a retired teacher, you deserved it. One thing I learned a long time ago, if you don't like the policies of the school, get out. Besides, the girl was breaking the law."

"I know. In retrospect, I wouldn't do it again."

"The question is," broke in Sue, how in the world did Justine know about this incident?"

"I don't know. That information was not in my folder. The superintendent promised to expunge that from my records if I resigned, and I certainly didn't give any of the people at my old school as a reference. Of course Justine did belong to the State Librarian's Association. Maybe a member from my old school was her source.

"One more thing, we three made up our minds to tell her on this trip that her blackmailing days were over. If she continued, we were going to the police no matter what it did to our careers."

"That was the most sensible decision you could ever make in a situation like that. I don't know how you've lived under the threat of exposure," said Nelda.

The music on the first floor came to a halt. A long line of vacationers in shorts and T-shirts were lined up on the top deck to receive snorkel gear. The boat neared its destination to Playa Sol. Nelda couldn't resist asking Doris one other question.

"Doris, how did you know Justine was blackmailing the others?"

"Winnie told us. She said Justine bragged about it to her. I don't know why the others are being blackmailed."

Standing, Nelda smiled, then reached out for Doris' hand and pulled her up. She laid her arm around the girl's shoulders.

"Let's forget about all this for now, Doris. Perhaps Celeste's grotesque joke is not important. We'll just have to see. We're here to have a good time, so let's do it. Why don't we join the line for snorkel gear? There are a lot of things to see underwater."

With spirits lifted, all three joined the exuberant party goers in trying on flippers, and finding masks that fit snugly on their faces. Of course Nelda had brought Lysol spray to make sure they didn't pick up the dreaded cruise virus from the face masks. After a lengthy wait and struggle to get the correct sizes, all they needed to do now was slip on their bathing suits before hitting the water. All three lined up at the rail looking toward a patch of green land dotted with palm trees and a white sandy beach.

"What are you going to do about your hair, Aunt Nelda?"

"Get it wet. I have a scarf and dark glasses to wear back. I'll probably look just like Jackie Kennedy."

"Oh sure, but no Jack waiting for you at home."

"Well, that old Sheriff Joe Coates may still be in Stearn when I get back."

Sue looked whimsical and sad. "I suppose there is a certain doctor there waiting for me. Hope I can find a quiet spot to use my cell phone when we get to the beach."

"Cheer up. I'm sure there will be. What about you, Doris? Do you have a male friend back home?"

"Yes, Doctor Donald Brown. We have a lot in common, but we're just good friends. Hey, everybody is rushing to the front. I think we have arrived."

*   *   *

There were people everywhere at Playa Sol Beach. Besides the party boat, chartered buses brought people in to swim and scuba dive in the blue-green waters of the Caribbean Sea. Steps led down into the water from the sandy white beaches in several places. The water was so clear you could see colorful fish darting in and out among the large rocks.

Doris and Nelda bent over to watch a small school of fish with bright red and white stripes swimming near the stairs.

"Look at that, Nelda; have you ever seen such beautiful fish?"

"No I haven't, but I see Sue breaking out in a sweat trying to get our attention."

Sue walked over frowning. "Now see what you'll have done. Everyone on that boat is ahead of us in the bath house. We're going to have a long wait changing into our suits."

"Well, I won't," Doris said smugly. "I have my bathing suit under my clothes."

"That's using your head, nursie. Don't be so upset, Sue, we're going to be here for hours. I'm sure if we went over and had a drink on the covered deck, by the time we finished, the crowd will be gone. Besides, I thought you were going to call Walter as soon as we got here."

"I did, but he was making rounds at the hospital."

"So that's why you're acting like you have a burr under your blanket?"

Sue grinned. "How do you come up with those quotes? I could swear you're from Texas."

Sitting on the dirty, wooden deck with some half-warm drinks was not Nelda's idea of an adventurous outing. There was no wind, so the ceiling fans just circulated hot air. Fifteen minutes of that was all she could bear.

"Alright everybody let's go. Doris, let me have your things, and we'll lock them up for you. Please find us a beach umbrella while we change. We won't be gone long."

As Nelda worked her way to the area where they could rent lockers, she and Sue talked about Doris' incredible story.

"What do you think about Doris' story, Sue?"

"Well, I've heard it said that truth is stranger then fiction, so I suppose this must be the case. Doris certainly sounds sincere."

"But why didn't Winnie object to sharing a cabin with someone who is blackmailing her?" Nelda asked, stepping around a group of children in the middle of the walk.

"I don't know about Winnie, Aunt Nelda. She seems like a spineless wimp to me, and Justine probably has total control over her. It would be interesting to know what bad thing she's done."

Nelda paused to shake sand out of her sandals. When she straightened up, she saw a flash of bright plaid colors on a young man standing on the beach. She could have sworn it was Daniel, but by the time she had a good view of the area, the man was gone.

Sue paid a deposit on a locker for them and they changed quickly. Nelda looked quite fit in her jogger suit with a striped top and nylon shorts, while Sue was mostly bare in her red Lycra spandex wrap. In her aunt's estimation, Sue's suit revealed too much cleavage plus everything else, but Nelda knew when not to nag.

It wasn't difficult finding Doris. She was wrapped up in a towel sitting under a beach umbrella very close to the blue-green water. They exchanged greetings, while she made room for them. Nelda found it so relaxing just to sit and look at the sunbeams dancing on the ripples made by swimmers and people on floats.

"This won't do, Aunt Nelda. I didn't come out here to sit on the beach. Let's go snorkeling out there by that group of rocks." Sue pointed to an area some distance away. "Do you think you could make it out there?"

"You're talking to an old tennis player here. I'm up to it. How about you Doris?"

Doris was not as enthusiastic about getting wet. She reluctantly took off the towel and stood up. Nelda couldn't believe it. Even the nurse's bathing suit was white, a one piece job that zipped up the front. It looked more like a wet suit than a bathing suit. Oh well, 'to each his own,' Nelda reasoned. Spandex in the suit's fabric did make her look thinner.

Snorkeling was not new to Nelda; she'd had a few tries at it with her late husband, Jim, many years ago when the Comal River in Texas was crystal clear. She looked forward to viewing a few ancient Mayan treasures and beautiful fish under the waters here.

Sue took the lead in the water, Doris next and Nelda followed close behind. They waited until they were away from the crowd before affixing their face masks. It was downright breath taking to see all the different colors of fish darting about. Nelda even thought she saw the remains of a Mayan god carved out of stone submerged in the sand, but wasn't quite sure.

"Let's rest a while on those rocks, before we explore anymore," Doris said, sounding a little winded.

"Suits me," Sue responded as she crawled up on the first available rock.

The rock butted up next to another large one, so there was room enough for all of them to sit next to each other with their feet, shod in flippers, trailing in the water. Nelda didn't realize how far out they had come. The people on the beach looked small. They all turned to watch a sailboat within hailing distance. It was making for a pier where several boats were tied up. A blonde girl on board who was seated in the stern quickly turned away from them to disappear behind the white sail.

"That girl looked just like Celeste," Doris said. I wonder if she and her gentleman friend rented that sailboat"

"Didn't she say anything about her schedule for today?" Nelda asked, stretching her arms over her head.

"Not a word. She's a pretty private person most of the time. However, she's the one that got us all together for this trip."

"Even Justine?" Sue asked, sliding back into the water. She hung on to Nelda's flippers because the rocks were slippery below the water.

"Yes, and Daniel too. We didn't like the idea of Justine coming with us, but Winnie said it was okay because she needed a roommate. She couldn't afford a private cabin."

Sue wiggled Nelda and Doris' flippers. "Let's snorkel some more. We only have an hour before we start back. I'd still like to find that old sunken boat the cruise newsletter said was out here."

"Fine," said Doris. You and Nelda go ahead and look for it, and I'll rest until you feel like heading back."

"How about it, Aunt Nelda, are you coming with me?" Sue treaded water while she waited for a reply.

"I'm not about to let you go off by yourself, Sue. We'll stay together in case one of us needs help."

"And how old do you think I am? You make it sound like I'm at summer camp."

"You know you'll always be my little girl, even when you're married to Walter and have a whole house full of kids." That said, Nelda started swimming slowly toward the next group of rocks.

"Ha, catch me if you can," called Sue as she passed Nelda, who was trying to follow a school of minute silver fish. Sue reached the rocks first and circled the area until Nelda caught up with her.

"I don't see any Mayan ruins or sunken boat, Sue, but my back feels like its burning. Don't you think we better rescue Doris and go ashore?"

"I suppose so; we have to get out of these wet things before we start back." Sue turned on her back and started doing the back stroke.

They swam slowly toward the rock where Doris was perched. Both had their faces under water part of the time to see if they had missed anything on their trip to the second group of rocks. Sue called Nelda's attention to an ancient mural mired in the sand. Only a corner of it was sticking out. Nelda lifted her face out of the water to locate the rocks where Doris was sitting. The rocks were bare.

"Doris is gone. She was there just a minute ago." Nelda started swimming faster.

She and Sue reached the location about the same time. They circled around all the rocks, but no Doris.

"Oh my God," whispered Nelda. "What has happened to that girl?"

Sue gave a whoop. "Here she is underwater. Come help me lift her out."

Rushing to Sue's side, Nelda helped lift the unconscious girl to the surface. Blood was pouring down Doris' back from a wound to her head. It stained her white bathing suit and caused the green water around her to turn pink. They braced her body against the side of a rock. Nelda held her there as Sue climbed on top of the rock and attempted to lift her by placing her hands under Doris' arms. After some pulling and pushing by both of them they hauled her up and placed her face up on top of the flattest rock. Sue began CPR, but Doris didn't respond.

Nelda looked toward the shore for help. Dozen of vacationers were swimming and using floats, but she could see only one snorkeler climbing out of the sea.

CHAPTER EIGHT

White Sand

Doris' body, along with Nelda and Sue, were transported from the water at Playa Sol by a team of shore officers in a small boat. The man in charge, Antonio Sanchez, took many photographs of the area where Doris drowned. In addition, samples of material on the rocks were scraped away and bagged.

The boat docked at an obscure pier in an effort to keep the public unaware of the accident. Nelda was grateful to Sanchez for that, because rubbernecking by the public always seemed crass to her. The body, in a zippered bag, was left with an officer.

Accompanied by Sanchez, they retrieved their belongings from their locker, and then he led them to an alcove off the outdoor restaurant for an interview.

"Please be seated," Sanchez said. "No need to be nervous. I need all your names and the circumstances surrounding this *accidente.*"

Names were easy, but the hard part for Nelda was trying to explain why they left Doris alone on a rock for an extended period. She couldn't explain, even to herself, why she felt so guilty about that.

Nelda was quiet for so long, Sue decided to answer Sanchez. "My name is Sue Grimes and this is my aunt, Nelda Simmons, we share a cabin on the cruise ship, *Liberation*. The woman that had the accident is Doris Hodge, a nurse friend I knew from Stearn, TX, our hometown. She was also on the cruise ship, but not in our party. However, all three of us came here on the Fiesta Party Boat."

"You have *documento* with you?"

Nelda rooted around in their beach bag until she found all their passports, then handed them over hoping they would get them right back. For some reason, she had never really considered Mexico a foreign country. While living in El Paso, they had walked across the border many times with only a driver's license for identification.

Sanchez pulled a small notebook from his pocket and copied information from the passports into the notebook. "Now, just tell me exactly what happened in the water?"

It was Nelda's turn. "The three of us swam out to the rocks. We climbed up on the rocks to rest, but after awhile Sue and I wanted to see if we could locate Mayan remains on the ocean floor. Doris was tired and just wanted to sit there. We were gone from her, maybe fifteen or twenty minutes."

"When you started back, did you see her—sitting there on the rock?"

"I did see her from a distance. But then we snorkeled on the way back. As we swam nearer, I looked up and she was gone."

"Was there anyone close to the area?"

"No, there was no one I could see."

"Thank you *Senora*. Here are your passports. If you wait by the road, I will drive you back to the *bote.*"

*   *   *

Nelda and Sue stood in the middle of the road looking at the dusty white ambulance. They were not alone. Curious bathing suit clad tourists crowded in around them to watch the body of Doris Hodge being loaded into the van. It seemed that Sanchez could only do so much to keep the gawkers away.

Sue wiped away a tear, while Nelda looked up at the sky with her eyes closed, for a moment of prayer. "Oh it's all so sad," Sue said, holding on to Nelda's arm. "If we just hadn't been here today, Doris would still be alive."

"I wonder," Nelda whispered, more to herself than to Sue.

"What? You can't believe murder? The blackmailer is already dead."

"Let's talk about this later, Sue. That shore patrol officer is over there waiting to take us back to the ship."

After picking up the beach bag, they made their way through the crowd toward the waiting car. Dark clouds blotted out the sun, making it several degrees cooler. Nelda shivered even though she wasn't cold. The whole beach area had taken on a menacing feeling to her. As if to back up her thoughts, she stumbled over a plastic bucket filled with sand. A small boy darted toward her, grabbed the vessel and ran down a path toward the water.

"Are you okay?" Sue asked, rushing to her aunt's side.

"I suppose so. Just anxious, disappointed and sad."

"I know what you mean. I'm glad Officer Sanchez offered us a ride instead of us having to face the party boat."

*   *   *

Sanchez stood beside his old car smoking a cigarette and watched Nelda and Sue with thoughtful eyes as they approached. He was a swarthy, handsome young man, native to San Miguel, the only town in Cozumel. Deaths from drowning that occurred on his watch were not good for his duty record. Sanchez resented these affluent Americans who could come over in ships and planes to enjoy the beauty and history of his country, while most of his countrymen were too poor to enjoy luxury travel. He wanted to frown at them instead of smiling, but it was not his nature. His clear thinking and gregarious attitude had landed him this job making it possible for his large family to benefit from his salary and prestige in the community.

*   *   *

When they were quite near, he threw down his cigarette, grinding the fiery end into the sand, and opened the back doors.

After they were settled, he slammed the doors and drove slowly down the road, making sure no tourists were in his path.

The interior of the car reeked of tobacco smoke, however since the car had no air conditioning, the windows were all rolled down, and the streams of air coming into the car from the openings kept Nelda and Sue from choking.

Antonio did not address them until they had left all traces of Playa Sol behind. "Senoras, you must believe me. I am so sorry your friend drowned. Those rocks they have, how you say? *Viscoso* stuff all over them. Very *malo*."

Nelda couldn't help herself. She jumped right in with what was on her mind. "Now Officer Sanchez—I know we've already been over this—but are you sure there were no signs of Doris being dragged into the water by her feet?"

"Senora, it was an accident. That is my *informe*. Why you think otherwise?"

"I don't know. Just a feeling, I suppose."

Sue wiggled in her seat, trying to avoid a broken spring while looking at her aunt with a worried frown. "Let it go, Aunt Nelda, don't conjure something up in your mind that isn't so. It's unfortunate, but she just slipped off the rock, hit her head and drowned."

Sanchez turned on the radio to some fast Mexican music, hung his left arm out the window and tapped out a steady beat to it with his hand on the door of the car. He did it with so much enthusiasm that Nelda's melancholy began to lift. Perhaps there was the possibility that both deaths were accidents. She chided herself for being a pessimist. Her late husband had jokingly said of her, "Once a detective, always a detective." She made up her mind to salvage what was left of their vacation.

"Sue, we can't pretend these deaths never happened. But I'll try to make the best of the time we have left on the ship."

"You want to shun the academy group?"

"Certainly not, Nelda smiled at Sue. Celeste doesn't need our friendship with her man around, and Daniel has no problem making friends, but Winnie is another matter."

Squinting her eyes at Nelda, Sue shrugged. "What a wimp she is. We'll do well to get her out of her cabin."

Antonio pulled up to the pier where the big white ship was anchored. He sighed with relief as he opened the car doors for them. "*Adios Senoras*, come back some more."

Looking tired, hot and disheveled, Nelda and Sue hurried toward the ship. Sue was thinking of calling Walter, and relaxing in a nice warm shower. Nelda's thoughts were on the distasteful job of informing Winnie of Doris' death.

"I'm going to call Walter again out here on the pier, Aunt Nelda. Surely he's seen all his patients by now and has time to take my call."

"Well go ahead. I'll see you back in the cabin. I can't wait to get these sandy clothes off." She ran a hand through her gritty tangled hair. "Just let this day end," she whispered.

Her niece sat down on the pier, before automatically pressing the telephone numbers of Walter's health clinic on a tiny cell phone. Nelda looked back to see a slow smile spread across Sue's face as she cradled the phone. A sure sign Walter was on the other end.

*   *   *

As Nelda showered, she thought about how she was going to break the news to Winnie about Doris' death. She knew it had to be done, and she wanted to beat the officials on board to that task. How would Winnie feel if a perfect stranger told her another one of their faculty members had died? Scared? Lonesome? Probably both.

It was the right thing to do. She'd ask Sue to come with her. As she dried her hair, she heard the cabin door shut.

"Sue, is that you," called Nelda, caught in the bathroom without a robe.

"Yes," sang out Sue rather dreamily. Then, there was a plop on the bed.

Nelda wrapped a towel around her body and found Sue spread out on the bed with a silly looking smile on her face.

"Aunt Nelda have you ever been so in love with a guy that you thought you would die."

"Never," countered her aunt. "When I was in love, I wanted to be alive so I could enjoy it. But I can tell your conversation with Walter went well."

"He'd die for me. That's what he said," Sue reported, rolling over to look at Nelda's reaction to that bit of news.

Nelda laughed out loud. "Wonderful, maybe you could die together. Now take a quick shower, while I finish dressing. We need to talk to Winnie, before someone else breaks the news to her about Doris' death."

"Alright, I'll go with you, but you don't have a romantic bone in your body." Sue struggled off the bed and stormed into the bathroom slamming the door. In ten minutes she came out all smiles. "I'm not going to let you get me down," she said dreamily pulling a blue cotton sundress over her head. "Walter is already planning our honeymoon for next summer."

Tired of Sue's prattle, Nelda didn't respond. She was sorry she couldn't show more enthusiasm for her niece's romance, but Doris' death had the highest priority right now. When she reached for her handbag to leave, she heard a faint tap on the door. Pulling the door open, Nelda found Daniel standing in the doorway with a somber look on his handsome face.

"I was hoping you and Sue would be in. I've just been told about Doris and I would like to hear what happened."

"Come in. We were on our way to break the news to Winnie. Do you know if she knows about the accident?"

"No, I don't," said Daniel walking into the room. "She didn't answer when I knocked on her door."

Sue offered a chair to Daniel, and then she and Nelda sat on the bed. Daniel's face and arms were red, as though he had had too much sun. He winched as he sat down in the chair.

"Well, let me tell you briefly what happened to Doris; then Sue and I are going down to Winnie's room. Maybe she'll be there by then."

"Here's the story. We all three signed up for the Fiesta Party Boat to Playa Sol. Sue and I didn't know that Doris was coming on that tour, so it was a surprise to us when we discovered she was on the boat. We invited her to be with us. After we arrived, we snorkeled out to a group of large rocks. We all climbed up on them and rested. After that Doris said she would sit there until Sue and I came back for her."

"How long were you gone?" Daniel leaned forward intently.

"Not more than fifteen or twenty minutes. When we came back, she was in the water at the base of a rock. We pulled her out and Sue tried CPR. It didn't work. We started calling for help. The shore police came out, took a lot of pictures and samples of slippery material from the rocks."

"Were they sure it was an accident?"

"The man in charge, Antonio Sanchez, seemed quite sure," Nelda said.

"Do the two of you think it was an accident?" Daniel stood up, looking down at them intently.

"We didn't see anyone in the area. The closest snorkeler was climbing out of the water near the beach." Nelda answered.

"Thanks, for telling me about it. It seems odd to me that two faculty members are now gone. Should I start worrying?" His clinched fists expressed frustration.

"Daniel, where were you today?" Sue asked him as he turned to leave."

He frowned. "So now I'm a suspect in two deaths?"

Nelda didn't smile. "Were you at Playa Sol?"

"Yes, I took the bus tour, but I didn't notice anything going on when I was there. We only stayed for an hour or so."

"Did you see Celeste at Playa Sol?" asked Sue.

Daniel looked surprised. "No, was she there?"

"We're not sure. Nelda and I saw a sailboat with a girl on board that looked like her."

"Look ladies, it looks like both deaths were accidental, so it might be better if you stopped all the probing. The happenings at Witherspoon Academy don't concern you anyway. Just enjoy your cruise."

"We'll keep that in mind, Daniel, but be sure to take care of that sunburn." Nelda opened the door and watched him as he disappeared down the hall.

"He certainly seems upset, Sue."

"I believe old Dan knows about the blackmailing. Maybe he was one of the victims too."

"Hum," muttered Nelda, "let's go. This has become a full fledged mystery."

"I was afraid of that," replied Sue, following her out the door.

*   *   *

Sue tapped lightly on Winnie's door. They heard a whirring sound inside the room, but no one answered the knock.

"You have to knock louder Sue. I think she's using the hair dryer and can't hear you."

Using her open hand, Sue tried again. This time the whirring stopped and Winnie pulled the door open. She was standing there barefooted in a white, terrycloth robe provided by the cruise line.

"Hello, Winnie, Sue and I thought we'd just see how you're doing. Could we come in for a minute?"

Winnie smiled and moved to one side so they could enter. "It's good to see you. I just got out of the shower and this room is a mess." She moved a pile of neatly folded clothes over on one of the beds. "Just sit there on Justine's bed. I'm almost through packing her things to ship back. The cruise line is taking care of it from there."

They sat on the bed, while Winnie stood stiffly in front of the dresser with her hand on the back of a chair. Nelda decided to get the bad news over quickly.

"Winnie, have you heard about Doris' accident?"

"Oh no, is Doris okay?"

"I'm afraid not. Doris drowned today."

Winnie sagged against the chair with her eyes closed. Sue and Nelda rushed over to her. They carried her to the bed, and then Sue began monitoring Winnie's pulse.

Nelda rushed to the bathroom for a wet washcloth. As she walked into the bathroom, her feet made a grating sound on the tile floor. Bending over, her hand felt sand, white sand.

CHAPTER NINE

Winnie Speaks Out

Winnie's green bathing suit was hanging on a towel rack in the bathroom. Nelda could see water dripping from it. The assistant librarian may not be the shrinking violet she and Sue thought she was. Where did she go swimming today? With a lot of unanswered questions on her mind, Nelda walked back to Sue with the wet wash cloth.

"She's coming around," Sue said as she placed the cloth on Winnie's brow. "Doris' death must have really been a shock to her."

Winnie's eyelids fluttered, and then her eyes opened. "What happened to me? I felt so lightheaded." She tried to get up, but gave up and lay still.

Nelda sat near her on the bed. "I guess the news about Doris was too much for you."

"What's happening to us?" She shook her head from side to side as the tears flowed.

"The authorities said Doris' death was an accident. Were you on one of those tours today, Winnie?" Nelda asked as Sue gave Nelda a funny look.

"I went to the beach. Why do you ask?"

"By yourself?"

"No, there were several of us that shared a cab. Why the interest in me, Nelda? You did say Doris' death was an accident."

NELDA SEES GREEN 75

"That's what they said, but I'm sure we need to all be accounted for at the time she died." Nelda patted the bed to give Winnie encouragement.

"Yeah, I guess it doesn't look good, two people dead from our group." Winnie found a tissue in her bathrobe pocket and blew her nose.

Nelda waited until she was sure Winnie had regained her composure before she continued. "Doris went with us on the party boat to Playa Sol. She drowned in the water there. But on the way over, she told us about your meeting at Sanders Bar and Grill. You want to give us your version of it?"

The assistant librarian sat up. "Why should I? I've been tortured enough." The tears started flowing again. She wadded the wet wash cloth up and threw it on the floor.

"We're on your side," Nelda said, comfortingly. "If Justine's autopsy comes back showing she may not have died accidentally, we're here for you."

Winnie looked from Sue to Nelda. "If something happened to Justine because of that meeting in the bar, I'll blame Celeste forever."

"Do you know who received the green dot?" Nelda's eyes never left Winnie's face as she waited for an answer.

Winnie slid slowly off the bed, retrieved her purse from a drawer, opened it and took out an envelope. She handed it to Nelda, who stared at its contents.

"Why did you keep this slip with the green dot, Winnie?"

Winnie's lips quivered. "To remind myself of how stupid I was to consider taking Justine's life."

Nelda thought there was a ring of truth to the statement, or maybe Winnie could be in line for an acting award.

"I'm sure Doris told you what Celeste said?"

"Yes, the person with the green dot would steal the EpiPen, so if she needed an injection it wouldn't be there."

Winnie's face was as white as the sheets on the bed. Her hands made clenched fists. "But it was all a joke. Celeste called us dummies. The joke was on us."

"That's enough talking for right now, Aunt Nelda. Let's go and let Winnie rest."

"One more question before we go, could you tell us why you were being blackmailed?"

Winnie worked on the knot in the end of the bathrobe belt—picking—pulling. She never looked up. Her voice was so soft, Nelda found herself bending over to listen.

"It wasn't right, I knew it wasn't right, but I helped the student's cheat on a state achievement test."

"Why did you do such a thing?" questioned Nelda.

"You wouldn't understand unless you've worked in a magnet school of last resort. These kids are so pitiful. I couldn't help myself." She finally untied the knot.

Nelda looked at the miserable, insecure girl on the bed and felt sympathy for her. "We won't abandon you, Winnie. Remember that."

They went out closing the door softly behind them. It was then that Sue gave an emotional response to their visit. "Aunt Nelda! What a sly fox Celeste is. I bet all three envelopes had a green dot in them."

*   *   *

Sue and Nelda, all dressed up for dinner, were seated in the Red Hot Piano Bar. They arrived early to unwind, something they needed to do badly. The same black man, whose name they now knew as Alex Tillman, who hailed from New Orleans, was playing a series of popular old numbers. He reached way back in his memory bank for this trio: Moon River, Stormy Weather and Star Dust. Songs even Sue could appreciate.

When Blackman took a break, Sue seized that opportunity to quiz her aunt about the interrogation of Winnie. She twirled her glass of white wine as she talked. "Aunt Nelda, I know you didn't want to talk about Winnie after we left her, but my curiosity has gotten the best of me. Do you suspect that weak girl of murder?"

Her aunt didn't answer right away. She took a sip of chardonnay, and discovered the taste was very nice with a just a hint of fruit and vanilla. Nelda knew she'd never be a connoisseur of fermented juices, but she did recognize the subtleties of a given wine. She had the same gift with people, the ability to look beyond the false fronts they presented.

"At this point, I don't know. But I think she's stronger than she pretends to be."

"You're not going to let go of these deaths are you?"

"No, can't do it unless I'm sure they were both accidents. I'm going to need help. Could you make an appointment for me to have a massage tomorrow? I want the same masseuse that Justine had."

"I'll do it. Guess you want all the gruesome details from her, huh?"

Nelda didn't smile. "Finish your wine and let's go eat. How does Bingo sound for tonight?"

"Very boring!"

*   *   *

When Nelda went to bed that night, she thought about how she'd get the masseuse to give her details of Justine's death. Perhaps she'd pretend she was a friend of Justine's, which really wouldn't be a lie. After all, she had set out to help her, even though her death came before she succeeded. She would also look for the massage oil she and Sue had given Justine for her birthday. As far as she could tell, it wasn't in the pile of things on Justine's bed; the ones being sent back home to Justine's next of kin. Of course, it could have been, and should have been, picked up by the detective, she rationalized. Finally, the whirling mass of faces, facts, and events took their toll. Nelda swallowed two aspirins before falling into a troubled sleep.

The next conscious moment Nelda experienced was Sue shaking her shoulder.

"Aunt Nelda, better get in high gear. You've got fifteen minutes to get to your appointment for a massage."

Her aunt groaned wishing she'd never made the appointment. She felt woozy and needed caffeine in the worst way. She sat on the side of the bed while Sue threw her some shorts and a shirt to put on. "Okay, okay, I'm moving, but if there's no coffee in that spa, I probably won't stay."

Sue was enjoying herself. Usually the shoe was on the other foot. "I bet they'll find something there for you. If not, you can just go back to sleep on the massage table."

Dressing in five minutes, which was a record for Nelda, she grabbed the room key and moved quickly to the elevators. Ordinarily she would have taken the stairs, but the spa was four decks up.

Stepping out of the elevator, Nelda went through double glass doors into the reception area of the spa. A pretty brunette looked up to ask her name, then pointed to a dressing room. There was a narrow hallway with dressing rooms for men and woman on one side. The massage rooms were across the hall. Nelda went into the dressing room area and was met by a rosy cheeked, blonde masseuse named Jane McDaniel.

The masseuse smiled as she looked at her slightly disheveled patron. "The top of the morning to you, Ms. Simmons, it's going to be a bonnie day. My name is Jane Mc Daniel."

"It could be, if I had a cup of coffee, and if you will call me Nelda."

"I'll see what I can do," Jane said as she handed Nelda a robe. "Take everything off except your panties and put your things in a locker. I'll be back in a few minutes."

Take almost everything off, with all those men around? Sue didn't tell her about the men across the way! Nelda guessed her niece was having fun with her, the prudish spy. Well so be it. She'd get this interview even if she croaked from over exposure and lack of caffeine.

By the time Jane returned, Nelda had removed her clothes and donned the terry cloth robe. The masseuse led her across the way to a massage room. It was dim, and small, however Nelda could smell coffee. She gratefully accepted a cup of Java while Jane adjusted the sheets on the massage table. There was Celtic music playing softly in the background.

"Jane, you're from Ireland?"

"Yes," I hope you don't mind the music. It brings a little bit of home to me."

Nelda was almost through with her coffee. She decided to make the plunge about Justine. "No, I don't mind the music at all, but there is something troubling me. I understand you were with my friend, Justine, when she died."

The Irish girl looked stricken. "Oh, it was such a horrible experience. In all the years at this job, nothing like that has ever happened."

"I know you've already told your story to the detective, but could you please tell me what happened? It would help me in so many ways."

Jane motioned for Nelda to get on the massage table. "Take off your robe, lie face down, and cover with the top sheet."

The middle aged sleuth obeyed, praying that Jane would describe Justine's final hour. The masseuse massaged Nelda's shoulders. She talked as she worked. Her speech had a tinge of the Celtic language.

"I swear on my mother's grave, Justine didn't show a trace of sickness when she arrived."

"Did you see her eating or drinking anything?"

"No! She didn't want to waste a minute of her massage time. Justine asked that I start with her arms, because her muscles were sore from some dancing she'd done."

Nelda pictured Justine gyrating in the Congo line the night they celebrated her birthday. "She was on her back when you started her massage?"

"No, I always start a massage face down, but I massaged her arms first."

"She was doing just fine, even though her muscles were like drumlins. Justine was enjoying the kneading, and pounding too."

"Drumlins?" questioned Nelda.

Jane explained. "Like hills, all drawn up." She waited a minute before she continued, moving her firm hands from Nelda's shoulders to her lower back. "The trouble didn't start until I asked her to turn over."

"What happened? Did she break out in hives or something?"

"Not that I could see. She started gasping for air. Justine was dying before my very own eyes." The masseuse stopped her circular motions on Nelda's legs to dry her eyes with a towel.

"Please don't blame yourself. I'm sorry you had to go through all that. Too bad Justine wasn't prepared for an emergency."

Jane's hands resumed massaging. "Thank you. Then this blonde American rushed over, from one of the massage rooms, to say Justine was having an allergic reaction. I called the doctor right away, but it was too late for him to help her."

Nelda was asked to turn on her back. When she flopped over, she could see a portable table with shelves holding expensive European products that you probably couldn't buy inland. Her eyes searched for the bottle of massage oil she and Sue had given Justine for her birthday, but couldn't locate it anywhere.

"Jane, my niece and I gave Justine a bottle of massage oil for her birthday. Did she bring it with her when she received her massage?"

The masseuse paused and briefly stopped her kneading. "I think so, now I remember, the oil wasn't absorbed by her skin very well, but it had a wonderful fragrance like outdoors. Things were so topsy-turvy I forgot to bundle it up with her clothes."

Nelda blamed the detective more, for that oversight, than she did Jane. "Do you have it on the shelf?"

"I'm not sure. Maybe one of the other masseuses borrowed it."

Nelda sat up, pulling the sheet over her chest. "Look my time is about up, how about seeing if you could locate that bottle."

Jane gave Nelda a worried look. "I don't see how the oil had anything to do with your friend's death."

"Probably doesn't, but let's see if we can find it." Nelda pulled on her robe, and then walked over to the shelves to see for herself. She went through the top shelf quickly before Jane could protest. Then Jane half-heartedly helped her look through the other two shelves. Nelda's persistence paid off. There was a bottle of Ocean Breeze on the third shelf behind a big fluffy towel. The sleuth was delighted to find it.

She held the bottle up to see how much was missing. The bottle was three-quarters full. Nelda unscrewed the top and smelled the contents, finding the same aroma as she and Sue had experienced in the gift shop. She carefully screwed the top back on the bottle.

"Jane, you need to inform Detective Moore right away about the oil, so he can pick it up."

"I don't see the reason for it," Jane said in an aggravated tone. "The oil was rubbed on her skin. She didn't drink it. Why don't you just take it and give it to him."

"Please do as I request, because I will ask the detective if you returned it. Everything surrounding an unnatural death is suspect. It wouldn't be proper for me to take it to him."

Nelda took one last look at the bottle's label, and then closed her eyes. Oh how stupid of me, she thought, now I remember. We didn't have a card for the gift, so Sue had written on the bottle label with a *permanent* ink pen, To Justine, from Nelda and Sue. This label is perfectly clean. The bottles of *Ocean Breeze* were switched.

CHAPTER
TEN

Bottle Dilemma

Nelda turned to Jane, "Has anyone else expressed an interest in Justine's death besides the detective and me?"

Jane thought for a minute as she pulled the sheets off the massage table. "There was one other person. I can't remember her name, but she said they taught together in the states."

"Could you describe her?" Nelda asked as she slid her feet into plastic slides.

"She was blonde and had the build of an athletic. Good muscle tone, very nice abs."

Nelda smiled. "Her name was Celeste?"

"Right, didn't ask as many questions as you." Jane pulled the door open and stood there with an armful of dirty linen. The bottle of ocean breeze was resting in her uniform pocket.

"Thank you for answering my questions. Your explanation helped me to understand what happened. Oh by the way, you give a great massage."

The masseuse made an impatient gesture for Nelda to precede her out the door. She seemed to be in a rush to leave. No doubt she was sorry she'd helped her patron find the bottle of oil. It might mean she'd receive a reprimand from the ship's detective for not mentioning the bottle.

"I'm going, I'm going," Nelda said, but don't forget to get the bottle of Ocean Breeze to Detective Moore or I'll send the banshee after you." She pointed toward the bottle in Jane's pocket.

Jane laughed out loud, "Female spirit indeed. Me thinks you've kissed the Blarney Stone."

The anxious sleuth hurried over to the dressing room before Jane decided to lock her in the small cubicle. She felt good about the information she'd obtained.

When she got back to the dressing area, she really hated to pass up the opportunity to use the big shower, fluffy white towels, plus soaps and lotions from a European company called Essence. It all seemed so glamorous, especially with the relaxing music in the background. But now she had a clue about Justine's death that had to be shared with Sue.

*   *   *

Instead of knocking on their cabin door, Nelda used her pass card to let herself in. She pushed open the door to find Daniel sitting in the only available chair chatting with Sue. Why was he here?—wondered Nelda. He didn't seem that happy to see us after Doris died.

"Aunt Nelda, have you finished your massage already? It seems you've only been gone a few minutes. But it's good you're here, because Daniel has news from Detective Moore."

Nelda now realized she shouldn't have passed up the shower opportunity at the spa. When she walked by the vanity, she peeked at herself in the mirror and saw a greasy creature with straight, stringy hair gazing back. Daniel's visit was not a timely one for the unwashed detective. If she was going to visit with him, she wanted the time set by her, not by him. However, her curiosity got the best of her.

"Forgive my appearance, Daniel. I need a bath the worst way, but before I jump in the shower, what did you find out?"

"Detective Moore said the autopsy proved that Justine died from an anaphylactic shock. They found peanut protein in her stomach."

"Any undigested peanuts?"

"No! And the authorities have documented it as an accidental death."

Nelda stood quietly for a few seconds. She licked her lips and could still taste the lemon balm that the masseuse had used on her. Most of her body was covered with it.

"Daniel, do you mind if I talk with you later about all of this? I've just got to get this sludge off my body."

"As a matter of fact, Nelda, I was wondering if you two could move to our table for the evening meals. Winnie is sweet, but not much of a conversationalist, and Celeste doesn't show up half the time."

Daniel turned his head toward Sue, showing his pearly whites. He was very handsome, with curly black hair that seemed to have a natural part. No, that wasn't it she realized; he had a long scar barely visible under his hair.

"Talk it over with Sue. Whatever she wants to do is fine with me." Nelda turned and made for the shower, checking to be sure her robe was hanging on a hook behind the bathroom door.

Now she had something else to worry about. Sue was a beautiful girl, was Daniel attracted to her? She knew Sue was vulnerable right now, not really sure of Walter's love. Maybe she should have insisted that they sit at their own table. Oh well, too late for second thoughts. She turned the shower on full blast. It will all come out in the wash, she mused.

When she came out of the bathroom, pretty boy had already gone. Sue was sitting there with a pleasant look on her face. Well what the heck, Nelda thought; it wouldn't hurt for Sue to have another young person around, as long as she remembered who she was promised to.

"Hurry it up, Aunt Nelda, in case you've forgotten, we're now in Cancun. We'll be gone all day on the bus tour to Tulum and Xel-ha."

"Slow down a minute," Nelda said, selecting shorts and a sleeveless shirt from the closet. "We have time for that chartered bus. I need one more cup of coffee and at least a sweet roll. Besides that, I'm just dying to tell you about the massage oil we gave Justine."

"Well, what about it? You don't mean it's still in the health spa?"

"I do and I don't." Nelda said, sitting down at the dresser, and brushing through her wet hair.

"What does that mean? The bottle was either there or not there."

Nelda continued dressing as she talked. "You might think so, but I imagine someone switched the bottles. I found a bottle labeled the same as the one we gave her, but it wasn't."

"How do you know?" questioned Sue.

"Do you remember me fussing at you for writing on the label of the bottle, because we didn't have a birthday card?"

"Sure, I used the permanent marker pen to write who the gift was from."

"Well," Nelda said, putting on her shoes, "your writing was not on that bottle."

"No big deal! I bet someone washed it off, so they could use the rest of the oil."

"Wrong," Nelda answered. "You just can't get that permanent ink off without destroying the label. Water or alcohol won't fade it. I know, because I've used the ink to mark towels and linens. Even with bleach in the water, it's steadfast."

"Okay, so you're telling me something in the bottle caused Justine's death?"

"Yes," said Nelda, "that's exactly what I think. Peanut oil was added to the massage oil and that's what killed her."

"Really, Aunt Nelda, that's pretty far out. You think Justine was so thirsty she took a slug of oil?"

"No, smarty, Justine didn't intentionally take the oil into her body. She either absorbed it through her skin or she had it on her face and licked her lips."

Gathering up their beach bag and towels, Sue mulled over what her aunt had said. "You know, you could be right. Even though the masseuse didn't put oil on my face, I put my head on my arms when I was on my stomach and got oil all over my lips. But it can't be proven without the bottle."

"How true, I'm sure it's disappeared forever."

"Let's hash this out on the bus. We've got thirty minutes and we still have to get you java and something to raise your cholesterol."

*   *   *

Sue and Nelda were comfortably settled on the air-conditioned bus ready for take off. The drive would take approximately forty-five minutes. Plenty of time to read the material they had brought along about the Mayan City they were going to visit.

Sue turned to Nelda. "The bus driver is selling sandwiches and drinks up front. I'll buy lunch for us before they're all gone. Chicken salad sandwich and coke okay?"

"Sure, and don't forget the napkins."

As soon as Sue left her seat, Nelda tried to concentrate on information about the Yucatan Peninsula and the Mayan culture, but her mind kept returning to the cause of Justine's death. Was there any chance of locating the bottle of oil she and Sue had given to Justine? Would the person that swapped the oils keep the stolen bottle? There were so many unanswered questions. To make matters worse, in giving the bottle of oil to Justine, she and Sue had provided the killer with a perfect vial for murder. But at least the syringe played no part in the librarian's death.

In a few minutes Sue came back with their lunch and a worried look on her face.

"Okay Sue, what's the problem, not enough money?"

"No, said her niece, settling in her seat. I just saw Winnie and her little old nose and eyes were red from crying."

"Now what? Did you ask her why she was in tears?" Nelda couldn't stand to see anyone distressed unless they deserved it.

"It didn't seem the thing to do with her seated next to the window. There was someone right beside her."

Nelda stood up. "Well, just let me out. I'll invite her to come back here with us. The seat next to me is empty."

"I was afraid of that," said Sue moving into the aisle.

When Nelda found Winnie, the young woman was sniveling into a tissue. Nelda spoke to her quietly. The petite brunette looked up through her tears and a small smile flitted across her face.

"Come sit with Sue and me," invited Nelda.

Winnie gathered up her belongings and apologized to the occupant in the seat next to her. She pushed past rapidly as though Nelda might disappear.

Trotting along behind Nelda, Winnie spoke in her whiney, shrill voice. "Oh Nelda, It's so good to see a person I recognize. Thank you for asking me to join you. I so wanted to see some of the places I've read about, but the thought of going alone got me very upset."

Sue had moved over to the window seat making room for Nelda and Winnie. She greeted Winnie with a big smile. "Glad you could join us, Winnie."

"You too, it's very lonesome in my cabin now. I never would have thought I'd say it, but I do miss Justine. Then, I laid awake all night thinking about the possible dangers we could be in."

"What do you mean Winnie? Do you think your life is in danger?"

Winnie squirmed in her seat. "Well, there are two of us dead already, and I also worry about this ship with all those foreigners working on it. I suppose it would be easy to blow it up. I stayed awake all night, scared about so many things."

Nelda put her hand on Winnie's arm. "I believe we're safe on the ship. Since 9/11 they've added additional measures to protect us."

"What about bombs, poison in our food or some group taking us hostage?"

"They use the same safety measures as the airlines," chimed in Sue. "Divers are sent down to examine the hull at every port."

"And all those foreign people that parade into our cabins have passkeys. That's why I haven't gotten out very much." Winnie's eyes teared up. One even made fun of me. He made a monkey out of a towel and put my reading glasses on it while I was out of the cabin."

Nelda laughed. "For goodness sakes, Winnie, they do that in every cabin. Sue and I have gotten a big kick out of the animals they make."

"Justine didn't like it either," whined Winnie. "She went back to our cabin the night before she died to put up her birthday gifts and the cabin steward was fooling with all the bottles sitting out. Maybe he poisoned her water when she went back out."

"Winnie, that's enough of that," Nelda said in exasperation. "Peanut protein killed her. That's what the autopsy showed. You just need to relax. Try to enjoy your trip, because we'll be headed back home tomorrow."

"That's true, the only time I really had a good time was the night before Justine's death."

"Well good, why don't you tell us all about the evening?"

Winnie's big brown eyes sparkled. "Didn't we have fun in the dining room at Justine's birthday party? The Congo line, gift giving and toasts were a blast. After that we all went to the casino."

"Who are 'we all'? Sue asked. "I thought you were going to split up and go to different places after dinner."

"We were, but I guess Daniel, Doris and Celeste must have felt bad that things didn't go well at dinner, it being Justine's birthday and all. They caught up with us after Justine left her gifts in our cabin and insisted we go to the casino with them. Daniel showed us how to play Black Jack. It was so much fun, because we were winning. Besides that, Justine loosened up with several cocktails bought by Daniel. The stories she told were hilarious."

"Sounds like a winner," Sue remarked. "Guess you were really late going to bed?"

"Justine was in bed before anyone else," snickered Winnie. "Celeste and Daniel insisted on taking her back to the cabin. That old librarian could hardly walk. Doris and I stayed in the casino another hour. When I finally went to bed, Justine was snoring loudly."

"Well it certainly seems you had a parade of people through your cabin that night," Nelda commented. She and Sue exchanged glances.

The middle-aged detective let her head rest on the back of the seat. Nothing comes easy, she reasoned. Now we have the cabin steward, Daniel, Celeste and Winnie, who could have poured peanut oil in our gift to Justine.

CHAPTER ELEVEN

Celeste Comes Clean

On the way to Tulum, the chartered bus stopped at a souvenir shop on the side of the highway. Everyone on the bus was invited to go inside and shop.

Nelda was still in the market for a straw-hat to wear when she worked in her flower beds. That thought made her think of home. She did hope Mrs. Marsh, who lives next door, was taking good care of her caladiums and roses. Nelda remembered how hard she'd labored over those flower beds to leave them in perfect shape.

Sue remembered she hadn't bought any little gifts for the girls in the clinic. Winnie decided she could use another box of tissue and maybe a few picture post cards.

As they trooped into the shop, Nelda lingered near a glass case filled with Mexican jewelry. She was enchanted with some of the pieces, but knew she wouldn't wear any of them. One item looked similar to the bracelet Celeste had worn at Justine's birthday party. It was made of square onyx stones mounted in heavy silver.

"Are you just going to stand there all day, Aunt Nelda? It'll be time for us to get back on the bus and you haven't bought anything."

"You're right." Nelda moved over to a rack of straw-hats hanging from a post. She selected a green one with a string tie that would allow her to keep it on her head even on a windy day.

"Aunt Nelda," Sue called. "You've just got to see this chess set. The pieces are beautifully carved from onyx. This precious stone must be plentiful here; so many things are made from it. Remember, you picked up a piece on the beach at Playa Sol?"

"That's it!" Nelda exclaimed. "What did I do with it Sue?"

"It's still in the beach bag. What's the interest in that?"

"That square piece could have come from Celeste's bracelet. She wore a silver bracelet with onyx squares to Justine's birthday party."

"You're really clutching at straws now. Tons of people were at the beach that day."

"That's true. I suppose I'll have to devise a way to find out if that piece is hers."

"Aunt Nelda, you are forever working on this case. Even the authorities haven't convinced you Doris' death was an accident."

Winnie walked up just in time to hear Doris' name mentioned. She clouded up again, but fortunately she had her new box of tissues under her arm.

"The kids are sure going to miss Doris," she whispered. They were always coming to see her, even when they weren't sick."

"Really? I didn't realize she was so fond of teenagers," Sue commented. "She complained about them when I was with her."

"Oh no, she had a list of favorites. Sometimes they asked permission to leave the library so they could visit with her."

"I guess there was a side of Doris I didn't know. We'll all miss her," Sue said.

"What did you get the girls in the office?" Nelda asked.

"Coffee mugs, you should see what they're drinking out of now, beakers and specimen bottles."

"Yuk," Nelda said and then laughed. "That's wanting coffee awfully bad. I hope they sterilized them first."

*　　*　　*

After settling down on the bus, Sue and Winnie took a nap, while Nelda opened up her guide book on Tulum. She needn't have bothered, because her mind was so full of details concerning the two deaths, there was no room for other thoughts. She put the book away and pulled a small notebook from her purse. What did she know about the circumstances surrounding these two deaths? Nelda decided to list the details in her notebook: Justine and Doris were faculty members at the Witherspoon Academy; Doris and Winnie said they were blackmailed by Justine; as a joke, Celeste passed out envelopes with green dots in them. Both Winnie and Doris received green dots, but no one stole her EpiPen; Justine died from ingestion of peanut protein; Doris died from drowning.

Nelda then listed things she needed to find out: What role did Daniel play in the deaths of Justine and Doris, if any? Was he also being blackmailed? Why was Celeste blackmailed? Who was responsible for switching the massage oil? Where were Celeste and Daniel when Doris' death occurred?

The bus jolted to a stop, causing Sue and Winnie to wake up. Nelda put up her notebook, but promised herself to visit Celeste and Daniel when she returned to the ship.

As they stepped off the bus a blast of hot air and dust enveloped them, but the sight of all those old buildings perched on top of limestone cliffs that led down to the turquoise waters of the Caribbean below, caused them to stare in awe. Winnie was the first one to speak as they entered the city through one of the five tunnels in the thick walls that surround the ancient city on three sides.

"I can hardly wait to hear what our tour guide has to say about all this."

"Well, I can wait," responded Nelda. "I'm going to be my own guide, with this book I purchased. Sue, maybe you'd like to join Winnie on the tour. I'm just going to wander around on my own."

"Okay with me, Aunt Nelda, I need someone to tell me about it, because I'll never take time to read your book."

There were several groups on the grounds of Tulum. Nelda watched her tour group gather in front of the large temple named El Castillo, before turning away toward the Temple of the Descending God. When she arrived, she walked up to the temple's platform, sat down and listened to the waves crashing below. Nelda wondered about these extraordinary people that lived so long ago. Their accomplishments rivaled those of the world's other great civilizations. Yet the exact origins of the Mayas remain unknown, a mystery that has never been solved. Nelda hoped she'd have better luck with her own mystery, the Witherspoon Academy Murder Mysteries.

Because of the relentless hot sun and crowds now gathering on the steps, Nelda decided to seek a shady, less crowded spot. She descended the worn steps slowly, but before she reached the ground, someone pushed her forward. Nelda threw out her hands as she braced for a fall. Her purses' contents scattered on the steps below. Two strong hands caught her on the brink of a major disaster. Nelda sunk to the next step and looked around. Celeste was already gathering up the items that had fallen out of her purse. She looked up and smiled as she handed them to Nelda.

"You'd never reach the water if you dove off here," she said.

"Oh my God, I could see my brains splattered all over those stone steps. Thank you for saving my life, Celeste. Did you see who pushed me?"

Celeste pointed toward a small boy scurrying down the steps with a plastic airplane in his hand. "I suppose the *chico* wanted to see you fly. Come sit here with me for a minute in the shade."

They found a spot out of the sun overlooking the ocean. The waves lapped against the ancient stones below while sea gulls circled in a cloudless blue sky. Nelda reveled in the scenery as they sat quietly away from the meandering crowd.

Celeste broke the silence. "I've not seen you since Doris' death, Nelda. I don't know if I buy the report by the police of an accidental drowning. Daniel told me how you said it happened, but I'd like to hear your version again."

Nelda looked at Celeste's beautiful face and saw a troubled weariness in her large, brown eyes. Perhaps this woman was not the self-centered, mischief making coach she had conjured up in her mind. Maybe Celeste could even be useful in giving her information she badly needed.

"I want to tell you everything about our outing with Doris, Celeste, even our conversation on the party boat before we arrived at Playa Sol. Some of that conversation concerns you."

Celeste smoothed her long, fly-away hair back from her face, and tied a folded, blue silk scarf around it, before giving Nelda her full attention. "Yes, tell me everything; I need to know."

"Well, first of all, she said you three girls had a meeting before leaving on the trip. It seems you wanted Justine dead because she was blackmailing all of you."

"Just wait a damn minute. That certainly wasn't my original idea. Doris came up with a plan before we even got there. She's the one that suggested it would be an easy way to put Justine away by getting her to eat peanuts."

"What about the green dots you passed out?"

"Okay, so that was a stupid joke. I didn't mean any of it, but I'm not sorry Justine's dead. She was bleeding us white for things we did that weren't all that bad."

"If it wasn't all that bad, why did you let her blackmail you?"

Celeste's eyes flashed anger as she turned away with her hands clenched. Nelda put her head in her hands, stupid me she thought; now I've blown my opportunity to get information. But the coach turned back with tears in her eyes.

"Each of us was asked to leave the public schools for minor infractions. Mine was for loving a married man, and I'd do it again in a heartbeat, even though you might think it's sinful.

"Yes, I do think it was sinful then and now too. I believe we saw you on a sailboat with that man at Playa Sol, the day Doris died."

Celeste stood up and put her hands on her hips. "So what! It's not my fault she drowned. I wasn't the one that left her-by herself—on a rock in the middle of the ocean. That is the correct version, isn't it?"

Nelda was wounded by her words, because she had spent a sleepless night dwelling on this very same blunder. She rose with tears stinging her eyes.

Celeste continued with her accusations. "Look, I'm sorry Doris died even though she was not the saint you and Sue seem to think she was. And as for Winnie, I've never seen a more pathetic, spineless sack of mush. I'm sure she filled your ears with gossip about me. But then again, she gossips about everybody. That's her middle name."

"Why on earth did you come on this vacation with them? Wouldn't it have been more pleasurable for you to book this trip by yourself?"

"I'm not going to say anymore. You can spy on me all you want to, but it won't do you any good. I'm not guilty of anything except loving my man." She walked down the steps and into the milling crowd below.

Nelda couldn't help but notice Celeste was wearing her onyx bracelet and there were no missing stones.

Sue found Nelda sitting on the bottom step of the Temple of the Descending God with her head in her hands. "What's wrong Aunt Nelda? This heat is getting to you, isn't it?"

"No, I'm fine. I almost fell from up there." Nelda pointed upward to the steps above her."

"Well, how did it happen?" Sue sat down beside her.

"Celeste said a little boy pushed me. She caught me just in time or I would surely have some broken limbs."

"So she was standing behind you when this happened?"

"Yes, I didn't know anyone was there, but she was, thank the Lord."

"Knowing you, this gave you an opportunity to talk to her. You feel like filling me in on what she had to say?"

"It's not very pretty. She admitted being happy that Justine was dead."

"That's no news. Tell me something I don't know."

"She practically accused me of letting Doris drown by leaving her on that rock. And believe me, Sue, I feel plenty guilty about that, if I had only been there."

"Nonsense, you're not guilty of anything except trying to help those people. What else did she say about Doris?"

"She said Doris was not the saint we thought she was."

"What did she mean by that?"

"For one thing she claims it was Doris' idea to feed Justine peanuts."

"She's lying, Doris wouldn't do that! Did Celeste admit to the sick joke with the green dots?"

"She did, and here's something else she owned up to. The reason she was dismissed from her previous school."

"I think I know already. She was sleeping with a married man, another coach."

"How did you know that?"

"Elementary my dear Nelda, I believe he's on this cruise. He's the man we've seen her with. Besides that, Winnie gave me that information a few minutes ago. The name of the Hunk is Richard Sinclair."

"Nelda laughed, "Good, old Winnie, she's probably still keeping some secrets from us. But I'm glad I talked to Celeste before I called Joe. He's just got to get me some background information on all of them."

"Daniel, the mystery man too?"

"I certainly haven't ruled anyone out. We know practically nothing about him."

"I do!" Sue gave Nelda a Cheshire cat grin and raised her eyebrows.

"What exactly do you know about him?"

"He's very good looking, has a winning personality, and Winnie said he's a great dancer."

"You're not attracted to him are you?"

"Relax, Aunt Nelda. You've got enough on your mind without worrying about me."

*　　*　　*

Nelda noticed their bus group was walking toward the exit. She and Sue hurried to catch up with them. After walking through the tunnel to the outside, they watched a troop of brightly dressed Los Olmecas Ototonacos de Veracruz Native Americans perform. The natives hung upside-down from a flagpole and presented a ceremonial dance. This exuberant performance lifted Nelda's spirits, causing her to make a generous contribution far exceeding the one dollar tip they asked for.

Nelda, Sue and Winnie were glad to board their air-conditioned bus, and greedily drank bottles of cold water offered to them by the bus driver. He assured them it would be cool when they entered the lagoons at Xel-ha.

"You didn't even bring your bathing suit, Aunt Nelda. What are you going to do while Winnie and I swim in the aquarium?"

"Look at fish and rest in a hammock between two trees."

"You're going to be talking to that good looking sheriff of yours aren't you?"

"When did you take up mind reading? I'll do that and then contemplate my next move."

Sue's eyes glistened as she gave her aunt a hug. "And if I were you, Aunt Nelda, I'd wonder about who really shoved you on the steps."

CHAPTER TWELVE

Trouble at Xel-ha

On the short trip from Tulum to Xel-ha Winnie sat between Nelda and Sue. She lectured on the accomplishments of the Mayan society in her little voice. "It's absolutely stunning, that's what it is. Why the Mayans' were the first people to cultivate chocolate, chili peppers, vanilla, papayas and pineapples. Their achievements rivaled other great civilizations of that day."

"Wow, chocolate," muttered Sue. "That's more outstanding then those old temples, pyramids or palaces."

Nelda reached over and tapped Sue lightly on the shoulder. "Don't be cute, Sue, what we saw today was called the Late Classic period, buildings built six to eight hundred years ago. It can't compare with their structures several hundred years earlier."

"Why no indeed," continued Winnie, referring to her guide book. "Besides all that, they had wonderful works of art and sculpture."

"Well, I'm sure you'll be able to use all that good information with your library students," Sue said yawning, "but let's concentrate on the future. What do you know about Xel-Ha?"

Winnie slumped in her seat. "All I know is what it says in the shore excursion description. It's a natural aquarium with two interlocking lagoons."

"Well I know something about Xel-Ha," said Nelda smiling. "It's a place where I can find a hammock hung between two trees, isolated from other people. And that's where I will chill out while you two swim or float down the river."

After that, Winnie closed her eyes refusing to continue any conversation. This gave Nelda a chance to relax, and figure out what information she wanted her sheriff friend, Joe Coats, to gather for her about the academy suspects.

There was some information she just had to have concerning each individual in the group. What previous high schools did they come from, and at what time did the academy employ them. She thought she knew the reasons Doris, Winnie, and Celeste were being blackmailed, but was Daniel a victim too? Joe could at least find out something about their backgrounds.

It certainly seemed obvious why Justine was killed—even how she was killed—but Doris was another story. Why was the nurse drowned? Could she be wrong about her death. The authorities thought it was accidental, was it? No way! So many unanswered questions. It was driving her nuts.

The more Nelda thought about the way Detective David Moore was handling the case, the less she thought of him as a detective. He should have personally gathered up all of Justine's things from the masseuse. Then, there wouldn't have been an opportunity for someone to exchange the bottles of massage bottles. That original bottle of oil would have proved it was murder. She needed to have another conversation with Moore about the bottles.

When Nelda looked over at Winnie and Sue, they were sleeping peacefully, their faces smooth and untroubled. She closed her eyes and was soon lulled to sleep by the hum of the buses' motor. Some minutes later she was awakened by Winnie pulling on her arm.

"Wake up, Nelda, we've arrived. I'm anxious to see the mangrove forest with the cool river flowing through it."

Nelda gathered by that statement Winnie knew a lot more about Xel-Ha than the information she gave Sue earlier.

*   *   *

Winnie and Sue headed for the dressing rooms. They changed into their bathing suits after deciding to take the wagon cart train to the entrance of the Riviera Maya River. They would journey down to the center of the park floating on inner tubes available to the tourists.

Nelda followed the beach on an unpaved path to a small inlet. There she found the perfect spot with a shaded hammock hung between two palm trees. Lush vegetation surrounded the area and gave her privacy from other tourists, but she still had a beautiful view of the crystal clear, turquoise lagoon. A few minutes after she had staked out her find, Sue and Winnie found her.

"Oh my Lord! Is there no place I can escape from the two of you?"

"Not on your life," answered Sue. "We need you to hang on to our belongings so we don't have to pay a locker fee. We're going to float down the river on inner tubes. By the way, we ran into Celeste in the dressing area. She's going to go with us."

"I'm happy for all of you. Now take your little, brown bodies off on your tube ride. I've got a phone call to make without you two hanging around."

Winnie didn't move, just stood there biting on her lower lip and twisting the beach towel in her hand. Her eyes swam with tears. Nelda thought sure she'd have to hand her a tissue, but the look faded and Winnie smiled. Now what brought that panic attack on? Nelda wondered.

"Grumpy old woman," Sue muttered under her breath, but loud enough for Nelda to hear. She laughed as Nelda set out to chase her with a piece of driftwood washed up on the beach.

After running out of gas, Nelda sat down in the hammock. "You girls stay with the others in the group. I've read about the fresh water sinkholes, so be careful."

They promised to be back in a couple of hours, and then set out to follow the path back to the group of tourists waiting for the wagon carts to take them where the river flowed through the forest. As Nelda watched them walk away, she had a small tinge of regret that she wasn't going with them. Should she watch over Sue like a mother hen? One of those girls going with her could be a murderer. As soon as she made her phone call she'd check on them. Her phone call to Sheriff Jim Coats was something she just had to do now. Their journey back home would start tomorrow.

Alone at last, she thought, lying here in this shaded hammock trying to relax, and thinking of how to word thoughts about the deaths to Joe. Memories of that old rough sheriff made her smile. Maybe, we could become serious about our relationship. All at once Nelda realized it had been a long time since she'd patted the empty bed beside her at night and cried of loneliness. The ghost of her husband was finally fading. Perhaps it was a good sign that she was putting the dead to rest, so she could enjoy living without guilt.

She jumped when she heard voices coming from the little inlet next to her. There was no one near her when she'd staked out her claim. The sounds were muffled by thick shrubs and palm trees that divided the coves, but one voice sounded so familiar she had to investigate. She carefully parted the bushes in one small area, so she could peep through them. There was Daniel in a blue bathing suit with a towel around his shoulders. The scar on his head was more visible now since he had acquired a tan. He was sprawled out on the sand talking to an older man in red shorts that looked like a bodybuilder. A big white ice chest sat between them. Mr. Muscles leaned against a palm tree and drank a can of Mexican beer. His sun-baked face sported a growth of shiny stubble. Above his dark blue eyes, his white yachting cap angled jauntily on his head exposing a golden mass of curly hair.

Listening through the small opening she had made in the shrubs, she could hear the conversation without too much difficulty. Daniel spoke with more than a little envy about the other man's sailing boat. "Richard, that's one gorgeous sailboat you have. Does that belong to you or did you rent it?"

"Ha, I wish. It belongs to a college buddy that spends his summers here. His salary is a little more lucrative than a high school coach."

"I can understand that. Where is Celeste? I thought I saw her headed this way."

"She left to ride the inner tubes with that little librarian, Winnie, and Sue somebody, who's on the cruise with them. They'll be back soon."

"That's some gal you have."

"She's a special part of my life and is always waiting for my call."

Daniel dug his fingers into the white sand, gathering the wet grains into a ball. "I had a wonderful girl too, but now she's gone. I don't know if I'll ever get over it." He threw the ball of sand toward the trail.

"Sorry Mate," he said quietly opening up the white chest. "Did she find someone else?"

"No, she's dead."

"That's really tough. I'm glad you recognized me and stopped to talk. Have one of these Mexican beers, they're not too bad." He reached out with a glistening, brown bottle."

"Thanks, I appreciate it," said Daniel accepting the drink. "Are you going to make Celeste an honest woman soon?"

"Not in this life time. I've got a wife and three kids to take care of. I'm sure not going to pick up another liability."

Nelda put a hand over her mouth and ran back to the hammock. What a low down sports jockey Richard was, leading Celeste on to think he'd marry her. This illicit romance was headed for troubled waters and she couldn't do anything about it. Of course Celeste had to take some of the blame. She was reminded of that old cliché, "It takes two to tango."

She shook her head and tried to concentrate on her phone call to Joe. Every time she used the small cell phone Joe had given her, she marveled at how her voice could be heard hundreds of miles away. Communication had come a long way since Bell invented the telephone in 1878. She didn't even want to keep up with the latest fads in cell phones; it was mind boggling.

Nelda walked to the other side of her inlet to make her phone call. She wanted to get as far away from Daniel and Celeste's lover as she could, eavesdropping could go both ways.

Unfolding the small, silver phone, Nelda proceeded to punch in Joe's cell phone number. She tried to hold the instrument by its edges so she wouldn't cut the phone off by accident, as she had done so many times before. She still found it very aggravating to use the thing. It gave a few half hearted rings and then Joe's voice rang out.

"Hello, Joe Coats here."

"Joe, this is your favorite snoop. Are you missing me?"

"Nelda! I was wondering when you'd call. It's been lonesome as the devil around here without you. You're coming home Saturday aren't you?"

"Yes, but it might be late. I'll call you when I get in. Could you scrape up a little information for me on the academy group?"

"I'm way ahead of you. I gathered information about all of them for that ship detective, David Moore. Has he shared it with you?"

"No, guess he figured he didn't have any reason to do that. Anyway he's convinced the two deaths were accidental."

"Two, are you saying someone else died besides that Justine Scales?" Nelda could hear the aggravation in his voice.

"Yes, Sue's nurse friend, Doris Hodge, drowned while we were swimming. I think someone pulled her off a rock she was sitting on. She hit her head and drowned."

"You shouldn't be messing around with those people. It's too dangerous. If there is a murderer in the bunch, he or she is not going to appreciate you sticking your nose into things. Come on home and let me handle it. They live in our county you know."

Nelda fought back the urge to tell Joe she could take care of herself. He always seemed to treat her as though she was fragile, not quite up to the job at hand. This was so different from her late husband Jim, who believed she could solve anything. Now, she was always proving herself.

"Joe, thanks for caring about me, but would you please give me the information before I go ballistic."

"Slow down, Nelda, here is the scoop. This is why those teachers didn't have their contracts renewed. Doris Hodge flushed marijuana down the toilet for a student. Celeste Fogelman shacked up with the head football coach; he is married with children. Winnie Speer had emotional problems."

"Emotional problems?" Questioned Nelda. "That's not what she told me. She said she helped some students cheat on the state achievement test."

"Well, that's what the principal from her previous school said. He said she was always crying and complaining about everything. She wouldn't seek help. He had no alternative, but to let her go."

"I wonder which version is true. Naturally he wouldn't want the state to know his students cheated. His school would be on the black list with low test scores. Did you find out anything about Daniel Hall?"

"You bet, you've got yourself a hero in that bad little academy group. He's an ex-Navy Seal, who was wounded in Iraq saving the lives of three other men."

"Oh, so that's how he got that scar on his head. Was he married?"

"No, and his parents live in Houston, they're retired teachers."

"What about Justine Scales, anything on her background?"

"Nothing really bad, she'd been the head librarian at the academy for the last ten years. Her teacher evaluations show that she's had some run-ins with some of the parents for being too strict, other than that they were good reports. In fact, the principal at the academy was very upset when he found out she was dead."

"Thanks, Joe, for the information. I'll get the names of those schools from you Saturday night. And don't worry, I'll watch my back."

"You better, I won't forgive you if you get hurt."

She turned off the power on the cell phone. In her mind, there was the image of Joe sitting in his office with a worried look on his face.

*   *   *

Time passed quickly, Nelda was stretched out in her hammock reading the ship's newsletter for Friday when Sue came running into the cove.

"Oh, Aunt Nelda, come quick. Something happened to Winnie. She was there one minute and gone the next. We've got to find her. This is terrible! Terrible! I can't believe she vanished so fast." Sue broke down sobbing,

"Hold on, Sue." Nelda rolled out of the hammock, sliding her feet into her sandals. "You were floating on the inner tubes and Winnie disappeared? I can't believe it. Weren't you all together? I knew I should have gone with you. It could have been you."

"It's not that simple, Aunt Nelda. We floated down the river, but each of us had our own inner tube. I was first, Celeste was second and Winnie was third. We were spaced pretty far apart. We rounded two bends and when we came out of the second bend, Winnie was no where in sight."

"There were other people on this float. Didn't they see her?"

"That's what I'm trying to tell you. She's disappeared. I'm afraid she might be drowned."

CHAPTER THIRTEEN

Unbelievable Catch

Nelda and Sue trotted along the shore of the river to the bend where Winnie had disappeared. Celeste, Daniel and Richard huddled together at the edge of the water. The trio turned toward them when they heard footsteps.

"Has Winnie been found?" Nelda asked, after taking several deep breaths.

"No," answered Daniel. "We've searched the two bends in the river and found nothing. Her inner-tube floated back without her. Someone went for help from the park employees."

"Come on Sue, let's investigate for ourselves. She might be under some vegetation floating in the river." Nelda's face was white, because she feared another death. How could all this be happening right under her nose? She shook her head and bit her lower lip, some detective she turned out to be.

Sue watched her aunt react to the news. "We'll do it, Aunt Nelda, but you've got to calm down. You're going to make yourself sick. You're not to blame!"

"You're right, blaming myself won't help one bit, just use up energy. We'll walk slowly along the shore and pay close attention to anything partially submerged or floating in the water. Also look for places where she might have come ashore. If she did, there'll probably be flattened plants where she stepped."

The banks of the river were fairly easy to travel, if they kept to the trail made for the wagon cart train, but if they deviated from the trail, the vegetation on the banks became a real obstacle.

Sue gave a shrill cry. "These vines and roots we're wading through are tearing my legs and feet up. I've got to stop and clear the stuff out of my shoes."

"I'll have to admit, rubber boots would be more fitting for this journey. We'll turn back after the next bend." Nelda said.

They had stopped next to a mangrove tree that had many roots radiating out on the surface of the mushy ground. Nelda searched the surface of the river with her eyes while Sue cleaned out her sandals. She thought she saw something pinkish on a log in the water near the bank; hurriedly she climbed down to have a better look. Something moved, was it a snake, frog or what? And then she heard a little moan causing her to lean forward. Her feet slid out from under her and she rolled down to the edge of the river. Sue rushed to help her up.

"I'm okay, Sue, look at that log; do you see anything on it?"

"Fingers! Small pink fingers. You've found her," she shouted.

Nelda was overjoyed. She hobbled the rest of the way to the log with Sue right behind her. When she located the hands holding onto the log, she leaned over for a better look. Winnie's little face was pressed to the other side of the timber with her eyes closed.

"Come help me Sue. I know she's alive by the way she's clutching that wood. We'll drag her over to the wagon trail." Nelda looked up in the sky and whispered "*Deo gratias.*"

"There you go again, Aunt Nelda, talking to yourself in that unknown tongue."

"Some people know it, Sue. I was just thanking God for helping us find her. Do you know if she'll need CPR? I heard her moan."

"We'll see about that after we pull her out of the water." Sue walked out on the log and sat down near Winnie, then tried to pry Winnie's hands loose but she couldn't budge them. "Her hands are clinging to the log like they were glued on. I'm afraid I'm going to break her fingernails off."

Nelda tested the water depth with a stick. It was shallow enough for her to wade out in it. Carefully she moved through the water until she was by the side of Winnie. She spoke to her in a quiet tone. "Let go of the log, Winnie, Sue and I are here to help you."

Winnie opened her eyes, lifted her head and looked at Nelda, then sighed, as though a heavy weight had been lifted from her small body.

"Try again, Sue. I think she knows we're here to help her."

This time Sue's tugging worked, Winnie's hands came off the log, and Winnie let Nelda put her arms around her shoulders, supporting her in the water. With Sue's help, they pulled her to the wagon trail and laid her down.

"Sue, I know you're tired, but would you mind going back to tell the park employees we've found her? They'll need to bring a wagon for her to ride back in."

"No, no, of course not, I'll be back as soon as I can find someone to transport her. And she's probably okay if she didn't swallow too much water." At first Winnie just laid there sprawled out on the ground, but in a few minutes she sat up. Nelda observed the color in Winnie's face was good and her breathing was nice and steady.

"Feel like talking, Winnie?"

"I'm so happy you found me, Nelda. I thought I was a goner."

"Well, you were practically on the bank. Why didn't you get out?"

"I ran out of energy. Someone tried to kill me," she sobbed. "It seemed like I treaded water forever."

"I'm so sorry, Winnie. Did they attack you in the water? I see you're missing your life preserver too."

"It's all so muddled in my mind," she said, squirming around with her hand over her mouth, then came the sniffling and more crying.

Nelda handed her a beach towel, and fought back her distaste for this slight librarian who seemingly used ever situation to shed tears noisily. How could this creature even hold a job? The constant leaking of her nose appeared analogous to a leaky faucet.

"Why don't you tell me what happened? Start at the very beginning of your float down the river."

Winnie twisted on the towel as she talked. "We were the last floaters in the water. At first Sue, Celeste and I were floating along together, and then we drifted apart. There were bends in the river, and if you were caught in a swirling current, you didn't move as fast. That's what happened to me. I found myself a couple of bends away from the others. I know it was foolish, but it was so warm I unfastened my life preserver and took it off." She paused, smoothing down the skirt of her green bathing suit. Nelda recognized it as being the same suit she'd found hanging in Winnie's bathroom the day Doris drowned.

"Go on," urged Nelda, "then what happened?"

"It's going to be hard for you to imagine, Nelda. Whoever was trying to kill me actually swam under my tube and pushed me out of it."

"Did you see who it was?"

"Oh no, whoever it was stayed submerged, using a snorkel to breathe."

Nelda couldn't picture that scenario. "Are you sure about the snorkel? It seems like the big inner tube would keep the person from using it."

"Well, maybe they didn't use it when they went under the tube. But I know I saw a snorkel above the water, before, who ever it was, forced me out."

"How did you escape from your attacker?"

"I'm really not sure. There was some debris floating around and I got in the middle of it. I continued treading water and swimming until I saw the log. Believe me, I was so tired by then, I grabbed hold of it like it was a life preserver."

"You poor lamb. What can I do for you until they get here with the wagon?"

"I know this is going to sound strange, but did you bring any bottled water?"

Nelda smiled, dug around in the beach bag and handed Winnie a half bottle of water. She reflected on Winnie's story while the thirsty woman drank the contents of the bottle. The events surrounding Winnie's attack were indeed baffling.

*   *   *

There was a note addressed to Nelda hanging on the door of their cabin when they returned to the ship. As soon as they had dumped all the wet clothes in the bathroom, Nelda tore open the envelope and found an invitation to meet Detective Moore in the library at 5:00 p.m.; no explanation was given for the meeting.

"What do you suppose that's all about?" asked Sue, when she found out the contents of the note.

"I think it's the prodding of that worry wart sheriff back home. I just know he's called Moore and asked him to share information with me."

"Do you think Uncle Joe would have that much influence over him?"

Nelda whirled around and frowned at Sue. "What do you mean Uncle Joe?"

Sue had an impish look on her face. She plopped on the bed and said, "Let's face it, Aunt Nelda, you know you've got a romantic thing going for Joe Coats, and you just won't own up to it. And I say it's about time. As far as I can tell, you've been a widow for too long."

"How about me deciding when I'm ready for romance? It's true, I'm attracted to him, but I want to spend my Golden Years enjoying them. That's why the man I choose to love will have a life philosophy similar to mine."

Sue yawned. "I sure wish we had a couple of hours for you to explain your purpose for living to me, Aunt Nelda, but it will have to be later. It's already 3:30 p.m.," Sue said with a grin.

Nelda tossed Sue a towel. "Okay, Featherhead, I'll take a quick shower first. I can hardly wait to see if the detective might have some information I don't have."

*   *   *

On the way to the ship's library, Nelda had time to think about Sheriff Joe Coats. She remembered the first time she met him; it was right after her first cousin, Laura Finch, was killed from drinking strychnine. Joe was the sheriff that took over the investigation. She could remember in detail the short, stout, moon-faced man with the ruddy complexion that made everybody aware that he was in charge and didn't need any help solving the case. Of course, she didn't pay any attention to that and solved it with little help from him.

Nelda didn't remember when their animosity had turned to friendship and then into a deeper feeling of affectionate regard. There certainly were many positive things about Joe. He was caring, tender, loving and above all, of good character, but his other traits made Nelda nervous. She remembered his tendency toward being in control of all situations, and he worked hard to restrain a bad temper. One thing Nelda had learned in her experience with people, it is difficult (if not impossible) to change them and especially those pass fifty. At this point in her life, Nelda took comfort in being her own boss, plus having complete harmony in her home. Now, who am I kidding, she thought, of course I love Joe's company. His kiss definitely sent a tingle down my spine. Sue is right; the romance will continue."

Her thoughts were interrupted by the sight of Detective Moore standing in the hall outside the ship's library. At the sight of Nelda, he stroked one side of his mustache while giving her his practiced, fixed smile.

"Ms. Simmons, it's good of you to take time out to see me. Please come inside, I've some additional information to give you about the deaths of the two ladies."

Moore was dressed like a tourist in a printed shirt depicting brightly colored birds of the rain forest, light weight slacks of pale green and leather sandals. He followed her inside carrying a large folder bulging with papers and a brown paper bag filled with something. They sat at a table near the row of computers. Nelda was not surprised to see the library empty; it was almost dinner time.

"Thanks for thinking about me. What additional information do you have?"

"You were right about two bottles of massage oil. They are now both in my possession."

Nelda was flabbergasted. "You have the original bottle that my niece and I gave to Justine?"

"Yes, yes we do. I'd like for you to identify it."

"Of course, I'd be happy to. I'm sure you checked it for fingerprints and the contents for peanut protein."

Moore smiled with his mouth, but his eyes were deadly serious. "Do not underestimate our skills, Ms. Simmons." He handed her some plastic gloves and pulled out the bottle of Ocean Breeze massage oil with his handkerchief.

It looked like the very same bottle, with their birthday message and signatures on the side of the label. Now it was only half full of the green liquid. Nelda pulled on the gloves and turned it over slowly in her hands. "I certainly believe this is the bottle we gave Justine. Where did you find it? And more important, was there peanut oil in the bottle?"

"It was located in one of the massage rooms. There was no peanut oil mixed in with the Ocean Breeze massage oil. And as for fingerprints, it was loaded with them, all belonging to the masseurs."

She handed the bottle back. "What do you suppose happened to our fingerprints?"

"Wiped off. Occasionally, the masseurs have to wipe off the bottles. They get so oily."

"I suppose we'll never know where the peanut protein came from that killed Justine."

Moore placed the bottle back in the bag and stood up. "That's true. I regret the accidents, Ms. Simmons, but that's all they are. Believe me I will be so happy when the rest of you are safe and sound back in the states."

He didn't mention the incident with Winnie. Nelda didn't know if he knew about it, but even if he did, she didn't see any point in discussing it with him. There was no way to prove Winnie's misfortune happened the way she told it.

She stuck out her hand and the detective shook it gently. "Thank you for sharing this information. I hope you're right about these deaths. The color of green has taken on an ominous meaning for me."

*　　*　　*

When Nelda arrived at the Red Hot Piano Bar, she discovered Sue, Daniel and Celeste seated in a booth. They stopped talking as she approached the booth. Sue moved over and made room for her aunt.

Daniel spoke up. "Did Moore comment on Winnie's mishap?"

"No, I don't know if he knew about it and I didn't bring it up. I'm not sure Winnie had her facts straight. Will she be at dinner tonight?"

"No," replied Celeste. "I'll bring dinner to her; she complained about being very tired."

"I can sure understand that," replied Nelda. "She said she treaded water for a very long time."

Celeste threw her head back and laughed. "Let me tell you something, Nelda. That little, old wimpy thing can swim circles around my swim team. The reason she's not here is not from swimming. It might be she doesn't want our company."

"Why don't we enjoy our last night on board?" Daniel asked. I for one am willing to forget all the unfortunate events for the time being."

Nelda was happy Daniel saved her from explaining why she had a conference with Detective Moore. However, all the happenings were whirling around in her mind. Winnie's mishap just added to the unsolved mysteries.

Even though Nelda had not known Justine or Doris well, she could not shake off their losses as easily as Daniel. A feeling of sadness filled her "happy hour."

CHAPTER FOURTEEN

Last Night Out

As they gathered around the dinner table for the last night on board, Adolfo, their waiter from San Salvador, was hovering over them with menus that listed dishes Nelda could not afford to order in the states. Her favorite seafood was lobster.

"I'll have the lobster dinner with all the trimmings," Nelda said.

"Do you know how high that dish is in cholesterol?" chided Sue.

"I don't give a fig," replied Nelda. "Put away your medical knowledge for one night and let me live it up."

Daniel observed the bickering between niece and aunt with a big grin. "And I'll order a bottle of wine to go with your lobster, Nelda; you've helped make this cruise bearable, even with all the bad things that have happened. You have a way of trying to help all of us feel better about ourselves and I thank you for it." He ordered a bottle of Napa Valley Chardonnay and for himself a rib eye steak.

Nelda was touched by Daniel's speech. She didn't know how she had helped him. He was still a mystery man to her, even though she now knew his military involvement. She'd try to learn more about him when they got home.

Sue and Celeste each ordered baked flounder, then an order to go, sautéed shrimp for Winnie.

The wine arrived before the food, so Daniel proposed a toast after Adolfo filled their glasses. "Here's to all the ladies present. May the rest of the year be filled with joy and contentment."

"What a wonderful toast," Celeste declared. "What are your plans for the summer, Daniel? I heard you were taking the summer off."

"I don't know. My life is in a bit of a funk right now." He looked down at the table, then excused himself. "I'll be back," he mumbled as he walked away.

"What was that all about, Celeste?" asked Sue, frowning. "You know him better than we do."

"He has a right to be depressed. He was wounded in Iraq, and still has terrible headaches from that. As if that wasn't enough, his girlfriend committed suicide while he was in the hospital."

Before Nelda had an opportunity to utter her dismay, Adolfo and his helper arrived with the food, and shortly after that Daniel returned to the table. His sinking spell seemed to have abated. He sat down with a lonesome look on his face.

Nelda watched the group while they feasted and visited with each other. What a good looking trio they were. Celeste's white sundress really showed off her bronzy tan. She seemed quite happy, unaware of the heart break she would face with her married lover. Daniel, whose smile masked the pain he must feel at the thought of his fiancée, was handsome in a navy blue jacket with white pants. It seemed he had a lot of mending to do, physically and mentally. And dear Sue-looking so young in her sky blue dress-could hardly wait to be with Walter. Nelda hoped this trip had made Sue realize that waiting a few months to marry wouldn't make a difference in the love she and Walter had for each other.

Her thoughts turned to Winnie, sniffling away her last night on board in her cabin. Could she have told that story about her attack in the water to bring attention to herself?

Why would she do such a thing? Nelda found herself drowning in all the unanswered questions. Her thoughts were interrupted by Sue.

"Hellooo, Aunt Nelda, from planet Earth. Could you beam down and help us make up our minds about how we'll spend our last night on board?"

Nelda laughed. "I was just watching all you beautiful people, and wondering why you'd want an old lady among you."

"Don't be absurd," Daniel said, "experience is what we need at a time like this. What's your vote, Nelda?"

"I cast my vote for the Mardi-Gras Party. Haven't been to one in years. It might bring back some good memories."

Daniel watched Sue and Celeste nod their approval. "Well, we can start out there and who knows?"

"Did everyone remember their gratuities for the waiters?" Nelda asked. "I for one would like to bring home our chef, waiter and cabin steward. They've been great."

Celeste pulled out her envelopes and laughed. "Right, especially that cute waiter from Brazil. And thanks for reminding us about the tips. I know how important they are. Tips from waiting on tables, helped me make it through school."

"Hey, we need some pictures with our waiters," said Sue. The grinning waiters gathered around the table, while a man from the next table volunteered to take pictures for them with Sue's camera.

Before leaving, Nelda made sure Celeste had Winnie's dinner to go. They all agreed to meet on the upper deck for the Mardi-Gras Party at 9:30 p.m.

*   *   *

After making the trip back to their cabin, Nelda deluged Sue with questions while her niece checked her makeup in the vanity mirror.

"I've been thinking about Winnie, Sue. Do you suppose there is any merit to her story about being attacked?"

"For heaven's sake, Aunt Nelda, how should I know?"

"You said Celeste was on a float between you and Winnie. Was there ever a time you couldn't see Celeste?"

Sue put down her lipstick. She leaned back and thought for a few seconds. "Yes, I couldn't see her when we rounded a bend in the river. But the time was too short for her to swim up stream and get to Winnie."

"Well, that settles that. It couldn't have been Daniel either. He was visiting with Richard Sinclair, Celeste's lover"

"How do you know that?" Sue asked, sitting by Nelda on the bed.

"I saw them and heard their conversation. They were in the next inlet on the beach. We were separated by some thick bushes."

"Aunt Nelda, you're incorrigible. I bet you towered over the bushes so you could hear them better."

"No, I didn't," answered Nelda, appearing to be insulted. "I just divided the bushes. I found out some interesting things."

"Like what?"

"Well, for one thing, I found out about Daniel's head wound."

"Is that it? You're keeping something back."

"Okay, I'll tell you this, but you're not to discuss it with anyone. Richard Sinclair is leading Celeste on, and will never divorce his wife and marry her."

"The whole affair is disgusting. Whatever she gets she deserves. After I'm married to Walter, if some woman came between us, I'd scratch her eyes out."

"Good grief, what a thing to say. Besides, Walter is not the type."

Nelda got up and stretched. It had been a long day, she thought. Maybe I shouldn't go to the Mardi-Gras Party. I've really had enough excitement for one day. On the other hand, Sue is displaying a surplus of energy.

"Another thing I've been dying to ask you, Aunt Nelda, why did the detective want to see you?"

"Another bummer. He found the bottle of massage oil we gave Justine. It was in one of the massage rooms. Finger prints were wiped off."

"As weird as it may seem to you, Aunt Nelda, there could be a chance that these deaths were both accidental." She hopped off the bed and looked down at her watch. "Let's go, it's party time."

"I'm really bushed, Sue. Why don't you go ahead and join them. I'll probably check on Winnie before I go to bed."

"Oh come on! You were the one that decided where we were going. I'm disappointed in you."

Nelda knew that disappointment would last long enough for her to join the others. "I really wouldn't be any fun, Sue. I'll visit with Winnie for a little bit then hit the sack. You'll have fun with Celeste and Daniel."

"I suppose so. But look, if you change your mind come join us, we'll be there for at least the next two hours." Sue bussed Nelda on the cheek before going out the door.

*   *   *

As she closed the door on her way to Winnie's cabin, Nelda saw her cabin steward. He smiled and gave Nelda a sheet stating that all the pictures taken by the photographers associated with the cruise ship were on display in the Photo Gallery. This would be the last opportunity for anyone to buy them.

"Thank you for reminding me, Juan. I'll go up right now and look at them."

Nelda walked up the stairs instead of taking the elevator. She would surprise Sue with a copy of all of the pictures they took together. It would be fun for her to add them to her scrapbook. It might help her remember the details of the trip, as if she could forget!

The Photo Gallery was not crowded. Pictures were displayed on screens set up in rows. They didn't seem to be in alphabetical order. Nelda smiled as she found the one of Sue and her with a pirate shouldering a parrot. After removing it from the screen, she located the two of them posing with the ship in the background. There was one taken at the Captains Cocktail Party, but she was having trouble locating it. Suddenly, she came upon a picture taken at Justine's birthday party. Nelda's eyes filled with tears. There they all were, so very happy: Justine blowing her candles out; Doris and Winnie pretending to help her; Sue clapping while Celeste gave thumbs up. Daniel was watching with amusement, and Nelda was ready with her cake plate. She decided she's get several of this one, so she could give Winnie one too. Giving up on the picture she couldn't find, Nelda paid for the ones she did find and hurried back to her floor. She wanted to talk to Winnie, before the girl retired.

Nelda stood in front of Winnie's cabin listening for signs of any activity inside. She didn't hear anything, but decided to knock anyway. To her surprise Winnie answered the door dressed as though she was going out. She was startled to see Nelda standing there.

"Hi Nelda, I thought you'd be out with the others."

"No, could I come in and visit with you?"

"Well sure, I was just going out to get some ice. I'm parched after my misadventure today."

Nelda walked into the room; the smell of shrimp was unmistakable. "Guess you got your dinner?"

Winnie looked at her wastebasket and laughed. "I'll be right back, Nelda. We'll have a drink together."

"Sure, go on. I'll just wait here for you."

Winnie had been packing; clothes were neatly stacked all over the room. Nelda moved a stack of clothes out of a chair so she could sit down.

It wasn't long before Nelda had as much of the shrimp smell as she could take. She walked over to the trash can and dug out the container holding what was left of the shrimp dinner. As she pulled it out, she turned over the basket scattering litter everywhere. "What a mess," Nelda muttered to herself. As she rushed to gather up the debris, she noticed Winnie had thrown away her receipts from using her credit card. Nelda was shocked by the carelessness of the young librarian. How would Winnie check the charges on her bill? After gathering up a handful of the slips, her hand remained motionless. The charge on top was for a massage the day after Justine died. She closed her eyes and took a deep breath. Was there also a charge for the massage oil? The door opened and Winnie walked in carrying a bucket of ice.

"What's going on, Nelda?"

"I've made a mess here. That shrimp you left in the waste basket smelled up the place, so I pulled out the container and accidentally turned over the basket."

"Well don't worry about it. Here let me help you."

Winnie turned around to set the ice bucket down. Nelda stuffed the receipts in her pocket, and gathered more papers off the floor. She waited for Winnie to pull the trash bag out of the basket, and then dumped the remaining litter in the bag. Winnie put the trash bag outside the door, before making them a drink.

"All I have is Coke, Nelda, is that okay?"

Nelda breathed a sigh of relief and sat down. "Sure, and I must say you're looking fine after your ordeal today."

Winnie handed Nelda her drink and plopped down on Justine's bed. "I was just tired and scared."

"That's one thing I wanted to talk to you about. Do you think it's possible that you ran into something submerged in the water, and you just thought someone was pushing on you?"

"What about the scuba diving tube. Could that have been my imagination too?"

Nelda took a big swallow of her drink. "I don't know, a reed maybe growing in the water. The only reason I'm suggesting these things is because our party was all accounted for. Who in the word would want to harm you?"

"That's a good question, but who would want to harm Doris?"

"You don't think her death was an accident?" Nelda got up and put her glass down on the vanity.

"Look, I know Doris was a friend of Sue's, but she wasn't exactly kosher. Those kids were going in and out of the infirmary with pills. She gave them out to teachers too: sleeping pills to make them sleep, pills to make them thin and pills to make them happy."

"That's terrible, why didn't you report her?"

"I warned her that I would if she didn't stop."

"So, you think Doris' death is drug related?"

"I didn't say that, I don't know what to think anymore." She put her glass down and started twisting on the sheet.

Nelda could not and would not stay to witness another Winnie melt down. She embraced her and said, "Look, Winnie, it's all behind you. I'm truly sorry our talk upset you. Just get a good night's sleep and when you get up in the morning we'll be home, debarkation at 11:00 AM." She quietly closed the door behind her.

*   *   *

On her way back to her room, Nelda saw Celeste in the hall. Now would be a good time to tell her about the pictures, she thought, and give her the one she'd bought for her.

"Hi, Celeste, you're not calling it a night are you?" Nelda asked.

"Heavens no, just wanted to get a wrap. It's chilly in the casino."

"Well, I won't keep you. I just picked up our pictures in the photo gallery, and bought one for you of Justine's birthday party."

"Thanks, Nelda. Come on in and show me the others too."

Celeste opened the door for her. As Nelda walked in she saw a towel rabbit on Doris' unmade bed with a red, ball point pen stuck through its heart. Red ink covered its chest.

Celeste followed Nelda's gaze. "Don't you see, Nelda? I had to take out my frustration about Doris' death on something."

CHAPTER FIFTEEN

Stormy Weather

Sleep wouldn't come easily tonight. She worried over the rabbit in Doris' bed with the pen in its heart. Celeste's attack on the rabbit seemed so senseless.

Once in bed, Nelda mulled over the information she had about the three academy suspects. But it was not nearly enough! Two of them were being black-mailed; was Daniel? She was too tired to think, her eyes closed and soon Nelda succumbed to a worried sleep.

Someone banged on the cabin door. It took Nelda a few seconds to get her bearings. "I'm coming, I'm coming," she shouted. "Give me a minute." She turned on the light and struggled into her robe and slippers, before asking who was there.

"It's me Aunt Nelda, let me in."

She found Sue standing outside by herself.

"Why didn't you use your key?"

"I don't know where it is. I looked all through my purse, but it's missing." Sue walked over to her bed and sprawled out. "I suppose I lost it. I'm too tired to think. Let's go to bed and work it out tomorrow."

"You have a good point."

"All I'm going to do is pull off my shoes, Aunt Nelda. Would you please turn out the lights?"

"That won't do, Sue. You'll rest better without those clothes, besides you need to wash that makeup off your face. You'll ruin your pretty complexion." Nelda threw her niece's brief night gown on the bed.

"Oh please," groaned Sue, brushing the gown aside, "Will I ever be my own boss?"

"Not at the rate you're going."

Sue sat on the side of the bed and removed her clothes, leaving them in a heap on the floor, before stumbling to the bathroom.

Nelda shook her head in exasperation. She placed a chair against the door in case Sue's key was floating around out there. The night was almost gone.

*　　*　　*

There were seagulls circling in a cloudy sky above the murky waters of the Gulf when Nelda woke up. There weren't very many times Nelda had slept pass 7:00 a.m. Sue, of course, was a different story. The only reason the girl ever got up early was to go to work. Looking at Sue asleep with an angelic look on her face made Nelda smile. Here was the adopted daughter she and Jim had raised from a child, a wonderful daughter with so much character and heart. Of course, she realized that there were a few superficial imperfections that maturity would have to care of. If only her late husband, Jim, had lived long enough to walk her down the aisle.

Enough of that, time to get going, lots to do. "Sue, it's time to get up. It's almost 8:00 a.m."

Rolling over, Sue looked at the bedside clock. "Oh no, I'm not even packed. They're supposed to pick up our bags in a couple of hours."

"And we haven't had breakfast either. You know I can't function without my coffee."

There was a flurry of activity in the cabin with Nelda and Sue dressing and packing. They didn't have time to talk about the previous night.

They placed their bags in the hallway on their way out to breakfast. Hoping to save time, they took the elevator to the grill located on the eighth deck. There were several passengers going through the breakfast line, but no sign of the academy group. After grabbing a sweet roll and cup of coffee, Nelda found a table near the window so she could look out over the water. Somehow, the water had a soothing effect on her nerves, even though the blue-green water had been replaced with water clouded with sediment.

Sue sat down with a clatter of food laden dishes. "Now, tell me what happened when you went to visit Winnie?"

"I visited the photo gallery first looking for pictures of us, and then I visited Winnie.

Sue crunched on a piece of crisp bacon before speaking. "Well, I was by myself for about an hour."

"Didn't you meet Daniel and Celeste as planned?"

"No they didn't show up at the Mardi-Gras Party. I found them later in the casino. Daniel said he was trying to shake a headache and Celeste was trying to shake a heartache."

Nelda smiled in spite of herself. Her niece certainly had a way with words. Well, I know where Celeste was for awhile. I was with her in her room."

"Why?" Sue asked, after drinking her juice.

"I purchased a picture of the group at Justine's party for her."

"That was nice of you, Aunt Nelda."

Nelda took a sip of her coffee. "You'll never believe what was on Doris' bed."

"What?" Sue asked, sitting up straight.

"A towel rabbit with a red, ball point pen through its heart."

"No kidding. What was that all about?" Sue picked up a slice of bacon.

"She said it was her way of showing frustration over Doris' death."

"That's totally weird."

"I thought so too." Nelda finished her last bite of sweet roll.

"You didn't tell me about your visit with Winnie. Was she still all shook up?"

"No, in fact she was going out to get some ice when I knocked on her door. While she was gone, I accidentally turned over her waste basket and found some receipts in there."

"What kind of receipts? Sue asked.

"There was one for a massage she received the day after Justine died."

"Proving what?"

"Proving she could have switched the bottles of massage oil, that's what."

"I don't suppose there was a receipt for the massage oil?" Sue asked, on the edge of her seat.

"No such luck, besides if the murderer has half a brain he or she would pay in cash, leaving no credit trail." Nelda stood up to leave.

Sue hugged Nelda as she left the booth. "Even with all the bad stuff that went on while we were on this cruise, I had a good time and thank you for taking me with you."

"You're welcome. Let's get off this ship, collect our bags and get on the road. Can't wait to see how my yard looks." Nelda's flower garden was the pride of her neighborhood. She worked out solutions to problems while digging in 'the good old earth,' as she called it.

"And maybe a certain old, weather beaten sheriff?" Sue put a finger to her lips.

Nelda nodded. "Him too."

*   *   *

As Nelda approached the pile of suitcases from their deck, she spotted Walter, with shaggy, brown hair in a rumpled, blue seersucker suit. Her face lit up with a smile. The young doctor was waiting in impatient anticipation for a glimpse of his love. Nelda waited to see Sue's reaction when she discovered Walter had come down to be with her when the ship docked. She didn't have to wait long.

Sue looked up; saw Walter, then literally jumped into his arms, almost knocking him down. He wrapped his arms around her in a passionate embrace, and then covered her mouth with kisses. The passengers, waiting for their luggage, applauded the act of affection.

Walter's face turned beet red with embarrassment. He finally acknowledged his old teacher and friend. "Nelda, thank you for inviting Sue to take this cruise. I know you enjoyed most of your vacation, but I just couldn't wait to have both of you back safe and sound. I've taken the day off to show you what Galveston has to offer vacationers."

Nelda hugged his neck. "That's sweet of you, Walter, but I think I'll drive on home. I'm really anxious to check on Sally, and see the condition of my house and yard. I bet you and Sue won't miss me in the least."

Sue's blue eyes looked concerned. "Are you sure you don't mind, Aunt Nelda?"

"Get out of here. Don't waste anymore time looking after me."

Walter loaded Sue's luggage into his car and they waved goodbye as they pulled away. Nelda stood waiting for the shuttle to take her out to the parking lot. She looked up to discover Daniel with a frown on his face.

"Hello," Nelda said. I guess we'll be shuttling together. Just wanted to tell you I've enjoyed your company."

"Thanks, Nelda, but we won't be using Doris' car to get home, because her relatives picked it up. I've called about a rental car."

"That's right! I had forgotten you came in her car." Nelda rubbed her face as she thought of the academy trios' predicament. In less than a minute she made a suggestion. "Look, Sue is going back with her fiancé. Why don't the three of you ride with me? I have to go right by the academy. Is that where you have your cars parked?"

"Yes, but we don't want to impose on you Nelda. We've got quite a bit of luggage."

"No problem, I bet we can fit it all into my Ford station wagon."

"That is so nice of you. I'll tell the girls, and then cancel the rental car."

Nelda was delighted that this had happened. She wanted to stay connected with them in order to solve the mystery.

Daniel hurried back just as the shuttle bus drove up. Winnie and Celeste were at his heels. He helped load the bags on the bus as Celeste canceled the rental car. Winnie stood to one side looking despondent.

"What's wrong Winnie?" Nelda asked.

"I've already started worrying about all the work I'll have to do by myself; now that Justine is no longer with us."

"No use borrowing trouble. I'm sure the academy will replace her."

Winnie sniffled. "Not until this fall."

Nelda decided that Winnie was a complete neurotic and needed help almost as much as Justine did. Maybe a four hour drive with this group wasn't a good idea after all.

*   *   *

The day was cool and cloudy, with a chance of rain. A salty mist caused droplets of water to form on Nelda's windshield as Daniel struggled to load their luggage. It almost took Houdini's magic to get the job done, but he did a magnificent job of placement. Now Daniel settled himself in the front seat with Nelda, while Celeste and Winnie occupied the back seat.

Once they were on their way, Nelda started a discussion about how they would spend their summer. "Are all of you working at the academy this summer?"

Celeste spoke up first, with a sense of resignation in her voice. "I guess so. It's only for six weeks. I've always helped with summer sports, track and swimming, besides I need to keep my girls in shape for the fall sports."

Winnie took her nose out of a romance novel long enough to answer Nelda's question. "I haven't planned any trips except this one. The library will be pretty quiet, so I'll probably have a chance to see if the books are where they belong. I'm really anxious about Justine's absence."

She didn't want to start Winnie sniffling, so Nelda directed her attention to Daniel, who was looking worriedly at the rain that started the minute they hit I-45. "Nasty weather huh, Daniel? I think the rain is picking up."

"So is the traffic, Nelda. This road is not safe when it's dry, must less when it's bad weather."

Nelda adjusted the speed of the windshield wipers and turned her lights on. "I'm going to drive carefully and if the rain is too heavy, I'll pull over until it lets up."

"Good," Daniel sighed. "And about this summer, I'll be looking to improve my health. I need more shrapnel removed from my noggin. These headaches are killing me."

"Sorry. I guess I'm too gabby." Nelda glanced over at Daniel and realized his expression was that of someone suffering from a migraine headache. There were deep lines in his face as he rested his head on the back of the seat with his eyes closed.

"It's okay. I've had a pill. It should be kicking in at any minute. With all the hell I've been through, I'm still glad I was a Navy Seal. I've had quite an experience, and someday I'll be able to tell you all about it. For now, it's a big secret."

Nelda started slowing down because of a red pick-up truck in front of her. She could see a white car coming up behind her very fast, with water spewing up in its wake. She pulled quickly over to the shoulder of the road just before the car slammed into the pickup. Now she thought she was safe, but a force from behind pushed her wagon into the water filled ditch.

CHAPTER SIXTEEN

Double Trouble

The rain came down in torrents as Nelda pushed away from the steering wheel. Her passengers were strangely quiet, except for Winnie, who gave a little moan. Nelda was grateful the air bags in her car did not inflate. The person responsible for pushing them into the ditch must have put their brakes on right before impact. She moved her arms, legs and neck before straightening up in her seat. When she was satisfied everything worked, she looked over at Daniel who was massaging the back of his neck with both hands. When he realized she was watching him, he reached over and placed his hand on her shoulder.

"I'm okay," he said, just a little shook up."

Nelda took her seat belt off, before turning around to look at Winnie and Celeste. "Are you girls hurt?"

Celeste answered first. "I don't think so, no bones broken. How about you Winnie?"

The librarian was huddled in the corner of the car with tears running down her face. "It's my elbow. I hit my elbow on the window when the car hit us."

"Can you bend it?" Daniel asked as he turned around.

"I think . . . so," she sobbed, "but there could be a . . . fracture."

"I'm so sorry," Nelda said. "I thought we'd be safe on the side of the road. I didn't know that lunatic would run into us. I'm sure help will come soon and they'll see about your arm."

"Look, Nelda," Daniel said loudly, "there's a man out there directing traffic around the wrecks. He's allowing the green car that hit us to get back on the highway. Hell, we didn't even get her license number."

"There's no use getting excited. I can't stop her. The only thing we can do is check on the other people in the pileup and make sure the police were notified."

Celeste had been subdued all morning, now she spoke quietly, "I don't think I'll get out, I'll stay here with Winnie." She rummaged around in her handbag, found two aspirins and handed them to the little librarian with a bottle of water.

"That's good, the 'Seal' and I will handle things. Daniel, there is an umbrella under your seat, pass it to me before you get out."

"Sure." He gave her the umbrella, slipped on his Navy Seal windbreaker, opened the car door and stepped out. "Good news! The water in the ditch is only a few inches deep and the rain has slacked up."

Nelda opened her door, then unfurled the umbrella, before plunging her leather sandaled feet into the water. She shook her head with misery, knowing her new shoes were ruined.

The parasol she opened was yellow with a black Labrador retriever painted on the side, and a thank you note from the Humane Society printed in red. Daniel took in the scene and suppressed a smile.

Nelda splashed around to the back of her wagon and flinched when she saw her bumper. It was badly bent. She couldn't tell what other damage her car had. Now, her greatest hope was that the wagon was drivable.

"Don't worry, Nelda, I'll get that car out of the water after the police get here."

"Thanks, Daniel. I'll trust you to do that. Let's check on the people inside the other cars. The guy directing traffic might know who needs help. He was probably involved in the pileup too."

Daniel and Nelda walked to the side of the road where a grey headed man dressed in a bright yellow raincoat and hat held a battery operated road torch. He waved it from side to side so cars would know there was an obstruction in their path.

"You're doing a good thing here," Nelda said. Were you in one of the wrecked cars?"

"Yes, I ran into the white car. Even though we were creeping along, I couldn't see the car stopped in the road."

"Did you call 911?"

"Right away. Help should show up in the next few minutes."

"Do you know if anyone was hurt?" Daniel asked.

"A couple of people, the guy in the pickup has a nasty cut on his head, and the woman who hit him is unconscious, but breathing. Her other passenger, a kid, is alright. My wife is taking care of him. Sorry I didn't have time to check on your passengers. I just had to get out here and direct traffic, before somebody else was hurt."

"I understand. We're okay except for a sore elbow. We'll look in on the two wounded," said Nelda. Right before they left, Nelda asked one last question. "Could you tell me what happened to the green Dodge that hit me."

"She backed up and went around us, then sped on off, but I've got her license plate number. I made a copy for you too."

"Good," she said accepting the slip of paper. I'll give it to the police when they get here."

"You won't have to wait long," said Daniel. I hear them coming."

They decided not to look in on the wounded, because the ambulance was right behind the police car, and it was followed closely by two wreckers. At least a wrecker would get her wagon out of the ditch, if Daniel couldn't handle it.

"We'll just be in the Medical Teams way, Daniel. Let's stand here on the side of the road and talk to the cops when we have the opportunity."

"Suits me. Do you have your proof of insurance and driver's license with you?"

"I have my driver's license, but the liability insurance card is in the pocket of the car. Do you mind getting it?"

"No," said Daniel. "I'll be right back."

The rain had stopped. Nelda closed up her umbrella then watched as the Emergency Medical Team arrived. The unconscious woman was loaded into the ambulance along with the man who had a gash in his head. Then, one of the team headed toward Nelda's car. She and Daniel met him at the wagon. He was a dark, young man dressed in a white coat with a stethoscope hanging around his neck.

"My name is James Craig. Anybody hurt in your car?"

"Yes, we have someone with a sore elbow," Nelda answered. She pointed toward Winnie in the back seat.

He quickly went around to the side of the car and opened the door. Winnie shrank back in the seat. "No, I'll wait until we get home. I'll go to my doctor."

"Are you sure Winnie? It will be a while until we get home," Daniel said.

"I'm sure." She reached out with her left hand and closed the door.

"Well, said the medic, we've got to get going. Make sure she gets help. Sometimes it takes a while for soft tissue to show signs of injury."

"I'll see that she visits her doctor," said Nelda. "Thanks for your concern."

Just as he left a beefy, middle aged police officer walked over with his notebook. "I'm officer McNabb, who's the owner of this vehicle?" he asked in a gravelly voice.

"I am officer," Nelda said, leaning against the car. Weariness had set in and she longed to be back home.

"Tell me who was driving, then your version of the accident."

"I was driving." Nelda said. "The pickup in front of me slowed down. I slowed down too, but the white car in back of me did not. I saw that she was going to hit me, so I pulled over on the shoulder of the road. After I stopped, a green Dodge car hit me from behind, pushing me into the ditch. The Dodge fled the scene of the accident. One of the ladies in the back seat hurt her elbow on the window when the car hit us."

The policeman wrote her description of the accident down. He then asked for her driver's license and proof of liability insurance. Nelda gave them to him and silently watched as he recorded the information on a pad. He gave them back before inspecting the damage to her car. After he made his appraisal of the rear bumper, he walked around to the front of the vehicle. He noted the stickers in the corner of the windshield.

"Your inspection sticker is out. I'm obligated to give you a citation."

Nelda was surprised; however the date on the inspection sticker was for the previous month. "I'm sorry officer. I didn't realize it was time to do that."

Daniel spoke up. "Look, Officer, could you just give her a warning? Having her car bashed in by someone that fled the scene is enough punishment for today."

The officer looked over at Daniel noticing the insignia on his windbreaker. "You on leave, son?"

"No sir, I'm out now, shrapnel in my head." Daniel put a finger on his scar.

"That's tough buddy. Got a boy in the Marines over there. Maybe I was a little harsh on the little lady here. After all, it's just a few days overdue."

"Thank you, officer. I'll see that she gets it inspected right away."

"Your insurance company will get a report about the wreck, Ms. Simmons. Don't forget to report it to them as soon as you get back home. I've got the license number of the car that hit you. We'll find them."

Nelda nodded as he left. She was a little put out with the 'good ol boy' system that was displayed by the officer, even if it did save her some money.

Daniel saw the pained look on Nelda's face. "You're a straight shooter, aren't you Nelda? He was just doing you a favor."

"No, he was doing you a favor, but I'm thankful he's giving me a chance to correct my mistake."

"Let's get back on the road, Nelda. I think our best bet is to have the wrecker pull us out of the ditch. The ground is soft from all the rain and we might bog down if I tried to drive it out."

It was no trick for the wrecker to pull Nelda's car out of the ditch. She then made sure the wagon was capable of being driven, before she let the wrecker driver go. Daniel took over the wheel; they had a lot of catching up to do.

*   *   *

It seemed to Nelda that she'd been gone for a month, not a week. She had never been happier than when she unloaded her passengers at the academy. Winnie wouldn't let her take her to the doctor, but assured Nelda she'd go as soon as she got home and had a bath.

Within a few miles of home, the cornfields Nelda passed were parched, brown stalks shimmering in the unrelenting sun, while the road side grass were blades of muted brown. Where oh where have the raindrops gone? No precipitation here in weeks. Thank goodness she'd asked Mary Watkins, her next door neighbor, to water her plants.

In the remaining few miles to her home in Stearn, she made plans for the coming week, it included having her car repaired, and staying in touch with the academy group. She would think of some way to stay in contact, perhaps through Winnie and the sore elbow.

As Nelda pulled into her driveway, the teenager from across the street ran over to talk to her. He was decked out in the cool clothes of a teenage tennis fan: electric blue shorts down to his knees, and a loose white T-shirt with a picture of Andy Roddick, 'The Rocket Man,' on the front of it. The tired sleuth was put out, not now she thought, rolling the window down. "How are you Tim? Did I miss out on anything while I was gone?"

"You sure did, that's why I ran over. Mrs. Watkins had a heart attack the day after you left. She's still in the hospital."

"Oh my goodness, thanks for telling me. I'll sure check on her as soon as I can."

Tim jogged away waving his right hand as though he had a tennis racket in it.

Nelda drove the car on up the driveway and stopped just outside the garage door, so she could unpack. Her first thought was of the plants she'd nurtured so lovingly since early spring. She gazed in horror at the sight of them. Her butterfly flower bed made up of butterfly weed, sunflowers, holly hocks and sweet alyssum were all wilted. Other plants that attracted humming birds had drooping heads and stems. She was afraid to look in the front yard at the caladiums and petunias. Would she be able to save any of them?

Nelda sank to the bottom step of her back porch and cried. Tears ran down her face in torrents. There was just so many bad things a person could take, after that a crash was inevitable. Her back was bent over with her head resting in her hands when she heard footsteps approaching. She could see two, black polished boots on the ground in front of her. With a tear stained face she raised her head and looked into the face of Joe Coats.

"Oh, Nelda, do I see a lady in distress? I came by four times in hopes of seeing your pretty face. What in the world has happened?"

The tired sleuth knew she was acting like Winnie, but she couldn't help herself. All the bad things that had happened to her came flooding out of her mouth. "This has been the worst day of my entire life. We were in a wreck, someone ran into my car; one of my passengers was hurt; I ruined my good sandals; my flowers have all burned up and the murderer is still out there."

More sobs racked Nelda's body. Joe reached down and pulled her to her feet. He gently put his arms around her, resting her head on his chest. "Nelda, Nelda, do I detect a chink in your armor. I think my girl is human after all."

"Forgive me, I'm such a baby."

"No you're not."

He lifted her chin and kissed the tears from her face. She couldn't help herself, she melted in his arms. Now she realized how much she needed him and knew the barriers she's built to keep him out of her life were almost gone.

"Now let's sit down here, Nelda, and we'll start working on those problems. I know you've got insurance, and it will be a nuisance using a rental car, but that should take care of that problem. Your sandals can be replaced. Maybe you can get those replaced by your insurance too. Now, as far as the flowers are concerned, they do look pretty far gone, but a good watering will do wonders for them."

Nelda had the ghost of a smile on her face. "I'm too tired to water."

Joe squared his shoulders and squeezed her hand. "I'll water while you take a shower and get dressed so I can take you to dinner."

Nelda pushed her damp dark hair out of her eyes. "I'm not sure I can make it."

"Oh yes you can. Over dinner we'll talk about the last problem you mentioned, the murder mystery."

All at once Nelda came alive. She saw in Joe the chance to have a sounding board for all her thoughts concerning the possible suspects.

While Joe started the sprinklers, Nelda played back her recorded messages. There were several advertisements, another message reminded her of a doctor's appointment and the last one had her laughing and crying. Sally was coming over with her new puppy the next day to spend the night.

CHAPTER SEVENTEEN

Shadowboxing

Joe and Nelda chose Red Lobster to celebrate Nelda's homecoming. She was thankful they could be seated away from the kitchen. The constant traveling of waiters from kitchen to tables bothered her. She looked forward to another good meal she didn't have to cook, plus a cozy talk with Joe about the cruise deaths. In Nelda's mind, the deaths of Justine and Doris were brought about by emerald green liquids, with the help of the killer. A mixture of peanut oil and Ocean Breeze massage oil for Justine and Western Caribbean water for Doris. Her thoughts were interrupted by a waiter hovering over their table.

The long haired youth fidgeted as Joe studied the wine list. "I'm not very good at this, Nelda. Why don't you make the choice for both of us?"

"Let's order a California Chardonnay. I think you'll like it."

"Good choice!" said the waiter as if he had personally tasted all the wines. He hurriedly disappeared with his pony tail flapping.

Joe held both of Nelda's hands across the table. "You look terrific, Nelda, even though you've had a lot of unpleasant things happen to you. The sun and water were good for you. They've given you a nice tan."

"Thank you. I needed that. You look pretty spiffy yourself, new shirt and haircut too. We need to spend more time together. You're good for me, and who knows when I might break down again."

"We can't let that happen." He withdrew his hands as the waiter brought their drinks. "We're not ready to order dinner yet." He informed the waiter.

"Yes Sir. Just signal when you've made your choice."

Nelda studied Joe from behind her menu. She knew, from his pleased expression, he had some news for her about the academy group. He was like a kid about to share his candy with someone he liked.

She took a sip of her wine. "All right, Joe, I've waited long enough. What news do you have about the academy employees?"

"I guess it's time to tell you, but I don't think it's going to prove anything. We checked the bank account of Justine Scales and couldn't find any deposits from the alleged blackmailing. The only deposit she ever had was her monthly check."

"You're right," Nelda said frowning, that doesn't prove a thing. She could have another account in a different bank, using a different name."

Joe took a long sip of his wine before speaking. "Or those flakey women made it all up."

"No, I believe blackmailing was going on. It probably wasn't for very much money. I'll find out how much. I bet Winnie will share that information with me. I don't suppose you could check the other women's accounts?"

Joe put his wine glass down, "Afraid not, we don't have any justifiable reason for that."

Nelda looked up from her menu. "Well then, is there anyway to get some background on the ex-Navy Seal, Daniel Hall?"

"Sure, but I'm starving. Let's forget about this for the time being and order our dinner. I'm having the sea food platter. What would you like?"

"Shrimp Caesar salad and a hot roll would suit me. Thanks again for the treat, Joe."

"My pleasure," said Joe smiling. He signaled the waiter.

*   *   *

After leaving the restaurant, Nelda climbed in Joe's shiny new pickup and leaned back with a weary sigh. She put her hand over her mouth and stifled a yawn. It had been such a long day with so many things happening. She hoped Joe wouldn't think her rude if she didn't invite him in.

As though Joe was reading her mind, he reached over and rubbed her shoulder. They were well on their way before he spoke in his low easy voice. "I'm sure you want to forget about this awful day with a good nights sleep. I'm going to let you rest a few days and then we'll paint the town red. In the meantime, I'll find out as much as I can about your Navy guy."

"Thanks so much. I guess it will be very difficult proving those deaths were not accidental. I keep making stabs in the dark"

"It's sort of like shadowboxing isn't it?"

"It sure is. Hard to figure out whom the bad guy is. I'll think of some way to keep tabs on the three suspects. For one thing the girls are teaching summer school at the academy, and I have a reason to contact Winnie. She hurt her arm in my station wagon."

Joe ran his hand through his hair in frustration. "That woman who hit you and fled will have to pay for that."

"Could you find out who that was? I'm sure the police have the license plate owner in their computer base."

"Anything for you, Nelda." Joe smiled as he pulled in her driveway.

He went around and opened the truck door. The air was heavily scented with the fragrant odor of honeysuckle growing on the wooden fence of Nelda's neighbor. Well, thought Nelda, at least someone in the neighborhood had flowers that were still living. A wave of determination surged through her body; tomorrow she would start reestablishing her flower beds.

Joe walked Nelda to the door then pulled her close. He stroked her hair and whispered, "I missed you so much, Nelda. Promise me you'll take me with you next time."

"I promise," Nelda sighed, "but I think you're going to have to wait a couple of years. It will take me that long to get over this trip."

Joe put his hand under Nelda's chin, tilting her head up before tenderly kissing her on the eyelids and mouth. She then laid her head on Joe's chest and heard the steady rhythm of his heart. How lucky she was to find this man.

Finally they parted. Nelda opened the front door, gave Joe one more farewell kiss then locked the door as he stepped away. She stood at the closed door listening to his receding steps. Some day she would have to make a big decision. Would she allow Joe to become a permanent part of her life?

*   *   *

As Nelda prepared for bed she heard the front door bell. She couldn't imagine who would be visiting her at such a late hour. All she could think about was Sue might be in trouble. Slipping on a robe, she hurried to the door. "Who is it?" She called.

"It's Richard Sinclair, Celeste's friend," said the voice through the door. "I was on the cruise ship. I've just got to talk to you, Ms. Simmons."

Nelda turned on the porch light, pulled the drapes back and looked out through a front window. Sure enough, the Hunk, as Sue called him, was standing near the door.

Well, thought Nelda, someone is definitely in trouble. I've got to hear what he has to say. She turned the key in the door.

As she swung the door open, she noted that there was no sign of the arrogant playboy in the character that stood before her. His yachting cap hung loosely in his hand and his face showed signs of deep stress. Tears stood in those deep blue eyes.

Nelda was a soft touch for anyone displaying emotional distress. "Come on in. Let's go sit in the kitchen and talk. I'll make you some hot chocolate and please call me Nelda."

They walked back to the kitchen with Nelda leading the way. She pulled out a stool from the bar for him, and then busied herself with making the hot chocolate.

"Thank you for seeing me at this late hour," he said, "I desperately need your help. I waited outside for a long time, before I worked up courage to ring your doorbell."

"I suppose this concerns Celeste," answered Nelda, placing the cups of water and hot chocolate mix into the microwave oven.

"In a way it does, but my wife is the one in trouble."

Nelda was baffled. What in the world was he talking about? Why was he coming to her with his domestic problems? Before she had a chance to answer the timer sounded. She removed the hot chocolate and handed him a cup, before sitting down at the bar with hers.

"What is this all about? I know you're having an affair with Celeste, but how could this get your wife into trouble?"

Richard's hand was shaking as he set the cup on the counter, the liquid spilled on Nelda's kitchen floor. Grabbing a napkin, he quickly cleaned up the spill. When he straightened up, he blurted out the reason for his visit. "My wife, Cindy, was driving the car that hit you."

Nelda opened her mouth in amazement, and then spoke. "Well tell me all about it. Give me the whole story, so I can make some sense out of why you're here."

Richard gulped his chocolate as though it would give him the courage to tell his story. "Celeste knew Cindy hit you. She didn't say anything to you, because she recognized my wife when she turned around after the accident happened. When you let Celeste out at the academy, she called me on her cell phone. I didn't believe her, but when I got home I saw the damage to our car. Cindy confessed. She suspected I was still fooling around with Celeste. She drove to Galveston and waited from a distance for me to appear. When she saw Celeste get into your car, she assumed I was in there too. That's when she started following you."

"Couldn't she see there was a brunette man in front instead of a blonde?"

"Guess not, she tried to stay several cars behind and then that awful storm hit."

"She didn't have to run away," answered Nelda. "I know she probably couldn't help but hit somebody, but she should have stayed there to see if anyone was hurt."

"I know," Richard's voice broke. "She panicked," he said, beating on the counter with his hand. "Cindy's guilty of hit-and-run and it's all my fault. I'm going to lose my family because I'm such a jerk."

Nelda took a sip of hot chocolate. "So how can I help? You already know you've messed up your family's life and Celeste's as well."

"Is there any way that you could help Cindy avoid the hit-and-run charge?"

"I'm afraid not, Richard, the state police have the license number, but I'm sure it's not as bad as you think. No one could see in that awful storm. She was bound to hit me or that line of crashed cars. I'm guessing she'll have a big fine and warning, but no jail time. No one was seriously hurt in my car; however, she needs to turn herself in."

"Oh, thank God," Richard whispered. "I'll take her down to the station first thing tomorrow. This whole episode has made me realize how much I love my family. I hope Cindy gives me *one more* chance."

Nelda drained her cup of chocolate and thought about Celeste. How will she survive this episode? Surely, in the back of that fair girl's mind, she knew what the final outcome of this illicit affair would be.

Richard got up to leave and Nelda followed him to the front door. She noticed the swagger was back in his steps. The tired sleuth wondered how this drama was going to play out. She thought Cindy's best move would be out. How many chances should a woman give a rat?

"Good night, Nelda," Richard said, opening the front door. "Thanks for listening and the good advice." He whistled as he ran to his car.

Locking the door, Nelda walked slowly to the bedroom and literally fell on her bed.

She was asleep before she could worry about how the children would survive with a part time father.

*   *   *

When Nelda awoke the next morning, she had a hard time adjusting to her surroundings. All that space in her old family ancestral home startled her at first. She looked up at the high ceiling and spaciousness of her bedroom and realized what a cracker box she and Sue had lived in on the cruise ship. It was good to be home.

The sun peeped through the middle of the drawn drapes. Oh goodness had she let the early morning get by? That was the best time to work in her garden. Nelda put on her robe and slippers, made a trip to the bathroom, and hurried to the kitchen for a cup of the dark brewed Columbian coffee. She loved the new coffee pot Sue had given her for Mother's day. It made coffee quickly and kept it hot.

Nelda easily fell into her old routine. After filling her coffee cup, she retrieved the daily newspaper off the front walk, and then made her way to the back porch. For some reason the coffee and newspaper just went together. Old habits are hard to change thought Nelda as she lowered herself into her favorite rocking chair.

As Nelda savored her dark brew, she scanned the headlines in the local news section, and then read with interest about the opening of Witherspoon Academy for the summer. She read the names of the teachers that would be on the staff during this period. Celeste was listed as the girl's P.E. Director and Winnie was listed as the librarian. Daniel's name, as she expected, was not mentioned. The first day of school was the next week.

Short time for them to get back in the school mode, Nelda thought. Later in the day she'd call Winnie to ask about her hurt arm, maybe even suggest she go with her to the doctor.

Nelda heard a big commotion as she picked up her empty cup for a trip back to the kitchen for a refill. A high shrilled voice screamed out, "Baby! You bad boy, get out of the street. A car will hit you."

A few seconds later a little brown Labrador rounded the corner of the house followed by Sally, Nelda's best friend. What in the world was she doing here so early?

"Oh Nelda," Sally screamed. "I can't catch the little booger."

The puppy scampered into a bed of lantana as Nelda joined Sally in the chase. There was only a brown tail peeping through the thick evergreen shrubs as Sally finally nabbed him.

Nothing else could happen to her poor flowers, thought Nelda, surveying the damage to red and yellow blossoms. Looking up at Sally, her consternation turned into a smile. Sally's face glowed with happiness as the fuzzy brown creature licked her face. Sugar lives on.

CHAPTER EIGHTEEN

Nelda Stays Close

Nelda caught Sally and the small brown dog in a bear hug, after a good squeeze she let go. "Sally, what are you doing here so early? I haven't even had my second cup of coffee."

Sally controlled the squirming pup by putting him under one arm before she answered. "And you're trying to sleep until noon, I guess. As for me, I haven't slept past four since your sweetie saw fit to give me Brownie. He insisted I needed a dog to replace Sugar, and maybe someday I'll forgive him."

Nelda laughed as the little dog squirmed out from under Sally's arm. She quickly opened the door to the screened in side porch. "Stick that little nuisance in here. Nothing he can tear up in there."

"You want to bet?" Sally answered, and then removed a red rubber ball from her pocket. She placed the dog in the screened enclosure, before sending the ball rolling across the floor. Brownie went bounding after it. "Just maybe, he'll be satisfied for the next few minutes."

Nelda found a clay saucer under a flower pot, filled it with water and then placed it in the corner of the porch. Brownie was so busy chewing on the hard rubber ball, he didn't acknowledge her presence.

Closing the side door, Nelda said, "I can't believe Joe gave you that dog without saying anything to me. I probably would have tried to talk him out of it."

"Well, I didn't want him at first, but now that I have him it has eased the ache in my heart. Of course no dog will ever take the place of Sugar."

"Of course not," Nelda said, as she led the way to the kitchen, remembering all the pets she, herself, had lost. What a shame they live only a short time compared to humans.

Sally rubbed her plump hands together after positioning herself on one of Nelda's kitchen stools. "I want to hear all about the cruise and the suspects in your newest murder case."

"I see my friend Joe has a big mouth. Is that how you found out about the emerald deaths?"

"Oh, is that what you're calling this mystery? You sure have a way with colors. Some day you'll be wishing you could only see in black and white."

"I'm really stumped right now, Sally. One accidental death in the academy group I could understand, but surely not two deaths."

She handed Sally a cup of coffee, then slid a tray with cream and sugar toward her. Her friend poured all the cream in her cup, dumped two heaping teaspoons and stirred briskly. Why Sally wanted to disguise the taste of good java never ceased to amaze her.

"Please start at the very beginning, Nelda. I'd like to know all about those people from the Witherspoon Academy and your thoughts on why two of them are dead."

"Okay, I'll do that. It will help me get the facts straight."

Sally savored her coffee milk. Nelda knew it was senseless to rag Sally about her diet. Her chubby friend didn't even take the advice of her doctor. Besides, she loved everything about Sally, especially her ability to listen and sort out facts in any mystery Nelda tried to solve.

"It all started before we left Galveston. Sue and I were sitting on the Fisherman's Wharf enjoying the sea gulls when these three women and a man appeared. One of the women stumbled and fell against our table sending my shrimp dinner to the floor. Then another woman, who was built like a tank, started chastising her for falling, and for leaving her passport in the car.

Sally slurped her coffee cream. "Big deal about the passport, couldn't they get that after they ate their lunch?"

"Not quite so simple, their car was already in the cruise ship parking lot. Fortunately for them, Sue recognized the besieged person as a friend employed as the academy's school nurse. She went over to their table and that's when we were introduced to all of them. The battle ax was Justine Scales, the head school librarian, who supposedly was blackmailing three of them and possibly all four. Winnie Speer was Justine's assistant. She's a mouse of a person, always whining. Celeste Fogelman, the women's sports director, is in love with a married man; and last was Daniel Hall, a good looking ex Navy Seal. We still don't know much about him."

"Wow!" Sally exclaimed. "What a list of characters. Joe told me the reasons they gave for Justine blackmailing them, but how did you stay in touch with the group on such a crowded boat?"

"Fate, I guess," Nelda said, refilling her cup and Sally's. "Our suite was on the same deck as theirs. They invited us to eat at their table in the dining room on several occasions."

"When did you get an inkling something was wrong about their relationships?"

"From the beginning, they were all so different and seemed to have nothing in common, except working at the same school.

"Justine was a head case, unhappy with herself and everyone else. I expected her to blow up at any time."

Sally squirmed on her stool. "I understand she died from an allergic reaction to peanuts?"

"Yes, but I'm not convinced she received peanut oil accidentally."

"Well, how do you think she got it?" asked Sally.

"I can't prove it, but I think it was added to a bottle of massage oil Sue and I gave her for her birthday. Somehow, she ingested the protein during the massage, because that's when she had the fatal attack."

"Humph," muttered Sally. "What were the results of lab tests on the oil?"

"It's not so simple. You see, when she first died, the detective didn't collect the bottle of oil. I went to the ship's health spa and found another bottle of the same oil. We knew it wasn't ours, because Sue had signed our names in indelible ink. Later, our bottle just happened to be found. At this point any evidence of foul play had long since vanished. Both bottles tested negative for peanut protein and fingerprints. The incompetence of that detective makes me want to tear my hair out."

Sally climbed off her stool, helped herself to a blue berry muffin Nelda had on the counter top and sat down again. She pushed her cup over to Nelda for another refill.

"Make yourself at home," Nelda said, laughing.

"Thought I would," Sally pinched off a piece of muffin and stuffed it in her mouth.

"I'll tell you about the other death, and then we'll have to make a couple of trips."

"Okay, Joe said you were really upset over the nurse's drowning, blamed it on yourself. Too bad you and Sue had to find her dead. Why don't you think that one was an accident?"

"I'm not sure it's not, but coming so soon after the other one makes me suspicious. When we left Doris she was contentedly sitting on a rock in the water. A few minutes later we found her drowned, and with a head wound."

"But that was all explained, wasn't it? Joe said the rocks were slippery and she could have easily hit her head while climbing down."

"Maybe so, but it just doesn't ring true. Anyway, I'm going to get dressed. I've got to see about having my car fixed, and apply for a job."

"A job! Whatever for? I believe you've gone bananas."

Nelda slid an advertisement she'd cut out of the morning paper over to Sally, who read it out loud. "The Witherspoon Academy is offering a part time summer job in the high school library. Please apply in person. No previous experience is needed, but must be knowledgeable in computer storage."

"What do you think about that? Nelda queried."

"Not much. I think you're desperate for some way to keep in touch with them. How do you know they're teaching summer school?"

"Winnie and Celeste told me they were teaching this summer. Daniel will be a little harder to catch up with. He may go into the hospital to have another piece of metal taken out of his head."

"Poor guy! Where did he pick that up, Iraq?"

"Yes, he's already had some pieces removed, but thinks there is a piece the surgeon missed. He has horrible headaches." Nelda could still picture the agony on Daniels's face when he was in pain.

Turning away from Sally, she loaded the dishwasher and barked out a command.

"Gather up that little dynamo on the side porch. As soon as I'm dressed we'll hit the road."

*   *   *

On the way to the academy, Nelda did her best to explain why Richard Sinclair's wife ran into her on the side of the road. "That cheating husband of hers had her so upset she followed me thinking Richard was in my car with Celeste. And then to top it off, that rat came to my home and asked me not tell my insurance company about her accident."

"For Pete's sake, Nelda, all of those people are unstable. How do you manage to get yourself in such a mess?"

"It's not easy," she smiled as she approached the academy parking lot. "Why don't you walk Brownie around under the trees? I don't think I'll be in there very long, but it's too hot to leave him in the car."

"I'll do that. He loves the opportunity to mark every blade of grass as his territory."

After leaving Sally, Nelda walked toward the administration office wondering if she was making the best decision. She didn't exactly relish six weeks of work with Winnie, even though she felt somewhat responsible for her elbow injury. Oh well, she could stand anything for that period of time. She was determined to find out the truth.

The front of the academy building was attractive; it had a colonial look with white columns holding up the clay roof of a wide porch. The building was built of red brick and had large windows with green shutters. There were a few small tables and chairs placed here and there on the flagstones of the porch. Having never worked in a private school, she approached the double doors with some anxiety. What made this school different from a public school? She wondered.

Once inside, she saw several glassed in offices. As she stood in the foyer trying to decide where the personnel office was located, a middle aged man in a brown suit approached her. Nelda thought he looked like an English college professor. He sported leather elbow patches on his jacket, and his face was covered with a small neat beard. She half expected to see a tobacco pipe sticking out of his pocket. But that was foolish, smoking these days was taboo, bad example for the kids.

"How can I assist you?" He inquired.

"I was looking for the employment office. I came to apply for the summer job in the library."

"Oh well, Mrs. Finley isn't here this morning. But I can talk to you about the position. My name is Phillip Witherspoon, headmaster." He smiles as he extended a hand as soft as Nelda's new foam pillow. She found herself comparing his hands to the rough, callous hands of Joe's. What a ridiculous thing to do.

"Nelda Simmons," she said, "retired high school teacher with some time on her hands."

"Great! Let's go to my office and we'll talk."

She followed him past the glassed-in offices to the end of the hall. He turned the corner and opened the door to an office that would make a bank president proud. The sides of the large room were lined with built-in shelves filled with books. A huge mahogany desk sat in front of a picture window. It gleamed from sun rays reflecting off the polished surface.

"This is a beautiful office," Nelda said.

She sat in an upholstered chair in front of him hoping this would not be an extended interview. There was Sally and the rambunctious, brown puppy to worry about.

"Thank you. This desk has been used by three generations of Witherspoons. Now about the job. We are short one librarian for the summer session, so we need someone to assist the one we have now. The hours are from eight to twelve and will last for six weeks. Pay will be fifteen dollars an hour. I assume you are familiar with the use of a computer." He drummed his fingers on his clean desk.

"Yes, I can write on a computer and understand how to load and use most programs."

"Great, just fill out this form," he said, opening up a drawer and handing her a sheet with several questions on it. "We have to run a security check, but that shouldn't take long. Work begins next Monday at 8:00 a.m. We'll call you after we receive the report."

Nelda was flabbergasted. "Well thank you for having such faith in a stranger. I know I can do the job."

"Not so strange," he said, while smoothing the hair on his chin. I knew your late husband, Jim, and have heard of your problem solving. I'm sure we'll be mutually happy with your employment."

Wasn't this an interesting development, she thought. Blackmail going on right under his nose, and he didn't know about it. Now, he hires me on the strength of what my late husband said about me. No wonder this staff is in trouble.

Nelda stood up and reached her hand across the desk. "I'll turn this form in on the way out."

He held her hand for a second then smiled. I must leave, but you're welcome to fill out the form here in my office, and leave it on my desk.

As he walked out of his office, Nelda sat down and pulled out her pen. What a gracious man, she thought, working here might not be so bad after all.

*   *   *

Nelda found Sally sitting on the ground under an oak tree, fanning herself with an old church program she'd found in the station wagon. The dog was lying next to her sleeping on his stomach. His little hind legs were still in motion.

"Heavens to Betsy, I thought you'd gone to work already. Brownie and I are roasted."

"Sorry about that," Nelda said, then pulled Sally to her feet. "I think I have the job, and the headmaster is very nice, charming even." She gave Sally a mischievous grin.

"Please," admonished Sally. "I was just getting use to your 'Good Old Boy,' Joe."

"No problem," Nelda answered. "But a girl can still look, can't she?"

"I suppose. I've quit doing that long ago. Now all I think about are my creature comforts, like eating. How about lunch?"

"My goodness, I didn't realize it was that late. Let's drop my car off at the Ford place, pick up a rental car, and then I'll make you the best soufflé you've ever eaten."

They were loading up when Nelda saw a figure running through the parking lot toward them. It was Winnie with a bandage on her right elbow. She waved with her good arm as she approached.

Winnie came to a halt and embraced Nelda with her good arm. "Nelda, I just heard you had applied to be my assistant for the summer. That's the best news anyone could give me."

"Thanks, it's good to know you care. Let me introduce you to my life-long friend, Sally Pennington."

"It's nice meeting you. Nelda and I were on the cruise together." Her eyes immediately filled with tears.

"I've been worried about you," Nelda said. "Now, what's with the elbow? I hope you finally had the doctor look at it?"

"Yes, I did, he said I have tendonitis in my elbow, and told me not to use my arm to drive for at least two weeks."

"That's terrible," Nelda said. "I feel responsible for that. Of course the insurance will pay your doctor bills, but who will drive you to work?"

"That's just it; none of the teachers live close to me." Tears rolled down her cheeks. "Please, Nelda, could I stay with you for those two weeks?"

"Don't cry," Nelda said. You can stay with me, if I get the job. Two weeks will fly by before you know it." She covered her mouth with her hand. Why in the world had she extended such an invitation? Only God could help her endure Miss. Whinette for two long weeks.

CHAPTER NINETEEN

One by One

Sally sat in Nelda's kitchen on the same stool she had occupied at breakfast. This time, she chomped on a piece of celery instead of a blueberry muffin. She watched Nelda unpack a bag containing the ingredients for the soufflé her friend had promised her.

"Now let's see," muttered Nelda, "I need butter, flour, milk, eggs, green onions, mushrooms and Canadian bacon. Do you want me to leave out anything? Maybe, the buttered bread crumbs."

Sally shook her head. "No, it sounds delicious just the way you planned it. It will make up for one of those meals I missed on the cruise."

Nelda bantered with Sally as she turned on the oven and greased a baking dish.

"Not my fault you weren't there. I begged you to go with me."

"I know, but I'm glad I didn't go. I might have missed out on my little brown gift." Smiling, she looked over in the corner of the kitchen where Brownie slept peacefully.

"That's true," Nelda said.

For the next few minutes, Nelda concentrated on the preparation of the meal, by giving Sally directions on how to stir the butter, flour and milk together. "When it's smooth, add the cheese, salt and pepper. Cook on low until it's all melted."

Nelda finished her part by sautéing the onions and mushrooms and adding the beaten eggs. Soon the two preparations were mixed together and put in the oven topped by bread crumbs, chopped green onions and paprika.

"We have thirty minutes to enjoy a glass of wine before we eat. What do you say, Sally? Let's go talk about my next move in solving the mystery."

The unflappable sleuth's latest, favorite wine was Riesling, a semi-sweet wine that she had discovered while searching through the numerous foreign wines found in the grocery stores. Nelda was drawn to it because of the beautiful blue bottle that housed it.

"Bought it for the bottle, Nelda?"

"Yes, at first, but now I love the taste. Let's go talk."

*   *   *

Nelda's living room reminded Sally of a long ago era. She never tired of examining the objects in the room. One wall had glassed in shelves lined with bric-a-brac: Hummels, Raimonds, and Royal Doulton pieces. Sally loved hearing how Nelda acquired them, because each figurine had its own story. Most of the figurines were gifts from friends or relatives that were now dead (gone to their reward) as Nelda put it.

On another wall stood a heavy, oak china cabinet with a curved glass door. It was lighted within, and the crystal, china and sterling silver pieces reflected light rays from their polished surfaces.

"I love all your beautiful things, Nelda. You do have them insured don't you? The prices have exploded in value over the past few years."

"There is no special insurance on them. I have a home owner's policy, but have no idea how much they would pay me if they were destroyed by a fire or stolen. Of course, not many thieves go after collectibles. They wouldn't know what they're worth."

"You're probably right. They would take your silver and electronic equipment."

Nelda laughed, "They're welcome to that old silver. It gives me no pleasure to polish it every few months, but I suppose I would get a little upset if they made off with my computer. What would I do without the jokes and spam?"

They settled comfortably on Nelda's old velvet couch facing the stone fireplace. Each was lost in their own thoughts as they sipped the wine. Nelda suspected Sally was tired from the drive and hot wait in the sun while waiting outside the academy.

"You feeling okay, Sally? After lunch, I'm going to visit my neighbor who had a heart attack, but you don't need to go. Would you like to just stay here and watch television until I return?"

"Thanks, but I have to head back this afternoon."

"You're kidding! I thought you were spending the night."

"Can't this trip, but I'll be back soon; I'm only an hour away. Having this puppy has certainly slowed down my activities. Now, what you got planned for the summer? I know it involves snooping around that school."

"That's part of it, but I have several days until next Monday, that is if I get the job."

"Yes, I know you're a big security risk. Their search will probably expose you as a double agent to outer Mongolia."

"Cut that out, Sally." Nelda took a sip of wine and licked her lips appreciatively. "I've got to find out if Daniel has checked into the hospital. He's really having a difficult time now, with his health and state of mind. Did I tell you his fiancée committed suicide while he was in Iraq?"

Sally shook her head. "Was it before or after he was injured?"

"I don't know, but somehow I've got to find out if he had any involvement in the deaths of those two women."

Sally put her wine glass down on the coffee table, with barely a drop left. "What about the other two? How do you intend to get the truth out of them?"

"At this point, I don't know, but I'll have six weeks to dig up something." Nelda glanced at her watch. "Times up, Sally, let's go eat."

As they walked down the hall, Nelda heard the phone ring. "Sally, please take that soufflé out of the oven. I'll get the call in the bedroom."

It was Sue, "Aunt Nelda, I found out Daniel is in Med. Center Hospital. He's going to have another piece of shrapnel taken out tomorrow morning. Why don't we visit him in the afternoon? You know the guy doesn't have any relatives in this area."

"I'd like that, but are you sure it will be okay?"

"I talked with him, and he seemed to think it would be minor surgery, and was pleased we would want to visit him."

"Well, I've got some news for you too, but it can wait. Sally is having lunch with me, and she has a new puppy. She'll only be here for the day."

"That's wonderful! Tell her hello for me. I'll pick you up tomorrow about noon."

When Nelda returned to the kitchen, Sally was already dishing up their plates. "Was that your lover checking up on you?"

Nelda laughed. "No, he's got better things to do. It was Sue; we're going to visit Daniel in the hospital tomorrow. He's going to have surgery tomorrow morning to remove some more metal."

"I'm glad you and Sue are going to see him. I tell you, I'm not much on hospital visits, they make me sad."

"I know, but what about your lunch? I need a little feedback here."

"It is yummy! Best I ever ate."

"Now tell me," said Nelda opening the door of the refrigerator. What do you think of my mystery so far?"

"You asked for my opinion, Nelda. I say go for it. You've had enough experience to know when something is wrong, clues or no clues."

She closed the refrigerator door softly. Exactly, what she needed to hear from her best friend. Sally's confidence in her gave Nelda new hope in solving the mystery.

*　　*　　*

By daylight next morning, Nelda was already out in her yard pulling up plants that died without water while she was on the cruise. She had scheduled a visit from Green Thumb Nursery to survey the damage and replace the lifeless plants. She grumbled as she stacked the wilted flowers in the corner of the yard.

Thinking of Sally made her feel better. Sally was confident there was a mystery, and her friend could solve it. The deaths of Justine and Doris were not accidental. In her heart, Nelda knew she was right.

Finally, Nelda was satisfied with the headway she was making in her yard. The surviving, flowering plants were thoroughly wet, and the sprinklers were busy watering the parched grass. She rushed inside to take a bath before Sue arrived.

*   *   *

"Let's have a report, Aunt Nelda," said Sue as they drove toward town. "What's happened since you've been home?"

"Some of it you probably don't want to hear, but the sight of all my dead flowers when I turned into the driveway made me sick."

"What happened? I thought Mrs. Watkins was taking care of them."

"She did until she had a heart attack the day after we left. Mary is one sweet friend. I visited her yesterday and she's going to be fine."

"I'm sorry, Aunt Nelda. I know how much those plants mean to you."

"My reunion with Joe was nice, but you'll never guess who visited me in the middle of the night?"

"Don't keep me in suspense, who?"

"Richard Sinclair! His wife, Cindy, was following us home from Galveston. She's the one who ran into us. He wanted me to help her avoid the charge of hit-and-run. As if I had any say so over that."

"That dirty rat. His wife must know all about his affair. When is she going to give him the heave-ho?"

"I don't know. About the only good news is that Sally has another dog and loves him."

"You had a good visit then?"

"Too short, but I must say I was happy with her opinion of my new mystery. She thinks I should keep investigating."

"Too bad the authorities didn't agree with her, Aunt Nelda."

"Do you suppose they would have thought any differently if they knew blackmail was going on?"

Sue shrugged. "I don't know. Has Joe found any evidence this was true?"

"No, there were no deposits in Justine's bank accounts, other than her salary. Why would they make up those stories if they weren't true?"

"I haven't a clue, Aunt Nelda. There is your mystery right there. If you find out the blackmail stories were all made up, then you'll have to find out why."

"Yes, and it's hard to interview them after they're dead, however there are still three living suspects. Now, for the good news, there is a strong possibility I'll have a job with the academy for the summer. I'll work half-days in the library helping Winnie. That will give me plenty of time for snooping."

"Aunt Nelda! Are you crazy? As much fussing as I heard from you about whiney Winnie, you're going to be with her constantly for six weeks?"

"I know, but that's not all. The doctor said she couldn't drive her car for a couple of weeks, so she'll be staying with me while she recuperated. She'll ride to work with me if I get the summer job."

Sue pulled into the Med Center parking lot, parked the car then beat on the steering wheel while she laughed. Wiping tears from her eyes she said, "I'm sorry Aunt Nelda, but that is the funniest story I've heard yet. You know what you are?"

"No, what?" Nelda asked in an icy tone.

"A glutton for punishment, but I love you anyway."

Nelda couldn't stay mad at Sue. She knew most of what she said was true. "Alright, so I'm a push-over." I'll survive and maybe Winnie will be a big help to me as I search for the truth."

"I don't think you've ever tried to solve a case where you weren't dead sure there was a crime."

"That's true, first time ever, just my past experience urging me on."

"Then go for it. Even the people you hound will be thankful they're no longer under a cloud of suspicion."

"Hope so, and the first cloud I'd like to remove is over Daniel. He's been through so much. I can't imagine any reason he'd have for harming those women."

"Let's go in and try to cheer him up. Promise me you won't grill him at the hospital."

Nelda opened the car door, and then stared at her niece while shaking her head slowly. "Really, Sue, what kind of person do you think I am?"

"Sorry I said anything." Sue walked over to Nelda smiling sweetly.

*   *   *

The hospital was new, with wide halls, high ceilings and comfortable furniture in the large lobby. Sue walked up to the elderly lady sitting in a small half-walled enclosure.

"Could you give me the room number for Daniel Hall?"

"Well now let me see, young lady." She pushed her bifocals up on her nose and gazed intently at the computer screen. "That will be room 440. The elevators are to the left."

As they walked away from the desk, Sue said, "It's so nice when older people help out at the hospitals. Don't you think so, Aunt Nelda?"

"Well I really haven't given it any thought, but I'm sure they enjoy helping, and they must save the hospitals some money."

They walked in silence to the elevators, behind two nurses headed in that direction. Nelda noticed that they didn't wear white uniforms and white shoes. They did have on pants with a long smock, but gone were the days when you could readily identify who worked in the hospitals. Both had tags pinned to their upper pockets, but the lettering was small. Times are changing thought Nelda. Was it for the better?

After arriving on the fourth floor, it was a long walk to room 440. Nelda knocked on the partially open door, then stepped back and waited for a response.

A rather weak voice responded, "Come on in."

Sue walked in ahead of Nelda. Daniel was propped up in bed watching television, with a dinner tray pushed to one side. The top of his head was swathed in gauze.

"Just your shipmates making a house call," said Sue.

"Come in. You are my second visitors and I'm glad to see you. Have a seat in those chairs by the window."

"You have quite a suite here," Nelda said after sitting down. "It beats the heck out of those state rooms on the cruise ship."

"You bet, but the foods not nearly as good."

"Are you feeling okay, Daniel? Aunt Nelda and I were concerned about you."

"I am disappointed that one piece of shrapnel is still in my head. It's too deep to remove."

"How about the headaches, think you're rid of those?" Nelda asked with her hands clasped together as though she was praying for a miracle.

"They're gone for right now. I'm sure hoping for the best. Friend of yours called on me earlier, Nelda."

"Really, who could that be? Someone we met on the cruise."

Daniel didn't answer. He removed money out of a billfold on his night stand, and then looked over at Sue. "Sue would you mind going down to first floor and get me some chocolate milk out of the machine? I really love that drink"

"Of course not, I've got a purse full of change."

After she left, Daniel looked over at Nelda sheepishly. "I needed to get her out of the room before I told you about Joe Coats visit."

"Joe visited you? She said, squirming in her seat. "I don't know why he'd do that?"

"Of course you do. You want to know if I had anything to do with those two deaths."

"It's true, Daniel. I asked Joe to find out as much about you as he could. Believe me, I like you, but I've got to find out if you knew anything about the blackmailing. And I think I saw you the day Doris died."

"I'm not proud of this story, Nelda. It was me you saw climbing out of the water, after Doris drowned."

CHAPTER TWENTY

Breaking Point

Nelda stood by Daniel's bedside with hands clenched. "Please tell me you had nothing to do with Doris' death."

Daniel gingerly sat up in bed, and then stuffed a couple of pillows behind his head.

"What kind of a monster do you think I am? When I saw you and Sue leave Doris on that rock, I did swim out to ask her a couple of questions. I wanted her in a place where she couldn't run."

"What's going on, Daniel? I want to know the whole story."

"Alright, here is the painful truth. My fiancée, Stephanie Williams, killed herself after she found out she was pregnant with my baby. But there were two people helping her to make that decision."

Nelda sank down in a chair. "How was that possible?"

"Stephanie wrote me a letter saying she was in trouble. But in the letter she also said the librarian was encouraging her to have an abortion, and the school nurse could help her."

"She wrote to you about her condition and you didn't have the decency to contact her?"

Daniel's eyes brimmed with tears. How could I? The impact from the head injury left me unconscious for two weeks, but the military informed her of my condition. By the time they let me read my mail she was dead."

"What did Doris have to do with her death?"

"That's what I wanted to find out when I swam out to the rock and confronted her. She told me all she did was give her a bottle of sleeping pills, because Stephanie was having trouble sleeping. It was that bottle of pills that killed her. She swallowed them all."

"Oh! How horrible. Didn't she have anyone to turn to . . . family . . . minister?"

"No, her family was the kind that saw things as either black or white, no in between, and no forgiveness. They would have disowned her if they had known. I don't know if she went to her parish priest or not. But she did believe very strongly in God."

Nelda turned away shaking her head. Surely Stephanie would have known the Roman Catholic Church's stance on suicide. Oh what a mess some people make of their lives. They act on impulse and don't think about the end results.

Both Nelda and Daniel were in tears when Sue entered the room. She looked from one teary eyed person to the other. "What's happened? Did you receive some bad news?"

"A long time ago," answered Daniel," wiping his eyes on his pajama sleeve.

"You want me to leave and come back?"

"No, it's okay," said Nelda. "Daniel was just telling me about how he was injured in Iraq."

"You're home now," said Sue soothingly, patting the bed. "Try to put it all behind you. Here's your chocolate milk, so enjoy. She put the bottle on the bedside table.

Daniel gave Sue a little smile. "Thanks, I might wash down one of those pain pills with that. I haven't taken any one of them yet. I just stick them here in the drawer."

"I know," Sue said. "A lot of my men patients are macho like that, but it doesn't make you a baby for wanting a little relief."

A shapely young registered-nurse with hair the color of copper wire sauntered in to administer a shot. "This will make you rest better," she said. She held his hand while waiting for the results.

After the nurse left, Sue and Nelda visited a few more minutes, before saying their good-byes. As Nelda turned to close the door, she could see Daniel's eyes slowly closing.

Once out in the hall, Sue turned to Nelda for an explanation of what went on after she left to buy the chocolate milk. "Daniel really looked upset when I came in. What did you discuss while I was gone?"

"Now don't start accusing me of grilling him. It was his idea to tell me why his fiancée committed suicide."

"No kidding, why did she?"

Nelda didn't mind repeating to Sue what she had learned from Daniel, because she knew the information would go no farther. "This is really a tragic story. The girl's name is Stephanie Williams. She was engaged to Daniel and working at the Academy before he left for Iraq."

"I remember someone saying she committed suicide. I guess his leaving was too much for her to bear."

"Yes, especially after finding out she was pregnant. Stephanie tried to contact him, but Daniel was in a coma."

"Oh no, she probably thought he was going to die, and that was the reason she killed herself?"

"Yes, but he thinks she had help with that decision."

Nelda unlocked the car door. A group of intern nurses could be seen in the distance. They were headed for the hospital entrance. The back of one of them seemed oddly familiar. Why was it on some days perfect strangers looked like people she knew?

Sue continued talking as she backed out of her parking space. "Who did he think helped her die?"

"Doris and Justine," Nelda said, adjusting her seat belt.

"That's just the most ridiculous thing I've every heard. Doris wouldn't hurt a flea. In fact, she was too good to the faculty. She was always offering medical supplies to teachers. She'd even stock up on things using her own money. I've heard her say so."

"Not good for Stephanie, according to Daniel. Doris furnished her the sleeping pills that killed her."

"Well, Aunt Nelda, I'm sure that was not Doris' intent. Now what part did Justine play in her death?"

"I don't know. He just said the librarian wanted her to have an abortion. Maybe it was because the school would fire a single teacher that got pregnant."

"That's a laugh, not in this day and time. Have you looked in the paper recently at the new born babies? It seems half of them are illegitimate."

"Perhaps, you're right, Sue, but remember Witherspoon Academy is a highly respected, top-rated school. Anyway, I really didn't have an opportunity to quiz Daniel about Justine. I was hoping I could eliminate him as a suspect in her death."

"Well, at least you know now, he was not sorry to see her die."

"Probably not, but I'm back at square one with three suspects fancy free. I'm ready to start school next Monday so I can pick up some clues. The trail is getting colder and colder, now that I'm on land."

Sue pulled up in Nelda's driveway. "Sounds like something Joe Coats would say. And when are you seeing that stud again?"

"Really, Sue, you sound like you're talking to one of your sex crazed friends. It's not any of your business, but we're going to a movie tonight."

Sue laughed as Nelda got out and slammed the car door. She rolled down the window and shouted, "Don't do anything I wouldn't do."

What an irritating person her niece could be, but what would she do without her? She was great fun, and made her feel young.

She stood for a couple of minutes enjoying the view of her flowers, now replanted, and her lovely old home. Sometimes you just have to put your worries aside and enjoy the good things in life God has allowed you to have. And if that included the stud, Joe Coates, so be it.

*   *   *

After coming home, Nelda studied the entertainment section of the paper and decided none of the motion pictures listed were worth her and Joe's time. She chose to cook dinner for him, and after a candle lit meal they would watch *Lonesome Dove* from her old velvet couch. Nelda was sure Joe would be delighted with her plan. He loved her cooking and never tired of watching that particular movie.

Nelda slipped a CD in her new DVD player Sally had given her. Sounds of Glenn Miller's big band playing *That Old Black Magic* filled her kitchen. She waltzed around the work island in the middle of the room to her refrigerator. In her opinion, the now generation was really missing out by not listening and dancing to these songs.

Humming away, she gathered the ingredients for their dinner. The main course would be her creation. It consisted of one large yellow squash, one half of a big green pepper, one medium tomato, a cap of Portabella mushroom and half a pound of medium peeled shrimp. The shrimp were set aside, while she washed the vegetables carefully and sliced then in thin slices on her built-in chopping block.

Her renovated kitchen was one of the remodeling jobs done after a pyromaniac decided to scare her away from a case two years ago, by burning up her kitchen. She didn't want to dwell on her escape from death trying to solve that case, even though solving the mystery brought her and Joe together. Nothing could spoil her good mood tonight.

In a large hot skillet she poured two tablespoons of virgin olive oil, and then added the vegetables, shrimp and Cajun seasoning. Cooking on medium heat she sautéed the contents until the vegetables were tender, and adding two tablespoons of cornstarch dissolved in a little cold water to thicken. "*Bonne*" she said out loud, after sampling her dish. It didn't take her any time to finish up by cooking long grained rice to go with her main dish. The green salad was already in the refrigerator along with a chocolate cheesecake, Joe's favorite.

Nelda rushed to the bathroom to shower, using a luscious body soap she'd found at Body Works. Dressing after her shower didn't take long, good thing because the doorbell sounded as she was putting the finishing touch to her hair.

She peeped out the side window before opening the front door. Joe stood there with a bouquet of mixed flowers. He was all polished and fresh looking, from his neatly combed hair to his shiny boots. Nelda felt a surge of affection for this rugged man, a sense of happiness she hadn't felt for several years. She hoped he was wearing Old Spice, and then the setting would be perfect.

Opening the door, she greeted him with a smile. "For me?" she said, grabbing the flowers. "You should have, because you know I'm worth it."

Joe laughed while pulling her close. Nelda nestled in his arms breathing in the smell of Old Spice. She sighed while thinking it's a good way to start the evening with someone she felt closer to at every meeting.

"Look at you, Nelda," Joe said taking a step backwards. "You look and sound like a teenager."

"Come in you handsome man. We've had a change of plans for the better if you're agreeable."

"You name it; what have you planned for us? I've got the whole night off, and I warned my deputy there would be no interference."

"Follow me to the dining room, Sir, after you close and lock the door. Your darling has good things planned for you."

"Humm, sounds too good to be true." Joe held her hand as they walked down the hall.

Nelda was enjoying every minute of the surprise for Joe. "I just decided we didn't need other people around us to have a good time. We can provide our own entertainment."

"*Bon appetite*," she sang out as she opened the dining room door. The table she had set for them was beautiful, with all the brilliance that fine china, silver and crystal can display. Most of the pieces on the table were considered antiques, and irreplaceable. A bottle of Riesling wine rested in the silver cooler Nelda had polished with great effort. Now she knew it was worth all the grumbling she'd done while cleaning it. Long tapered candles in silver candlesticks glowed softly on either end of the table. The aroma of fresh baked yeast rolls wafted in from the kitchen.

"You are a sweetheart," he said whirling her around. "What a beautiful table. You've cooked a wonderful meal for me haven't you?"

"I think you'll enjoy it. You sit right there while I bring in the food." Nelda pointed to the chair at the head of the table.

"Oh no, I'm going to help you in the kitchen and with the cleanup too."

You're scoring a lot of points with me, Joe. Being responsible for the yard and house can be a burden.

They worked together well, and soon the table was laden with food. Nelda placed the flowers Joe had brought in the center of the table. He poured the wine without spilling a drop, hesitating before offering a toast.

She looked up at Joe, bowed her head and said, "Thank you God for all our blessings and watch over those who need your help."

"Amen," said Joe, "a message straight from the heart. I suppose you were thinking about that young Navy Seal, Daniel?"

"I was, he told me about your visit, and then he told me his sad story. Let's drink a toast to his better health," she said.

"And our continued closeness," Joe added.

*   *   *

While seated on the sofa with Joe, Nelda had the urge to know more about him. They really didn't know very much about each others background.

"Before we start the film, Joe, why don't you tell me about yourself?

"My life growing up was pretty uneventful. I was the oldest of three sons. My father always told me I should be an example and not get into any trouble."

"I suppose you followed those orders," smiled Nelda, taking his hand.

"Pretty much. There weren't too many things to get into out in the sticks."

"I know you served in the Vietnam War. I guess the war was an eye opener?"

Joe's eyes misted over. "It's something I would never want to repeat. Wars are so senseless. You'd think in this day and time leaders could work things out, before it came to death and destruction."

"I'm sorry I asked about it, Joe." Nelda said, rubbing his arm. "But the military training does make me wonder about Daniel. He was a Navy Seal with special training in killing. Do you think a man trained to do that would find it easier to murder someone after he came home?"

"Now we're back to the academy deaths, aren't we?"

"I guess we are." Nelda shook her head in disgust with herself. Boy I've really messed this romantic evening up, she thought. Why can't I just let it alone for one evening?

Joe didn't stay silent long. He grabbed her and pulled her close. "Its okay, Nelda, I know you have a one track mind. But I really don't know the answer to your question. What motivates one man to murder may not affect another, with or without training. Right now my mind is on love not hate.

He tenderly pushed her hair back, before covering her face with kisses. Nelda returned his embrace. She had almost forgotten how wonderful it was to be loved.

Somewhere in the background the phone rang, but she ignored it. Finally, Sue's voice came on the recorder.

"Aunt Nelda, I know you're out, but I just wanted to tell you Walter is fighting to save Daniel's life. They think he overdosed on pain killers. Call you . . . later," Sue sobbed as the recording stopped.

CHAPTER TWENTY-ONE

Close Call

As much as Nelda was enjoying her loving embraces with Joe on the sofa, her maternal and detective instincts won out when she heard Sue's tearful call from the hospital.

Nelda jumped up and pulled Joe up too. "I'm sorry about this interruption, Joe, but I'm worried about Daniel's condition and also Sue's involvement in this. I don't know why she and Walter are even there."

"Well, he's a doctor isn't he?"

"Yes and he does have patients in that hospital."

"There you go; I don't see the worry there. What we need to be concerned about is why he took so many pills. Come on, we'll drive to the hospital and see what's going on."

While waiting for Joe to open the truck door, Nelda looked up in the sky to check the weather, as was her habit. What a beautiful panoramic view greeted her, with a luminous half-moon surrounded by celestial brilliance. The perfume of her neighbor's flowering honeysuckle vine filled the air causing her to groan over a missed opportunity to sit in the swing with Joe.

Joe sped down the street with Nelda seated close beside him. Traffic was light and they made good time, arriving at the hospital in thirty minutes. There were plenty of places to park, now that visiting hours were almost over.

"I wonder if we're going to have a problem finding Sue, and getting information about Daniel's overdose." Nelda asked Joe as they entered the reception area.

"Don't worry," Joe replied, "if Sue's not here, I'll get the information you want."

When they passed the reception desk, the same silver haired lady was sitting there.

Nelda paused to speak to her. "My goodness you're putting in some long hours here."

"Yes, but I went home and rested for a while before coming back. The woman, who was supposed to take my place, didn't, so here I am. I remember you were here earlier with that pretty blonde."

"I was. Do you remember seeing her later?"

"Sure do, she came dashing in here with a nurse's uniform on, but didn't even stop for the elevator. She turned and went up the stairs. I haven't seen her since."

"Thanks, Mrs. Price," Nelda said looking at the name tag penned to her blouse.

Joe and Nelda took the elevator to the fourth floor in silence. Nelda could hardly wait for the elevator door to open. She walked ahead of him to room 440 and found the door open with no one there. They hurried back to the nurse's station on that floor. Two nurses were carrying on a quiet conversation while flipping through papers attached to clip boards.

"Excuse me, could you tell me where Daniel Hall is?"

The nurse looked startled. "Are you a relative?"

"No, close friend. Is he going to be alright?"

The older nurse gave Nelda a sympathetic look. "You need to go down to the waiting room on second floor. He's just had a procedure that requires him to be under observation. You'll find out more information down there."

"Thanks, I will. Has a nurse named Sue Grimes been up here?"

"Oh, sure," said the younger nurse smiling. "Sue will be there, too."

Nelda was relieved to hear Sue was still in the hospital. There were so many unanswered questions to this story.

While making their way to the second floor, Nelda discussed Daniel's predicament with Joe. "Daniel wasn't taking the pain pills the nurse gave him here in the hospital. He was sticking them in the bedside table drawer, but I don't know how he could have collected enough of them to kill himself. He's only been in the hospital for two days."

"You don't know how many he brought with him. Did he seem depressed when you left him?" Joe asked.

"Somewhat. They couldn't remove all the metal from his head, so he doesn't know if his headaches will stop or not."

Joe shook his head. "He's in a bad situation alright, but that guy's got grit. I can't see him as a potential suicide victim."

"I'm afraid, someone made a choice for him," Nelda whispered.

They had arrived at the waiting room. It was a small enclosure with the outside wall made up of glass windows. Nelda could see Sue huddled in a corner next to a soda machine with Celeste keeping her company. There were only a few seats occupied in the room.

When they entered, Sue rushed over to Nelda and embraced her. She acknowledged Joe with a weak smile. "Oh, I'm so glad you got my message. It seems like Walter will never come to tell us if Daniel is okay. I called Celeste to tell her about him and she wanted to wait with me for the news."

They walked over to Celeste and Nelda introduced her to Joe. "Celeste this is my friend, Joe Coats."

Nelda was shocked by Celeste's appearance; she no longer had the glamorous model semblance. Her hair was scraggly and her clothes had a thrown-on wrinkled look. Immediately, Nelda suspected Celeste's illicit relationship with Richard Sinclair had ended. The young woman's pain would be with her for a long time.

Joe acknowledged the introduction and then suggested they sit in seats opposite each other, so Sue could explain what she knew about Daniel's situation.

"Walter was making his rounds at the hospital when they found Daniel unconscious in his room. He was the only doctor in that area of the hospital, so he took charge and it's a good thing he did. Daniel had swallowed sleeping pills in the chocolate milk I bought for him."

Nelda spoke up, "Sue, you said it was pain pills when you called.

"I did, but they ran a check on his stomach contents, and what was left of the chocolate milk in the bottle too. The contents of both tested positive for pentobarbital, a compound sold as sleeping pills."

"He dissolved the pills in the milk or somebody did it for him." Joe said.

"What a mess," Celeste said bowing her head. "I think we're still having repercussions from that cruise. I wish I'd never taken the trip; I wish I'd never been born." She sat down sobbing.

Joe and Sue stared at her with pity, but Nelda knew just what to do. She put her arms around her. "I promise things will get better," Nelda said soothingly. She knew that Celeste was thinking about herself as well as Daniel.

Walter finally walked through the door. His tired, but happy expression on his face told the good news. "Daniel's going to make it, but he's still pretty much out of it. He did manage to say no, when asked if he swallowed the pills on purpose."

After that there was a lot of hugging going on. Nelda gave thumbs up. "I'm so grateful you saved his life. The chocolate milk was a perfect vehicle for the sleeping pills. I guess the guilty party found Daniel sleeping, placed the crushed pills in the milk and returned the bottle to the bedside table . . ."

"Probably so," Walter answered. The chocolate covered up the taste of the pentobarbital, and in powder form the drug is absorbed faster. Now, the police will be interested in the people who had access to that bottle of chocolate milk."

"Have the police been notified, Walter?" Joe asked.

"A detective is on his way here now. I imagine he'll want to talk to any visitors Daniel's had today, and the nursing staff too.

I've got to go now, but I'm really glad we got to him in time. From what Sue's told me he's had a lot of bad luck."

Sue put her arm around him. "I'll walk you to the elevator, Walter."

After they left, Joe excused himself to use his cell telephone, and Celeste walked forlornly down the hall.

"I'll see you Monday at the academy," Nelda called after her.

*   *   *

Joe, Sue and Nelda waited in the reception area on the first floor for the city detective to show up. It was growing late and the night cleaning crew had already started their chores.

"After finding Daniel unconscious, I wonder if the staff handling the milk bottle had sense enough to wear gloves," Nelda said.

"I'm sure they did, there is no shortage of rubber gloves around here." Joe responded. "You've got to relax, Nelda. I called the Chief of Police a few minutes ago and I know the man they're sending out. His name is George Garfield; he's been a detective for a long time. I'm sure he'll question them about the details."

Sue got up and started pacing the floor. "The thought just occurred to me, Daniel's and my fingerprints will be all they will find on that bottle."

"You don't know that," Nelda answered.

"Yes I do, Aunt Nelda. Whoever tried to kill Daniel would be careful not to leave any evidence that pointed to them. So where does that leave me?" Tears welled up in Sue's eyes.

Joe watched the drama played out with some concern. He didn't have any jurisdiction in the city limits. "Nelda, I'll have a talk with Detective Garfield in private when he gets here. I need to fill him in on what happened when you'll were on the cruise."

Nelda squeezed Joe's hand. "Thank you, Joe, for staying with us. I guess it was just fate that Sue and I met those academy people, and now we're tangled up in their lives."

*   *   *

Detective Garfield was short, blocky and very bald. His looks, however, did not diminish his ability to take charge. The meeting with Joe, Nelda, Sue and the head nurse, would be conducted in the deserted cafeteria. Those nurses that had finished their shifts by 4:00 p.m. would be interviewed the next day.

Sheriff Joe Coats and Detective George Garfield finished their little tête-à-tête, before the session began. This gave Nelda time to study Mrs. Gaspard, the head nurse on the fourth floor where Daniel had occupied a room when he drank the sleeping pills. She looked like a no nonsense person, who would take her duties very seriously. Nelda didn't see the red headed, registered nurse who'd given Daniel the shot. Her shift must have ended before he was found unconscious.

With everyone seated, Detective Garfield adjusted his black rimmed glasses, and opened up a spiral notebook. "I'm sorry to call this meeting so late, but I need to get some information about Daniel Hall's overdose of sleeping pills while facts are fresh on your mind. We'll start with Ms. Grimes' statement about buying the chocolate milk. As I understand it, Ms. Grimes, you are a nurse in a Stearn health clinic, but you were visiting Mr. Hall here at Med. Center earlier."

"Yes, I suppose it was about 2:00 pm when my aunt and I arrived."

"Why did you buy the chocolate milk for Mr. Hall?"

"Shortly after we arrived, Daniel asked me to go downstairs and buy the milk for him. He said he was very fond of chocolate. Then, when I returned, I put the milk on the bedside table."

"How long were you gone?"

Sue rubbed the side of her face. "I would say about fifteen minutes."

"Now, Mrs. Simmons, did you stay in the room while your niece was gone?"

"Yes, Daniel and I talked about the cruise we'd been on together."

"Did he seem upset or depressed about his medical condition?"

"He knew that the doctor hadn't removed all the metal from his head, but he certainly wasn't in a suicidal mood, as far as I could tell."

The detective then turned to the head nurse in charge of the floor. "Mrs. Gaspard, do you know how many visitors Mr. Hall had today?"

"No, we generally don't keep track of the visitors. Usually they acquire the room numbers at the receptionist desk on first floor, and don't need our help to find the room."

"What medications were administered to Mr. Hall today?"

"He was given antibiotics in the early morning through an IV tube and a shot for pain in the afternoon."

"Did you know he wasn't taking the pills handed out to him for pain?"

"Yes, one of the nurses was aware of it and told the day, head nurse about it. She reported it to the doctor. That's why he was given the injection at 2:30 pm. I was the only one on the night shift here when Mr. Hall was found unconscious at 4:30 p.m. We change shifts at 4:00 p.m. except for the head nurses on each floor. We come early to make sure all the personal are accounted for on the night shift."

"What was the name of the person that found him unconscious?"

"Shelia Watts, she's normally on the shift from 8:00 a.m. to 4:00 p.m."

Garfield closed his notebook. "Thank you, Mrs. Gaspard, for your help. Please make a list of the day shift personal on fourth floor, and their telephone numbers. I'll be back tomorrow to talk with them."

After Mrs. Gaspard left them, Detective Garfield turned his attention back to Nelda. "Mrs. Simmons, Joe told me about the blackmailing, deaths and near death on the cruise. He says you think the murderer is one of the three academy survivors from the cruise. After this episode, do you feel the list has been narrowed down to two?"

"I don't know what to think. But I do feel all the misfortunes have not been mere accidents. They were made to happen."

The detective seemed weary and stifled a yawn as he talked. "We'll talk some more after the fingerprint results come in from the bottle of milk, and hear Daniel Hall's side of the story. Thanks for waiting for me."

Joe Coats and George Garfield shook hands, and did some back patting before George headed out the cafeteria door. They were brothers of the law, always living in an element of danger. Nelda understood their camaraderie because her late husband, Jim, had been a sheriff. She had wonderful memories of holidays celebrated with keepers of the law from all parts of the state.

Sue stood up. "I've got to go. The clinic will be closed tomorrow, but I promised to take inventory. I guess I'll be hearing from that detective again, but you keep me posted too, Aunt Nelda."

"Please wait; Joe and I will walk you to your car, as soon as he answers his phone. There is a maniac running loose now and I want you to be extra careful everywhere you go. Maybe the culprit thinks I'm getting close to their identity."

"What about it, Aunt Nelda, have you been able to eliminate anyone?"

"I could probably take Daniel off the list, if he swallowed those pills with help."

Joe walked up in time to hear the last remark. "You might feel sorry enough for him to take him off your list right now."

Nelda spun around. "What's happened?"

"I just got word Daniel's apartment has been ransacked. Everything he owns is in a pile on his apartment floor."

I know why, Nelda thought. Excitement overcame her fatigue. "I bet the culprit was searching for the letters from Daniel's fiancée, Stephanie Williams. Now, the guilty one would want to make sure her name wasn't mentioned in any of them."

"Did you say her?" Sue gasped with the significance of Nelda's statement.

"I'm saying the list may have suddenly become smaller."

CHAPTER
TWENTY-TWO

Nelda Draws a Blank

Sunday afternoon Joe and Nelda sat in her dining room going over the strange happenings of the academy group.

"My back is to the wall, Joe! I'm puzzled as to what my next step should be to solve this mystery."

"What do you want me to do, just listen to you talk about what happened on the cruise, so you can get the facts straight in your mind?"

Nelda had her notes in front of her, and a large chalk board on an easel with the names of the academy group on it. She'd write information about each one by their names. This would help in working out possible clues.

"More than that, I want your opinion too. As problems happened on my trip, I jotted them down in this notebook."

Joe smiled. Let's see what you can put on your chalkboard."

Nelda picked up a piece of chalk and walked over to the easel; Justine was listed first.

"Justine was accused of being a blackmailer by Doris, Winnie and Celeste." She wrote, possible blackmailer, death by peanuts.

"Why are you writing possible?" Joe asked."

"We have no proof she blackmailed them, except the trio saying so." Nelda replied.

By Doris' name she wrote, death by drowning, and possible murderer.

Joe looked surprised. "Do you really think Doris might have killed Justine?"

"I don't know. If she was being blackmailed by her, and had access to the massage oil, maybe so."

By Winnie's name she wrote possible murderer. Before Joe could ask she said, "Because she was being blackmailed and had access to the massage oil."

"Was Winnie capable of killing Doris too?"

"Maybe, if she had a reason for killing her. She was at the beach that day. When Sue and I went to tell her about Doris' death she had a wet bathing suit hanging in the bathroom and white sand on the floor."

Celeste's name was next; by it she wrote possible murderer and instigator of scheme. "She's the one that passed out the green dots when they had the pre-cruise party and both Winnie and Doris received one. The person who received the green dot was supposed to steal Justine's *EpiPen.*"

"But no one did," added Joe.

"Right, she said it was all a joke. All three decided to talk to Justine before the cruise ended and convince her to stop blackmailing them or they would go to the police."

"Only sensible thing for them to do, they were crazy to let her do that in the first place."

Nelda patted Joe on the back. "Stated like a true lawman."

"You got one name left. I'm anxious to see what you put by Daniel's name since you seem to be so fond of him."

The sleuth smiled, "Do I note a little tinge of jealousy, even though he's decades younger than I am?"

"No," Joe grinned. "I'm just anxious to see if you treat him like one of the girls."

She wrote on the board next to Daniel's name, possible murderer of Justine and Doris.

"Great guns, how do you figure that, especially after his near death in the hospital and ransacked apartment?"

"To me, he had the best motive of all. He believes that Justine and Doris were responsible for his fiancée's suicide."

"How so? I haven't heard this before."

"Daniel told me that Doris furnished Stephanie with the pills that killed her, and Justine wanted her to have an abortion. So he had both motive and opportunity."

"But you can't bring yourself to believe it?"

"Right," smiled Nelda. "Let's take a break and I'll make you some coffee. I might even find you a cookie or two."

"Why not? I've got two hours before I have to leave." He led the way into the kitchen holding her hand.

While Nelda fixed the coffee, she continued talking. "Daniel seemed so sincere when he told me he swam out to the rock where Doris was sitting, so he could talk to her about her role in Stephanie's death."

"What did Doris tell him?"

"Doris told him she provided Stephanie with sleeping pills, because Stephanie complained about not getting any sleep."

"Did he confront Justine too?"

"I don't think so. He did say the librarian encouraged her to have an abortion."

"I guess you're right. He could have thought, 'eye for an eye.' But what about someone trying to kill him, and then there's that big mess in his apartment."

Nelda poured coffee into mugs and set a plate of oatmeal cookies in front of him before she answered. "Could have all been staged. The nurses go in and out of their rooms every few minutes; so maybe he thought someone was going to find him before he died of an overdose. As for his apartment, it's possible that he messed it up before going to the hospital. He might have thought these things would cast suspicion on someone else."

"It sure worked with me," Joe said as he picked up a cookie and his coffee mug.

"Anyway," said Nelda, "This is the predicament I've gotten myself into. No one, but me, is convinced a murder has even taken place, and I haven't eliminated any of the three remaining academy members."

"What do you intend to do about it, wait until one tries to kill you?" Joe got up and paced, then sat back down.

"No, I'm going to be on my guard, but at the same time I'll have close contact with them at the academy. I'll just fish around until I find some clues."

Joe wiped his mouth on a napkin. "When did you find out the girl's were being blackmailed by Justine?"

"Doris was the first one to tell us about it."

"Did the others volunteer to tell you too?"

Nelda massaged the back of her neck. "Well, it was hardly a volunteer, more like a squeeze. You verified their reasons for being black-mailed by talking to the principals of their previous schools. The reasons all fit except Winnie's. The principal at her school said she was too emotional, instead of Winnie's claim that she helped the kids on the state test."

Joe drained his mug and set it in the sink. "It's like I told you before, the principal could have made up that story. They'd be in serious trouble if anyone found out Winnie helped the students on their tests."

"That's true," Nelda said, "he certainly wasn't lying about her emotional state. I've never seen such a crybaby. She keeps the Kleenex people in business. Of course there were times she needed to cry."

"I'm sorry I haven't been more help, Nelda, but my cases are so much simpler. Our murders are usually solved at the time they're committed or at least in the next few days. What you have here are some cold cases. You don't have any clues to go on."

"Right, but I've been thinking. How did Justine approach them about collecting blackmail money? Did she send the girls e-mails or contact them in person? And how did she receive the blackmail money, in cash or checks? And lastly, did they hand the money to her or mail it to her?"

Joe grabbed his hat, stood up and laughed. "I suppose there's only one way to find out. Why don't you ask Winnie or Celeste?"

"You can't go, I'm just getting started."

He pulled her up and close, then kissed her before she could protest. After a long embrace they walked down the hall to the front door.

"Let me borrow your notebook, Nelda. I'll read through it and see if I can come up with some way we can smoke the killer out. You're worrying too much, and I'm afraid it might affect your health. Which brings up another point, are you sure you want Winnie staying with you? It's enough that you'll be working with her for six weeks."

"Now who's worrying? You go catch those cattle rustlers and be careful doing it. I'll just hang on to my notebook until I see you again."

After Joe left, Nelda closed the door smiling. She wondered how he would feel reading her thoughts about him in her little blue book.

*   *   *

Nelda didn't have time to sit around thinking deep thoughts. Winnie would be arriving in a taxi four hours from now. The guest bedroom and bath had to be spotless for her. Preparing for a guest gave Nelda a feeling of pleasure, a trait she'd inherited from her mother, a born hostess.

As she erased the chalkboard in the dining room, a feeling of panic took over. There was so much to do, and so little time to do it in. Having retired three years ago, her wardrobe was sadly outdated. There were few occasions new clothes were needed. Her clothes mainly consisted of sports wear and several suits for church. The things she'd bought for the cruise wouldn't do at all for a librarian. Tomorrow she'd make amends.

She rushed out the door to start the sprinklers going on her parched lawn. It would be sometime before the grass would be nice and green. Needless to say she was still in mourning for her beautiful flowers that died from lack of water, while she was on the cruise. Next time she'd have a backup person to take care of her yard. There was no way she could have foretold that Mrs.

Watkins would have a heart attack, and not be able to take care of her precious plants.

The phone was ringing when she entered the house. Joe was calling to give an update on Daniel's apartment break-in.

"Nelda, you sound breathless. Hope I didn't interrupt something important."

"If you think scrubbing a bathroom is important, then you interrupted. I just finished watering the dead grass, and am on my way to the guest quarters."

"I'm not going to keep you. I realize you'll be a working woman for the next six weeks and need to get ready."

Nelda laughed. "I think I denote a bit of sarcasm in your pretty little speech."

"Not me, sweetheart. I just called to tell you that Daniel reported only one thing missing from his apartment, his gun."

"What! I don't know what to make of that. I still think it was the murderer looking for Daniel's letters from his fiancée."

"Maybe, but you watch your back. Lock up everytime you leave your house or go to bed. I'll be cruising your street a lot until this mystery is solved to your satisfaction."

Nelda was touched by Joe's concern. Her affection for him was growing stronger every day.

After she hung up, Nelda rushed to the guest bedroom to see what shape it was in. As she surveyed the room, she noticed her blue Wedgwood vase needed dusting, as probably everything else in the room. Hurrying to the utility room, she brought out a bucket of cleaning materials, and a vacuum cleaner. She suspected Winnie would think she was moving into a museum, but at least it could be a clean one. For the next thirty minutes Nelda cleaned until she was satisfied with the results. The bathroom just needed a minor cleanup, and an addition of fresh towels and soap.

As Nelda headed toward the kitchen to prepare the evening meal, the doorbell sounded. Had her guest arrived early?

She peeped out the front window, there stood Sue and Celeste dressed in old jeans and T-shirts. Their attire didn't keep them from looking beautiful, even if they did appear tired. She pulled the heavy door open and stood to one side.

"Well, what have we here? It's a little early for trick or treat. Would you settle for a glass of lemonade?"

Sue hugged Nelda's neck as they made for the kitchen. "That's just what we need. You can't guess what we've been up to."

"From the looks of you it could be sandlot football."

Celeste, looking in better shape than she did the previous night spoke up. "We went over to Daniel's apartment and straightened it up as best we could."

"Yeah," Sue said. The police made a bigger mess of it looking for Daniel's gun. He told them where to look, but that didn't stop them from tearing the place apart."

"Bless both of you. What a thoughtful thing to do. When will he be going home from the hospital?"

"Tomorrow," Celeste said. "I'll pick him up when school is out."

Nelda raised her eyebrows. What's going on here, Nelda wondered. Maybe, the beauty queen is coming to her senses, and has dropped the rotten apple.

They sat at the bar while Nelda got a frozen can of lemonade from the freezer. She had a lot of questions to ask Celeste, but wouldn't do it. She was afraid Celeste would be offended if she opened up the blackmail charges at this time. Her self confidence still seemed a little shaky.

"Why don't you girls stay and have dinner with Winnie and me. She'll be here in an hour or so. Celeste, in case you don't know, Winnie will be staying with me until the doctor gives her permission to drive."

"I know that, Nelda, and she's very lucky to have the invitation. If you can humor her, you'll get along fine."

Sue shook her head and laughed. "Auntie has more gumption than anybody I know, Celeste. I'm sure she's already stocked up on tissues from Sam's Club."

Celeste grinned. "Wish we could stay, but I've got plenty to do for tomorrow and Sue has a date with a certain doctor."

They drained their lemonade and let themselves out while Nelda pulled a meat casserole from the freezer. She was busy chopping up a green salad when the doorbell sounded again. This time it really was her guest standing there like Little Orphan Anne on the front porch with luggage all around her, and her arm in a sling.

Nelda stepped out on the porch and gave her a careful hug. "Winnie I'm happy to see you, I'll call the bellboy and see if we can't get that luggage in the house."

There was a quizzical look on her face, her eyes quenched up for a possible shower."

"Oh, Nelda, I didn't know you rented out rooms."

"Don't be silly Winnie. I'm just teasing you. We'll have these bags in your room in no time. Why don't you carry something light with your good arm and I'll get the rest."

Winnie seemed relieved. She followed Nelda inside, her eyes taking in all the bric-a-bracs. "What pretty things you have. I'm going to enjoy you telling me about them."

"Thanks, Winnie, but most of it has become a burden, just accumulating dust. If you didn't have a sore arm, I'd let you clean the pieces for me."

There was no sound from Winnie. Nelda knew she would not be able to joke with Winnie as she did Sue. This girl was just waiting to take offense at everything. Oh well, she sighed, 'this too shall pass,' a saying she'd heard her aunt use from the Bible.

When Nelda finally opened the guest bedroom door, Winnie was all smiles. "This is a great bedroom, Nelda. I just love antiques."

"Good, you just wait here and I will get the other two bags." Nelda started out of the room.

"Oh no." said Winnie. "I'll help you."

She rushed ahead to the front porch, and picked up the smallest bag. That's strange, thought Nelda, shaking her head. What could she be hiding in that bag?

CHAPTER TWENTY THREE

Baiting the Trap

Nelda got up early to dress for her first day of work. No sound came from Winnie's bedroom. That was okay with her. She'd have time to sit on the back porch, read the paper and have coffee. She hurriedly dressed in a blue pant suit, one she often wore to church. Sliding into her slippers, she padded down to the kitchen and used the big mug she'd brought home from her cruise to hold her coffee. It held enough java to give her a jump start for the day.

After settling in a rocking chair on the porch, Nelda looked at her flowers, trees and then at the sky. The new summer plants were in full bloom, mostly lantana in several different colors, couldn't be prettier. Only the mulberry tree showed signs of an early fall. A slight breeze stirred its branches causing beautiful, yellow leaves to float gently to the ground. When she looked at the sky, cumulus clouds like piles of giant cotton balls were tinged pink by the rising sun. There was nothing more beautiful than the morning sky.

She was in a cheerful mood until she opened the paper. In the regional news, there was an article stating the date and time of a memorial service for Justine and Doris at the academy. Of course Nelda was pleased that the students and teachers would have a closure to these untimely deaths. She shook her head in disgust knowing the murderer would probably be attending this farewell eulogy. But she had a plan to catch the culprit. It had come to her in the middle of the night, with one simple sentence Joe had said earlier. "Watch your back, Nelda."

The back door opened startling her, Winnie stood there smiling. She wore blue jeans, red t-shirt and old sneakers.

"Good morning, Nelda. My goodness you're all dressed up. You know we're having a workday today. The kids aren't going to be there until tomorrow."

"Really! No one told me."

"Didn't you receive a letter from the school?"

Nelda put her hand to the side of her face and thought for a few seconds. "Yes, but I can't remember reading that."

"The information was there. It was just a form letter, so I don't imagine you paid much attention to it."

"That's true," Nelda replied. "I'll run in and put on my jeans. If you're having cereal, there's a box in the pantry." When she got up to change clothes, she handed the newspaper to Winnie. "I'll see you in the kitchen."

A few minutes later both crunched on wheat bran flakes. Winnie ate the cereal slowly with a sour look on her face, but gobbled up the toast smeared with strawberry jam.

"We'll grocery shop today, Winnie. I know you must have some preferences in your food. Right now, I think we better get a move on. I wouldn't want to be late on my first day."

"You're so dependable, Nelda. I suppose you have a set pattern you follow for everything."

"I try to; it certainly makes life easier when you don't have to wonder what to do next."

When they were ready to go, Nelda went to the utility room to get her car keys and purse. She always placed them on a hook in a broom closet along with extra keys to the house. The car keys weren't there. Winnie watched her search the closet, every hook and even on the floor. Finally, Nelda grabbed her purse and slammed the closet door.

"Well, it seems my organized life has a flaw. I can't find my keys."

"Maybe you laid them down in the kitchen or put them in your purse."

Nelda opened up her purse and there they were. She shook her head, grabbed the keys, shaking them in frustration.

"My goodness, they were hiding in my purse. Now, we can hit the road."

A smile flitted across Winnie's face. The look of snugness in Winnie's demeanor after the key incident irritated Nelda. Winnie followed her to the car making sure her sore elbow didn't bump into anything.

The teacher's parking lot was almost filled when they arrived at the academy. Nelda parked in Winnie's spot, next to the entrance. She felt strange walking into this building that would be her work place for the next six weeks. Of course the job would take second place to solving the mystery. She needed a lot of information, and perhaps she'd find it here.

Winnie gave Nelda some inside information about the agenda for the day. "The first thing we'll do after everybody grabs a cup of coffee is to meet with the headmaster, Mr. Witherspoon. He runs a tight ship here, and makes your business his, or tries to." She gave a shallow little laugh.

Nelda would make up her own mind about Phillip Witherspoon. He seemed a decent guy to her, and she was quite sure he didn't know all the business of these people, but maybe enough to help her find a clue to the murders.

The faculty lounge was crowded with about thirty faculty members. They were in all shapes and sizes, casually dressed with an air of excitement about them. Celeste stood in a corner dressed in shorts and a T-shirt she'd purchased on the cruise. The shirt featured the green waters of the Caribbean and a sailboat. The coach seemed very animated in the presence of a circle of young teachers. Nelda hoped the sailboat on Celeste's chest didn't indicate she was back with the weasel, Richard Sinclair.

"I'm going over to speak to Celeste," she told Winnie. "Be back in a minute."

As Celeste made her way to refill her cup, Nelda joined her at the coffee pot. "Good morning, Celeste, you look bright and cheery this morning."

"Thanks Nelda, it's good to see you too. Are you excited about your first day of school?"

"Yes, it seems like old times. I came over to tell you again how nice it was for you to help Daniel when someone trashed his apartment. I know he appreciated it. I wonder how he's doing now."

Celeste bit her lip and then smiled. "No need to wonder, Nelda. He was feeling great when I left him last night."

"What? Do we have a new romance on the horizon?"

The beautiful coach hung her head for a moment. When she looked up there were tears in her eyes. "Let's just say we were commiserating together. It will be awhile before I can trust again."

Another teacher headed toward them. Nelda quickly asked, "Do you suppose I could come to your office and visit you sometime today?"

"I'll be available at two. Come on over."

Nelda acknowledged a greeting from a middle-aged woman heading in Celeste's direction. There were so few people she knew here, but she recognized the secretary from her previous visit. Her last name was Pruitt, but Nelda couldn't remember her first name. Secretaries are important to teachers and she'd found them indispensable when you needed information about what was going on in the school.

She made a mental note to visit Ms. Pruitt soon.

Nelda needed to get back to Winnie and learn some of the names of her fellow educators before they met in the library. However, her house guest had vanished. Maybe she had already headed for the library. She pulled out the new teacher's packet she'd received through the mail and located a floor diagram of the school. The library was located in the middle of the main building, with the infirmary across the hall from it. A good location she thought. All the classrooms had easy access to both places.

As Nelda made her way down the hall, Mr. Witherspoon turned a corner, colliding with her. There she stood, face to face with her new boss, actually nearer than she wanted to be. He was dressed in tan trousers, blue plaid shirt and loafers, not quite as informal as his faculty.

"Ah ha! Just the lady I wanted to run into."

"Well, you succeeded in that," Nelda said as she bent over to pick up her purse that had fallen in the collision.

"Sorry, it's just a madhouse the first day back. Tomorrow the students will be back and we'll be more in sync."

"I'm sure that's true. Why were you hoping to see me?"

"It seems our new nurse will not be able to start school this week. I would like for you to take her place until next Monday."

"As long as this doesn't require doing anything but treating scratches, bruises and handing out aspirin. I know nothing about the duties of a nurse," Nelda said.

"Not to worry. Send them home, if they're sent to you. I'd appreciate you finishing the inventory that Winnie Speers started in the infirmary."

"You're the boss, Mr. Witherspoon. I suppose you'll break that news to Winnie?"

Phillip smiled, "I'm on my way to the library now. Our faculty meeting is in five minutes."

The library was buzzing with conversation when Phillip and Nelda entered. She saw Winnie seated at the first long table and went to join her. Most of the faculty was already seated, while others rushed in to find a seat. The headmaster stood behind the podium waiting to begin the meeting.

After clearing his throat, Philip said, "Good morning. First of all I want to thank you for spending part of your summer with us here at the academy. This will be a short meeting to pass out your schedules, class rolls and a sheet telling you what to expect this week. Ms. Pruitt will give those to you as you leave the library.

"Next, I just wanted to express my sorrow about the accidental deaths of our faculty members, Justine Scales and Doris Hodge. There will be a memorial service for them on Friday, last period. I'm hoping the students and their parents will have closure from this service.

"Ms. Nelda Simmons, retired Latin and Science teacher, will be the nurse for one week until the new nurse arrives, and then she'll be giving Winnie Speer a hand in the library for the summer session. Stand up Ms. Simmons; I'm sure we'll all help you to have a pleasant, productive six weeks."

Nelda stood up smiling, scanning as many faces as she could. When she looked at Winnie, she saw frustration written all over her face. Now what was she upset about?

Witherspoon ended the meeting. "Now, faculty, if you have any questions about your assignments, I'll be in my office all day."

The headmaster walked out quickly with a few of the teachers tagging along behind him. Nelda sat there not speaking to Winnie until the line of teachers picking up their packets had dwindled down to a few.

"What's wrong, Winnie? It wasn't my idea to be in the infirmary you know. Mr. Witherspoon advised me of that this morning."

"Oh I'm not mad at you, Nelda, but I can't unpack all those boxes of new books with my arm hurting. That's why I didn't finish the clinic inventory last week."

"Wait on the books until next week. Now, give me your inventory sheet and the keys to the infirmary."

"I don't have them. Mrs. Pruitt had me hand them in last Friday. You better catch her before she goes back to the office. I'll see you at lunch time."

Winnie got up and walked to her desk with a shredded tissue in her hand. Nelda could see another crying mode coming on. She didn't want to witness that, so she hurried over to Mrs. Pruitt, who explained to a small man with thick glasses, why his social studies class was so crowded.

"Sorry, Jack, not enough students signed up to have two classes. Mr. Witherspoon said you can handle thirty students. That's all I can tell you."

Grabbing the student list out of her hand, Jack whirled around and disappeared down the hall. No doubt Witherspoon was in for a long day.

Pruitt acknowledged Nelda's presence with a smile, "Hello, Mrs. Simmons, glad you're helping us out. Here are the keys you'll need to get in the infirmary and the supply cabinets. I've also included a tablet and pencils for the inventory." She handed Nelda an envelope. "If I can do anything else to help you, let me know."

"Thank you, do you have the inventory list that Winnie Speers started?"

"Yes, it's in the envelope too, but she was just getting started. Mr. Witherspoon wants you to rearrange the contents of the cabinets. It seems as though some of the supplies are all mixed up. Put like things together and label each cabinet as to what's in it. This will help us see what we need to order."

"I believe I can handle that. Are the keys labeled?"

"Supposed to be, these are duplicate keys we had in the office. Doris didn't turn her keys in because she was going to teach summer school."

Nelda gathered up her belongings and walked across the hall to the door of the infirmary. She tried the largest key in the envelope and it opened the main door. Stepping inside, she found one huge room divided into five small ones: The nurse's office with storage cabinets covering one wall, two bedrooms (each containing a single bed), one bathroom, and a small kitchenette. Everything in white: the walls, floors, bedcovers, even the floor mats in the bathroom. She had to smile thinking of Doris and her fondness for white.

Nelda decided to start the inventory with the lower cabinets and work up. She worked steadily for a couple of hours emptying the individual cabinets and putting the contents on a utility cart she found in the closet. Her idea was to take everything out, stack it on the counter in the kitchen and then she could group like things together and put it back. Doris may have been a wonderful nurse in some areas, Nelda thought, but orderliness was not one of them. She couldn't believe the jumbled mess in the cabinets. Finally she came to one cabinet that none of the keys could open. Now what? She supposed Winnie had forgotten to turn the key in. She spent the next two hours grouping things together on the kitchen counter. Some of the medications needed to be discarded, way past their expiration date.

Someone knocked on the door. Nelda turned around to find Winnie standing in the office staring at the clutter.

"My word, Nelda, looks like a cyclone passed through here. Did Witherspoon really mean for you to do all this?"

"I don't know, but you can't take inventory when everything is mixed up. It's hard to believe that Doris was so disorganized. How did you get anything done without taking things out?"

"I didn't, it's not my job to be janitor."

"Winnie, did you forget to turn a key in? I couldn't open the cabinet by her desk."

"Does it show the number of keys on the outside of the envelope?"

"Four," said Nelda, holding the packet, "that's the number I received, but I can't open one of the cabinets with any of these keys."

"Well, let's go to lunch. You can figure it out when we get back."

"I could use a break. Let me get my purse and I'll lock up."

*   *   *

Winnie, Nelda and an English teacher, Amelia Brite, walked down to a sandwich café several blocks away. After ordering their sandwiches and drinks, they sat in a booth. Amelia, with a somber look in her eyes, spent most of the time praising Doris. Her auburn curls seemed to sway in time with the movement of her mouth, which never stopped.

"I've never seen a person so knowledgeable about every phase of medicine. The kids adored her, and her clinic was always full of them just wanting to talk to her, you should have seen her solve their problems."

After thirty minutes, Nelda and Winnie left Amelia with another group of teachers, and hurried back to school.

Winnie groaned out loud. "Thank goodness for the solitude of the library"

"She was just getting started," laughed Nelda.

When they arrived at the school, Nelda stopped at Pruitt's office. "I've got to see about getting that cabinet open. I'll see you later, Winnie."

The librarian wavered for a minute as though she wanted to follow Nelda, but then turned and went on down the hall.

Pruitt was working in her glassed in office. Nelda tapped on the door. The secretary motioned for her to come inside.

"How are you getting along, Ms. Simmons?"

"It seems I'm short one key. I can't get into one of the cabinets with the keys I have."

Pruitt drummed her long fingers on her desk. "That's strange. Maybe the lock is rusty and that's why it won't open. I'll send our head janitor, Ron Cole, to get it open."

"Good, I'd appreciate that. I don't know if I'll finish the inventory today. Things are really in a mess."

"Take your time. It only took ten years for them to get that way. That's when the cabinets were installed. We've employed four different nurses during that time and not one cleaned out the cabinets."

The secretary called the janitor as Nelda walked out. She hurried back to the infirmary so she would be there when Ron Cole showed up.

Twenty minutes later a gray headed man dressed in blue overalls and carrying a tool kit walked in.

"Ms. Simmons, I'm Ron, I heard you had a problem."

Nelda smiled acknowledging the greeting. His wrinkled face and crippled gait indicated he'd faced problems of more severity then this one.

She walked behind the nurse's desk. "I can't get this cabinet open. None of the keys will open it." Nelda handed the keys to Ron.

With large calloused fingers, he tried all the keys. "The key is not here. The old lock has been changed out."

"Can you open it?" Nelda asked.

"There is never been one I couldn't open." He took a funny looking gadget out of his pocket, placed it in the key hole, and with a few twists opened the cabinet.

"Thanks, Ron, I appreciate your help."

"That's what I'm here for," he said gruffly, picking up his tool kit. Without a backward glance he hobbled out of the infirmary.

She opened the cabinet expecting a jumbled mess, but this one appeared orderly, mostly bottles of pills and small boxes stacked neatly. Nelda took a closer look, not believing what she saw. The cabinet was filled with prescription drugs: Retin-A, sleeping pills, tranquillizers, diet pills, and other medicines she couldn't identify. There were also boxes containing prophylactics.

Out of curiosity she opened several bottles of pills. The pills came in various sizes and shapes. She noted the sleeping pills looked a lot like her favorite mints. Closing the cabinet, Nelda sat down heavily in a chair. She covered her eyes with her hand, while her mind was spinning with the knowledge that Doris had provided all these drugs to teenagers.

CHAPTER TWENTY-FOUR

Gathering Clues

The prescription drugs Nelda found in the cabinet caused her great concern. She had no chose but to tell Mr. Witherspoon about them. Now she was troubled about the stain on Doris' character, and what it would do to the reputation of the school. She wondered if any of these drugs had harmed the students.

She looked at her watch and saw that it was nearing the time she would meet with Celeste, so she locked up the infirmary and made her way to the coach's office. The office door was open with several young girls gathered around Celeste, who was sitting at her desk. They were all laughing at something Celeste said. At any other time, Nelda would have enjoyed the scene, but now she wanted the coach alone for a serious talk.

Celeste looked up and smiled at Nelda. "What do you think of these athletics, Ms. Simmons? They're ready for volleyball season to start."

"Terrific! But do you think we could have a few words in private?"

The coach stood up and pointed toward the door, "Okay girls, I'll see you later. I have some business to take care of."

The well muscles girls left the office giggling and throwing around a volley ball. Celeste closed the door behind them.

"Sit down, Nelda; could I get you a Coke?"

Nelda sank down in a folding chair. "No thanks, Celeste, Winnie and I just ate a sandwich. The reason I'm here is for your help in solving Justine's and Doris' deaths. I guess you know I'm still looking for the killer. That's one reason I've accepted this job, to find clues."

Celeste leaned back, massaging her shoulders, "I knew it had to be something like that. Daniel said you wouldn't give up until the mystery is solved. My conscious is clear, but I'm afraid to help you. I need this job now more than ever. If you find someone killed them, all the blackmailing will come out in the open. Do you understand my position?"

"You're in more danger if we don't find the murderer. You could be next. Besides, they aren't going to fire you for an affair in the past. You're no longer dating a married man are you? And you are the best coach this school has ever had."

Celeste became animated. "You bet I'm the best, with boys and girls. I have a winning boy's tennis team too. However, I have bigger plans for coaching. My feelers are already out for a university position." Suddenly, her smile turned to concern. "You really think I could be in danger."

"I do, so please work with me."

"Okay, what do you want to know?"

"It would certainly help if I knew how the blackmailer contacted you, how much you paid the culprit, and how the money was delivered?"

Celeste rolled a soft ball back and forth on her desk as she talked. "I was only here two weeks before I received an e-mail. The writer didn't actually identify herself, but I knew who it was when I received instructions on what to do with the money. To most people the sum would be insignificant, but one-hundred dollars meant a lot to me, with all the bills I have to pay."

"What did the message say?"

"You've messing around with a married man and I have pictures to prove it. If I don't receive one-hundred dollars every paycheck your head will roll."

Nelda frowned. "Do you think the blackmailer had pictures?"

Celeste rubbed her forehead. "She could have. We tried to meet in larger towns, but other people travel too."

"Well, how did you get the money to the blackmailer and was it in cash?"

"I have a homeroom at the beginning of the day. The teachers are asked to collect money for overdue books, put it in an envelope, and then place it in the librarian's mail box. The money I paid in cash was placed in this envelope after I received my monthly school check."

"Did you ever see anyone get the envelope out of the librarian's mailbox?"

"No, my conference period is in the afternoon, way after everyone has picked up their mail."

"Did you keep the blackmailer's e-mail?"

"Certainly not! I didn't need to be reminded."

"One more question. How well did you know Doris?"

Celeste got up and looked through a window adjoining the gym. "Just had to check on what was going on in there. Even though school doesn't start until tomorrow, some are eager to be here. Can you believe that?"

"Of course, but let's talk about the nurse. Did you know very much about her life?"

Celeste talked with her back to Nelda while she played with the Venetian blind pull.

"The facts about Doris' early life haunt me now. Last fall she went to some volleyball tournaments with me, and the team. One weekend we had to spend the night in a motel together, and that's when she told me what a miserable childhood she had."

Nelda waited for her to continue. Finally, Celeste whirled around with tears standing in her eyes.

"She said she was a fat, pimple faced teenager with stringy hair. Her whole adolescence was a nightmare. She didn't blame her parents, who just didn't know how to help her. There were six children and not enough money to go around for them to live decently."

"How in the world did she get into nurse's training?"

"Doris was smart, very smart. She got a scholarship and worked on the campus. She told me that the only thing she wanted to do when she graduated was to help kids in school be happy."

"And did she?"

"All the students adored her. She tried to solve problems for them that their parents didn't bother with. Sometimes the students just went in to talk to her."

"Did she ever charge students for medication she gave them?"

"Good heavens, no. That woman spent money out of her own pocket for things they needed. Believe me, not anything stays hidden from Coach."

Nelda stood up. "I'm happy to hear such good things about her. Guess I better get back to the infirmary. Lot's of inventory left to do."

As Nelda turned to leave, she noticed a half-dead mouse in a sticky trap by a file cabinet. "What's with the mouse, Celeste? Why don't you get it out of its misery?"

"Why? It's given me plenty. The exterminators couldn't catch it, but I did."

Nelda shook her head in disgust. "Even a mouse has feelings."

"Okay, okay, I'll get rid of it. And speaking of mouse, how are you and Winnie doing?"

"So far, so good. I hope I can be of some help to her in the library."

"That's another story. Winnie is so organized it's sickening. The kids hate to go in the library, because Winnie is always on their backs about keeping the books in order. Sometimes Justine had to intervene for them. I guess she'll be that way in your home too."

"Hope so, Nelda said with a smile. "I might have to put her to work in the pantry," she said as she went out the door.

Nelda didn't want to report what she'd found in the cabinet with the new lock, however she had no choice. She realized Mr. Witherspoon needed to know the situation in the infirmary, and get rid of the prescription medicine plus other things that were not suitable for school nurses to dispense. In spite of the laws Doris had broken, she couldn't help but believe that Doris' intentions, though misguided, were to help the students have a better life.

As she neared Witherspoon's office, a woman in a brown suit came out slamming the door behind her. She barreled past Nelda without even a nod. No doubt the woman was disturbed about something.

After the second knock, Mr. Witherspoon opened the door. His neat appearance from that morning had vanished and his face was flushed from anger. He composed himself before escorting Nelda to a chair, and then plopped down in his seat with his eyes closed.

"I cannot tell you how happy I will be to see our counselor, Mr. Edwards. If I have to listen to one more complaint from a teacher or parent, I will explode.

"Please forgive my ranting, Ms. Simmons, how is your inventory going. Ms. Pruitt said you found the cabinets in a chaotic state. I'm sure you'll remedy that for us. We shouldn't have let this go on for so long."

Nelda hated to pour fuel on a day that was going badly for Witherspoon, but she had no choice. "The inventory is going okay, but I ran into a problem only you can handle."

The Headmaster sat up straight. "Tell me about it, couldn't be any worse than I've been through today."

"Doris had a cabinet filled with prescription drugs, and things she shouldn't have been handing out to the students."

He twisted in his seat. "Could be we have a perfectly innocent reason for the drugs. Students brought their prescriptions to the nurse and she kept them until they were used."

"Not these. There are no doctor's names or patient's names on them, only the names of the drugs and their uses, mostly the kind that might benefit teen-agers.

"How would it help them?"

"Get rid of pimples, lose weight, get some sleep, make them less nervous when taking a test, and there were also boxes of prophylactics."

Witherspoon got up. His face turned red and he worked hard to control his breathing. "The school has never ordered any of those drugs. Furthermore, there was not one complaint about her from students or parents, always glowing reports about how she's improved the lives of their children."

"I'm sure that's true. I'll put all the prescription drugs in a box and you can take care of it. No one knows about this, as far as I can tell, but me."

"Please call me as soon as you've done that and I'll personally get rid of it. Thank you for handling this in such a discreet manner."

"You're welcome. From what I've heard about Doris from faculty members, she only wanted to help people."

Witherspoon shook his head in assent as Nelda walked out the door.

*   *   *

Nelda couldn't wait to get home for several reasons; her feet, head and back were hurting. She whizzed on past the grocery store to Winnie's dismay.

"Hold up," Winnie said. Don't you remember we're going to stop at the grocery store; your pantry holds nothing but health foods.

Making a u-turn at the next intersection, Nelda turned into the parking lot of an HEB grocery store. "I tell you what, Winnie, you run in and get whatever you want and I'll wait for you here. Take your time. I'm simply not up to grocery shopping."

"I guess I can manage with one arm," Winnie said and sniffled.

"Get one of their electric carts. They'll show you how to use it."

Winnie got out of the car. "That's okay. I'll manage somehow, anything to get my sugared cereal," she then laughed.

After watching her leave, Nelda almost felt guilty, but something told her that Winnie's injury was not as bad as she made out. The librarian had used her right arm when she didn't think anyone was watching. She had watched her unload a book cart using both arms, after lunch.

Opening her purse, Nelda got out her cell phone and called Sue. She told her all about the secret cabinet in the clinic, stressing some of its contents. Then she outlined a course of action she would take in the next few days. After she finished, she pulled the phone away from her ear.

"Sue, don't holler at me; I will be careful. I've been taking care of myself for a long, long time. And please call, Joe, make him understand my plan, that's the only way I can carry this out. Gotta go, here comes Winnie."

She folded up her cell phone just as the young man from the grocery store opened up her car trunk to put Winnie's grocery bag inside. The librarian climbed in and soon they were on their way. As they neared the house Winnie asked a question Nelda knew she was going to ask sooner or later

"What was Mr. Witherspoon doing in the infirmary near the end of the day? I saw him carry out a big box." Winnie squirmed as she waited for a reply.

Nonchalantly, Nelda adjusted the AC before answering. "Oh, he just removed some outdated drugs and things that didn't belong in the infirmary."

Winnie chewed on her lip, but didn't ask what things; instead she let out a whoop causing her tired hostess to slow down.

"Why did you do that?" Nelda asked with irritation in her voice.

"Because, you passed up your street. Has your memory been giving you problems."

"As a matter of fact it has, but that's not for publication."

Winnie gave Nelda a quizzical look. "Aren't you going to do anything about it?"

"No, can't fix it. Not much you can do." Nelda glanced over at Winnie. The librarian had a ghost of a smile on her face.

They finally arrived home, but Nelda was not in the mood to put Winnie's groceries up or start dinner. She marched to the refrigerator and decided to have a small glass of wine on the back porch, hoping Winnie would find something to do elsewhere. As she passed Winnie's bedroom she noticed her Wedgwood vase was missing from the dresser. Even though Nelda took all her beautiful inherited things for granted, she loved every piece. Now what had Winnie done with that piece she wondered. Only one way to find out, she'd ask.

She made her way to the kitchen where Winnie was supposed to be unloading her groceries. As she neared the entrance, she heard Winnie talking on the kitchen phone in a low voice. Curious, she stopped to hear what Winnie had to say.

"I'm very concerned, Sue. Nelda has been very forgetful and I think it's getting worse every day." There was a pause and then Winnie continued, "No, I promise not to mention it to her. I'll let you handle it."

Tiptoeing back down the hall, Nelda decided now was not the time to pursue the missing vase.

CHAPTER
TWENTY-FIVE

Saying Good-bye

Nelda was up with the sun. She gathered all the soiled linens and towels from the hamper and headed for the utility room. After filling the washing machine, she opened the cabinet to find her Wedgwood vase sitting next to the detergent. Why in the world would she put this valuable vase in such a place? Before Winnie arrived, she remembered cleaning the guest bedroom. The vase was dusty, so in Nelda's haste she put the vase away in here and *forgot* about it. Or, *maybe*, someone up there was punishing Nelda for trying to fake memory loss.

*   *   *

The next few days went smoothly enough. Nelda and Winnie were in a routine, with the summer school and household activities. Although, Nelda found time to escape from Winnie by claiming she needed to visit her family doctor for a thorough physical, since she hadn't had one in the last few years. And of course these visits included a few specialists. Joe and Sue accompanied Nelda on these trips that ended with dinner at one of the restaurants, insuring them time to speak on confidential matters relating to the "Green Murders," as Nelda referred to them.

After ordering dinner in The Tea Room restaurant, Nelda brought Joe and Sue up to date on her life with Winnie. "It seems that Winnie has turned out to be fanatical about neatness. I even caught her in my bedroom adjusting the drapes. She claimed that they just didn't hang right." Nelda laughed. "As soon as she has thoroughly cleaned my house, it will be time for her to leave."

Sue spoke up. "Now what's all this business about losing your memory? I know it's not so, but you've convinced Winnie it is."

"Why are you doing that?" Joe asked.

"I want Winnie to think I'm vulnerable. She'll spread the word about my memory loss."

Joe had a frown on his face. "I don't like it."

Nelda rubbed Joe's arm. "I'll be fine, I promise. Now tell me the latest on Daniel. Are you satisfied he didn't try to kill himself?"

"Yes, I'm satisfied. And by the way, he let me read those letters from his fiancée, the ones she wrote before she died. Stephanie mentioned the school nurse and librarian, but not by name. The school nurse gave her the sleeping pills, because she wasn't sleeping well. The librarian encouraged her to have an abortion. She told Stephanie that she'd be fired if Witherspoon knew she was pregnant.

Nelda, didn't you tell me that Daniel talked to Doris right before she drowned, but didn't have an opportunity to speak with Justine about Stephanie?"

She looked over at Joe. "Yes and I believe him. I sure can tell you're convinced he's innocent of those murders."

"I am. I think he wanted Justine and Doris to tell him why Stephanie took her life without waiting for word from him."

"Any leads on who stole his gun and trashed his apartment?" Sue asked.

"No, nothing, not one clue. Whoever did it wore gloves and must have had something over their shoes or walked on air."

"We haven't discussed Celeste yet," Nelda said.

Joe saw the busboy headed their way with their dinner. "Time out! We've got to eat this healthy meal you ordered for us. I'm starving and it better be good."

Nelda smiled at Joe. "Okay, we'll have a break. You're going to love this mushroom and brown rice soup. The chicken salad is delicious too."

The busboy with spiked hair and earrings in both ears just happened to be one of Nelda's ex students. He set the tray down on a stand with a flourish and then proceeded to serve the dishes, without even a hello.

"Pierce," Nelda said. "You're not going to speak to me?"

"Ms. Simmons, I'm sorry. All I had eyes for was the sheriff."

"Why, did you do something wrong?"

"No Mam, not since he showed me the way."

Joe put his hand over his mouth to cover a grin before he spoke. "Mr. Pierce Adams here, just got a little out of control at a concert, but now he's an outstanding citizen, aren't you, Pierce?"

"Yes sir, you did a lot for me and I appreciate it. Saved me from a jail sentence. I won't forget it, no sir." He put the food down and hurried back to the kitchen.

"He's scared to death of you, Joe." Nelda commented.

"No, he's not. If he was he'd quit sticking his finger in an electric outlet to get that hairdo and stop wearing girl's jewelry. I wonder how he got his job, looking like that."

Sue and Nelda both shook their heads. The next few minutes were taken up with enjoying the cuisine. The looks of the waiter didn't detract from their appetites.

"You're right, Nelda, it's all delicious," Joe said, "especially these yeast rolls. You know they don't make TV dinners that include fresh rolls."

It was only after dessert was served with fresh coffee that Nelda talked about Celeste. Between bites she told them what she'd learned from Celeste, how the blackmailer contacted her, how much the culprit wanted, and how the money was to be delivered.

Sue held a fork up in mid-air. "And none of that can be proven, right?"

"No, she didn't keep the e-mail and she paid in cash."

Joe wiped the pecan pie off his lips, while setting his coffee cup down slowly. "I wonder if Winnie saw Justine take money out of the envelope."

"I'm not ready to quiz Winnie about that. There are some other things I need to nail down." Nelda folded her napkin. There was so

much ground work left to do, before her house guest went home.
Now was not the time to discuss it with Joe and Sue. They would
object to her methods.

Joe called for the bill and got up. "You ladies will have to excuse
me. It's back to work now. I'm helping the night crew and have to
run. Nelda, you won't forget our date this weekend?"

"I'm looking forward to it. Be careful; don't let the cattle
rustlers get you."

"I won't." Joe, slowly brushed his lips across Nelda's
cheek, hugged Sue and headed out. Nelda watched him leave,
remembering their last date. Those memories caused her heart to
beat a little faster.

*   *   *

Nelda's walk-in closet was huge. Several years ago, she'd had
a carpenter box in a portion of the side porch to make it. At the
end of the closet was a window that allowed daylight in and was
used by her to air it out.

She stood in the middle of the closet trying to decide about
her wardrobe. As she stroked the sleeve of a green, wool jacket, she
recalled fun times on a skiing trip with her late husband, Jim. He'd
bought her the jacket especially for that trip twenty years ago.

Her train of thought was interrupted by Winnie's voice. "Nelda
where are you?"

"I'm in my closet," answered Nelda.

Winnie walked through Nelda's bedroom and stood next to
her. "Good grief, I feel like I'm in the Goodwill Store."

Nelda laughed. "That's not very complimentary. I just couldn't
bear to part with all these old clothes, hoping they'd come back
in style."

"I'm sure they will by the end of the century," Winnie said,
wrinkling her nose at the smell of moth balls.

"Okay, you've made your point. As soon as summer school
is over, I'll get rid of everything I haven't worn in the last five
years."

"Harrumph," muttered Winnie. "You know you'll be too cowardly to make a clean sweep. I'll help you."

"No thanks, right now I'm going to call it a night, go to the kitchen and wash all my pills down with some milk. You want to join me? You could have a bowl of that sweet stuff you call cereal."

"Thanks, I suppose so."

When they arrived in the kitchen, Nelda took out her seven-day pill box, pouring out several pills and capsules in her hand. She then washed them down with soy milk.

Winnie watched her with fascination.

"Nelda, those are really a lot of pills. Don't you find them difficult to swallow at one time?"

"No, right before bedtime is the best time to take them. Then, you're finished for the night."

"If you say so," her guest said shaking her head.

*   *   *

Having finished her inventory in the infirmary the day before, Nelda was helping Winnie in the library by unpacking new books. Her mind was not focused on the monotonous job. She was thinking of the memorial services scheduled for Justine and Doris at 1:00 pm that afternoon. What a sad event this promised to be. In a way she felt as though she could have prevented their deaths. Both might still be alive, if only she hadn't given Justine the bottle of oil, and if only she hadn't left Doris resting on the rock.

Her self incrimination was interrupted by Winnie. "Nelda, I hope you don't mind taking the weekly report of students using the library to the office."

"No, not at all. It'll give me a chance to stretch my legs. Why do they need that report?"

"Witherspoon thinks this is one way to make sure the teachers are using the facilities in the library."

"Good idea," said Nelda, grabbing up the folder. "Be back in a jiffy."

She looked through the folder as she walked down the hall, and found out why she'd had so many books on sports to put back in their rightful place. Celeste had had her students in the library two mornings in a row.

Nelda was delighted that Winnie was sending her to the office. She'd been trying to think of some excuse to visit the secretary, hoping Pruitt could provide another clue that would help her identify the killer.

The secretary seemed surprised to see Nelda. "I thought Winnie was bringing me that folder, so she could order some programs for her new computer."

"You mean we have a new computer?"

"Sure do. I'm not talking about the ones the students use. This one is just for the librarians use. It seems some student destroyed the other one by pouring water on it. Claimed it was an accident."

Nelda shook her head. "I didn't know that, but while I'm here let me ask you a question."

Pruitt got up to file the folder. "Sure, I'll answer if I can."

"Are there handbooks with duties for the various departments?"

"Yes, I'm sorry I didn't give you one. I just assumed that Winnie would tell you what your assignments are. There's one in this file cabinet." Pruitt opened the top drawer and handed Nelda the booklet."

"Thank you. I just want to make sure, I'm fulfilling my duties."

"I understand." Pruitt turned away to answer the phone. "I'll see you later at the memorial."

Nelda could hardly wait to look through the booklet. She quickly opened to the page that gave the duties of the assistant librarian. Looking through the list made Nelda smile. It seemed that Winnie was taking on more than her share of duties. Perhaps she'd point that out to her when the time was right. For now she tucked the booklet under her arm and returned to the library.

*   *   *

The academy gym was also used as an auditorium with the stage at one end. Folding chairs were set up on the hardwood floor. Winnie and Nelda settled on sitting several rows back from the front near the aisle. Nelda wanted to make sure Sue could find her and sit with them. She was surprised when Joe, Sue and Celeste walked in several minutes before the ceremony started. They found seats in front of them.

On the stage several speakers sat on either side of a podium. Down below on the gym floor were floral arrangements, mostly of white lilies. Nelda smiled through her tears knowing Doris would have liked that. A small table held portraits of both Doris and Justine. They were unflattering school pictures that someone had enlarged, making Justine look like a tusk less walrus. Nelda passed Winnie another tissue.

Someone forgot to turn the school bells off. At one o'clock after the bell sounded, Witherspoon made his way to the podium. Thumping on the microphone several times to make sure it was working, he began his speech.

"Good evening, we are gathered here today to remember our two faculty friends, Justine Scales and Doris Hodge. The unfortunate accidents they incurred on vacation have caused all of us to grieve. They will be sorely missed, not only as gifted faculty members, but also as beloved friends. We encourage all of you to write one page of remembrances about them. These pages will be bound into a book for the library."

After Witherspoon's brief welcome, a prayer was said by a local minister, and several faculty members got up to express the sterling qualities of both faculty members. The last speaker was a physician, one of Doris' friends. Nelda sat up straight in her chair and gave full attention to Dr. Donald Brown. Doris had mentioned him the day she died.

Dr. Brown was grey headed and had a goatee that he stroked after each positive statement he gave about Doris. "My friend was on a mission," he said, "to eliminate all the bad things that students incur as they mature. She was their friend, when they were in trouble or pain. I commend Doris for making the high school years of many students more enjoyable, mentally and physically. I've seen her dig into her own resources to help the students at this academy. The academy has a better learning environment because of her existence. She's raised the bar for all school nurses."

Nelda was impressed by the doctor's statements about Doris. It inspired her to double her efforts in unmasking the killer.

*　　*　　*

When they got ready to go back home, Winnie discovered her purse was missing. She always put it in the bottom drawer of a filing cabinet near her desk. They searched the library and finally found it under some newspapers. Winnie couldn't understand how it got there. However, there didn't seem to be anything missing.

On their way back home, Nelda discussed her duties at the library with Winnie. "Now that I'm in the library with you, Winnie, I'd like to go over my duties. There is no sense in me not doing my share."

"How do you know you're not doing your duties?"

"Ms. Pruitt gave me the booklet today that specifies what I'm supposed to do."

"Oh, well I thought during the summer-time it wouldn't make any difference."

"I suppose you're right. I'm sure we'll both have plenty of work. By the way I saw Celeste bending your ear. How are things going with her?"

"Mostly, she was asking about you. I think she's nervous about your snooping. She wondered if you would ever believe the deaths were accidental."

Nelda didn't know what to think of Celeste's remarks to Winnie. She thought she had made it clear to her what her intentions were."

"Don't look troubled, Nelda, Celeste has always been a selfish one. She thinks you spoiled her love life, but she'll probably forgive you."

Gears were shifting in Nelda's mind. How could she have been so foolish to overlook the obvious? It would take motive, opportunity and nerves of steel to carry out a double murder.

CHAPTER
TWENTY-SIX

Show Time

Saturday was a gorgeous day. Nelda saw real progress in her yard's appearance. All the new plants were blooming and the grass was almost all green. A few weeks of watering had worked wonders. She savored her coffee while making plans for her daily activities.

She had an appointment to visit Dr. Brown at 10:00 am. Nelda didn't know exactly how to question him about Doris' stash of illegal drugs. He wouldn't incriminate himself by saying he gave them to her, and maybe he didn't. Would this information even help her solve the murder mystery? It was worth a try.

The screen door opened with a bang, and Winnie came out with clothes draped over one arm. "Nelda, I'm moving out today, because my elbow doesn't hurt at all. If you could help me, we'll only have to make one load to my apartment."

"My goodness, when you make up your mind about something, you don't fool around. What's the rush, Winnie?" Are you sure your doctor will approve of this?"

"I'm sure he will. Besides, you've got your own life, and I should get out of it."

Of course Nelda was pleased to hear she would get her privacy back, but wondered why the abrupt change in Winnie's plans. "I hope I haven't done anything to offend you?"

"No, I appreciate your help. I just feel this would be a good time to move."

Nelda got up stretching, "Well, I'll get dressed while you pack. Have you had your breakfast yet?"

"No, I'll eat in a few minutes. I'm already packed, except for a few loose things that I could put in your laundry basket if that's okay."

"Sure, I'll bring it home after you unload it."

They both walked back in the house. Nelda worried about Winnie's sudden exit. She hadn't said a word about it before they said good night. Winnie had received a phone call after Nelda had gone to bed. Could that be the cause of this sudden move?

The sleuth dressed in clothes she'd wear to the doctor's office: navy blue slacks, white blouse and her new comfortable, Clark shoes. She would be pushed for time, but if Winnie didn't start one of her crying jags it would work out.

Walking briskly to the kitchen, she found that Winnie had finished breakfast; her cereal bowl was in the sink. Nelda ate a bowl of instant oatmeal then joined Winnie in the guest bedroom. Two suitcases were packed and Winnie was folding dirty clothes to go in the laundry basket.

"You're folding dirty clothes?" Nelda shook her head and didn't wait for an answer. "Did you get everything out of the bathroom?"

"Yes, this is all I brought."

"Let me roll this big suitcase out and load it while you finish up in here."

"Thanks, Nelda. I couldn't have made it through the last few days without you."

"No problem. I'm just glad you mended so fast."

She quickly rolled the suitcase outside and put it in the luggage compartment of her Ford wagon. This was not the bag that had something heavy in it when Winnie moved in. Nelda still couldn't imagine what Winnie packed in the little bag to weight it down.

Winnie came out struggling with the small suitcase. Nelda took it from her, but found it was very light. When they returned for the clothes basket, she saw a heavy object that probably had been in the smaller bag when she moved in. It was a weight, a ten pound weight.

"What are you doing with that weight? You weren't supposed to be lifting anything."

Winnie squinched her eyes. Nelda just knew a flood was coming, but Winnie held back. She struggled to pick up the weight to lower it into the basket.

"Weren't you trying to convince everybody that a murderer was loose? I believed you." Winnie said. "That weight was for self-defense."

Nelda struggled to keep from laughing. She could just see Winnie using the weight as a weapon. "Do you think you'll feel safer at home by yourself?"

"Safer than with you. I'm no dummy, Nelda. Your meddling makes you a sure target."

"Are you keeping information from me that could help me solve this mystery?"

"I've told you everything I know for sure. I'm not going to point a finger at someone just because I'm not fond of them."

Nelda stood very still looking over Winnie's head out the window. The librarian was not going to give her any more help. It seemed entirely possible that this detective might have her first unsolved mystery. She was running out of time on this cold case.

"Let's go Winnie, you grab one end of the basket and I'll handle the other."

They loaded up and were soon on their way. They didn't have much to say on the drive to Winnie's apartment. After they unloaded her things, Winnie returned the keys she had to Nelda's house, and the laundry basket.

As Nelda drove away, the sense of relief from losing her house guest was replaced with anxiety over Winnie's sudden move, and the late phone call her guest had received.

*   *   *

Dr. Brown had his office in an old house in downtown Stearn. Nelda liked the idea of fixing up old homes and using the buildings instead of tearing them down. There was a Texas plaque on the wall near the front door, indicating the stone and wooden home was built in 1905. When she opened the door, there was no trace of odors that normally escape from old dwellings; paint and antiseptic cleansers covered up the past.

Nelda heard a chiming sound as she closed the door. There was no one at the desk in the small lobby area. She sat in a comfortable, cushioned chair waiting for someone to appear. Hanging on the walls were several documents attesting to the doctor's assistance in many charitable organizations. Now, she understood why Doris and the community minded doctor had so much in common.

Finally, a grey headed woman in a blue smock appeared. "Are you Ms. Simmons," she asked, smiling.

"Yes, Dr. Brown said he could visit with me at 10:00."

"Good, he has fifteen minutes before his next appointment. He's in the coffee room and wants you to join him."

The woman, who introduced herself as Carolyn, led Nelda down a long hall to a kitchen and dinette area. The doctor was seated at a small table drinking coffee. He wore sneakers with an open white lab coat covering jeans and a T-Shirt. It was hard for her to accept a medical doctor dressed so casually. He got up to shake her hand.

"Ms. Simmons, it's nice to see you again. Please sit across from me and I'll pour you some coffee." He poured coffee in a paper cup, than sat back down, placing the cup in front of her. "I suppose you're here to see me about a donation for Doris' memorial scholarship fund."

"No, I'm not, Dr. Brown. I didn't know about the scholarship. That's an admirable thing for someone to start."

He gave her a quizzical look before glancing at the wall clock. "What is the purpose of your visit?"

"I'll be frank with you. I was hired by the academy and asked to inventory the clinic cabinets. I found some prescription drugs in one cabinet that didn't have the patient's or doctor's name on the labels. Granted they were to help students with problems that occur to adolescents, but they were obtained illegally. Do you know how she acquired them?"

Before Brown spoke, he stroked his goatee and took a long sip of coffee. "I did a little snooping of my own, Ms. Simmons. I know your reputation as a detective. What business is it of yours what happened at the academy? Doris is dead now." His eyes misted over. "Why are you doing this? You'll only blacken her name."

"I don't intend to blemish her memory. My concern now is that her death was not accidental. I'm trying to find out if her possession of the drugs had anything to do with her drowning."

Brown stared at Nelda with anger showing in his green eyes. "You must believe me. I did not give her those drugs. She did ask me what would be suitable for a given condition. I told her, but warned her to have the student's parents take them to a doctor. There is no way I would jeopardize my medical license, even though I knew she had good intentions."

"I believe you, but did she give you any information about how she received them?"

"No. Doris did mention that someone from school told her they could order the drugs from Mexico for her."

Nelda was too upset to finish her coffee. "Did she mention who it was?"

"No, and I didn't press her. The less I knew about this the better."

Nelda stood up. "Thank you for your time, Dr. Brown."

"Sorry I couldn't be of more help. Doris was my special friend. If she didn't die accidentally, I hope her killer is brought to justice."

He walked her to the door and made one more tug on his goatee.

*   *   *

Nelda spent the afternoon doing laundry, cleaning floors and moving things around in her walk-in closet. She opened the window in the closet to get rid of the moth ball odor.

About 4:00 pm there was a call from Joe. Plans were changed for their date. It seems they were going to an awards banquet sponsored by the Sheriff's Association of Texas instead of a movie. He had failed to put it on his calendar. Nelda really didn't care where they were going. All she wanted to do was bend Joe's ear about what had happened today. Winnie's sudden plans to move out, and learning Doris had help in obtaining drugs had given her a headache.

At 5:00 pm, Nelda took a shower, dressed in a navy cotton suit and brushed her hair. She applied makeup with care, covering up the dark circles under her eyes with a light base concealer. Sleepless nights were taking their toll on her appearance. Minutes later she stepped back to look at herself in the full length mirror on the inside of the bathroom door, and decided she'd pass Joe's inspection.

*   *   *

Joe and Nelda drove slowly down Harvey Rd. to the Hilton. Joe didn't want to go to the sheriff's banquet for two reasons. He knew Nelda would be seeing some law enforcement officers that she had known when she was married to her first husband, Jim. Maybe, this would rekindle memories of her late husband, and Nelda might start comparing the two. Jim Simmons had been well liked throughout the state. Another reason, Joe was to receive an award. He didn't like bringing attention to himself. As they neared the entrance to the hotel ball room, he put his arm around Nelda's waist and pulled her close, as though she might slip away from him.

"Are you still in touch with any of the people your husband used to work with, Nelda?"

"No, I'm afraid not. So many of them have retired or found something else to do. It would be nice if I could recognize a few faces when we get to the Hilton, but I'm not counting on it. I guess they have the same format as they used to, a few speeches and a few awards?"

"Yes, we should be finished by 9:00, if they're not too long winded."

"Good, I need to go over a few things with you about what happened today when we get back."

Joe smiled; it was good to be needed even if she didn't take his advice. What a strong willed person Nelda was, they'd make a hell of a team. He'd pressure her about marriage when the time was right.

*   *   *

There were at least fifty people seated in the ballroom of the hotel when they arrived. Nelda purposely sat next to one of the few people she recognized, Steve Henry, a narcotics investigator. His specialty was rooting out the sellers of illegal drugs. Needless to say, she was very eager to find out if he knew anything about drugs coming in from Mexico. After catching up with news of various law officers, she turned to a question that was bothering her; how do U.S citizens receive drugs from a foreign country.

"Steve," Nelda asked, "Is it difficult to buy prescription drugs from Mexico?"

"Not if you have a prescription from a doctor in the U.S. and a computer with e-mail. Why do you ask?"

"Oh, I've heard the drugs are a lot cheaper there. Have you had a lot of trouble with forged prescriptions or anything like that?"

"I'm sure that we have some of that going on, but it would be pretty hard to catch a person forging a prescription or a dishonest physician writing them for someone. I don't know how closely those prescriptions sent over the internet are monitored."

"Thanks, Steve, I'll stick to the drug companies closer at home."

*   *   *

Nelda's face lit up with pride as Joe received his thirty years service award plaque. He was the last person to receive an award that night. Everyone stood up and the clapping went on for sometime. Nelda could tell his peers were proud of his record as a law man, and considered him a true friend. She listened intently as Joe gave a short speech.

"Thank you. I feel like I'm receiving this award for all the officers who came before me and all of you who work with me. I learned to do my job by example from the great sheriffs who are no longer with us. And of course I couldn't do justice to my position without the help of those working for the state now. I also want to thank all of you who were involved in planning this awards dinner. It is certainly one of the highlights of my career."

Nelda placed a hand on Joe's arm when he sat down. Humility was a great trait to have. One that Nelda had to struggle with constantly.

*　　*　　*

"I was so impressed with your career record, Joe," Nelda said as he drove her home. "It was a wonderful affair and I'm glad you asked me to attend."

"I'm always embarrassed by these things. I'm just doing what I'm paid to do."

Nelda smiled in the darkness. "Well, I'm glad to hear you say that. I've got a little scheme going, and maybe you won't fuss about helping me with it."

Joe's hands tightened on the steering wheel. He knew this plot was going to put Nelda in danger. She had mentioned using herself as bait before. The idea caused a knot to form in his stomach.

"Alright, what do you think is going to happen?"

"I believe the killer is coming to visit me soon. Winnie has suddenly healed and moved home. She's not coming clean with me about what she knows, but I've pressed her all I can."

"Either my deputy or I will be guarding your house at night for the next few days. We'll be in an unmarked car."

"I'll leave it up to you. I'll have my cell phone handy and will call you if I hear or see anything out of the ordinary."

By this time they were back in Nelda's driveway. Joe faced Nelda with his lips making to straight lines. "Please, Nelda, don't take any chances with whoever this deranged person is. They might harm you, before I can even respond."

"I promise to take all precautions. I'm not going to trust any of the academy group."

He got out of the truck and walked around to help her out. Part of the full moon was covered with a thick layer of clouds making Nelda's front porch a patch work of dark and light areas. A brisk breeze caused the porch swing to move with a clanking sound.

Joe helped her out of the truck and kept his arms around her. "I'm going inside with you Nelda and check every room and closet. We're not going to skip any part of your house."

Nelda had to admit the gloomy exterior of her home made her leery of what might be waiting for her inside. She put on a false front for Joe. "You really don't need to do that, but if it makes you feel better, let's do it. And I'm happy to say, Winnie left it very clean."

Joe didn't laugh; he led Nelda to the front door, and stood to one side as she opened the door. After they entered, Nelda turned on the lights and they started their thorough search of every room, including behind drapes and in closets. When they got to Nelda's bedroom, Joe stepped in Nelda's walk-in closet and found the window unlocked.

"For heaven's sake, Nelda, why is this window unlocked?"

"I thought I had locked it. I aired this closet out this morning, because it smelled like mothballs."

Joe shook his head in frustration. "I think I'll check all the other windows too. Please do not open any more windows. The culprit could come in quiet as a mouse if you left one open."

Nelda was tired and just wanted Joe to leave so she could go to bed. "Okay, I'll help you. We both have to get up early tomorrow and I'm pooped."

Joe reached over and massaged Nelda's shoulders. She felt it was wonderful to be treated in such a nice way. The Sheriff was making more and more inroads into her affection.

For a moment they forgot where they were, just enjoying the moment, but Joe's cell phone ringing brought them back to earth.

They stepped out of the closet. Joe listened for a few seconds shaking his head in disgust, and then answered with, "I'll be there as soon as I can."

"What's wrong, Joe?"

"Someone set old man Sam Johnson's pasture on fire. He has fifty head of cattle in there and a barn that's right in the fire's path. I've got to help battle the blaze and get those cows to safety. He started down the hall with two final requests, "Check the windows and call me if you need help. Someone will come right away."

Nelda quickly responded. "When I call, don't call me back; just get somebody here as fast as you can. You'll know I'm in trouble."

She ran behind him for one short embrace, slipping the key to the front door in his hand. He responded with a kiss that she wouldn't soon forget.

CHAPTER TWENTY-SEVEN

Finale

Nelda checked all the windows to see if they were locked. She knew that a few wouldn't come open even if they were unlocked. On occasion she'd tried to open them without any luck. Her next trip was the bathroom to methodically get dressed for bed. When she finished, she grabbed her cell phone, sugar mints and a bottle of water before getting into bed. Then she carefully programmed Joe's number into her cell phone.

As was her habit, after lying down she opened up a mystery book and read until she had trouble keeping her eyes open. At that point Nelda tucked a book mark in her mystery and laid it on the bed beside her.

* * *

Tim Calloway, rookie deputy sheriff, was sulking in his own personal car parked down the street from Nelda's home. What a crappy assignment Sheriff Coates had given him when all the excitement was on the edge of town where Johnson's pasture was on fire. It was 1:45 a.m. and not a thing had moved in this neighborhood for hours. He slouched a little lower in his seat and closed his eyes. His eyes popped open when the short wave radio informed him to proceed to a convenience store around the corner. The burglary alert signal had just come in from the central office.

The excited rookie checked the gun in his holster and made his tires squeal as he raced down the block.

*   *   *

Joe was quite confident his deputy was watching Nelda's home and would inform him if anyone approached it. Nelda had told him about her security light in the back yard, so she would be aware of anything happening there.

It was hard for him to keep track of time; Johnson's fire was a little like how his childhood minister had described Hell. The wall of fire was several feet high consuming everything in its path. Animals squealed as the yellow fingers of the blaze moved across the land. Volunteer firemen from the county were using brush trucks that carried water, and slap sticks to fight the blaze. With the high, swirling wind it appeared to be a losing battle.

Two hundred acres of scorched grass, burning Mesquite trees and singed cows made one forget about anything else. The barn was a smoldering skeleton, but there was a slim chance some of the cows could be saved. The fire crews needed all the help he could give them. He was using the slap stick, which was nothing more than a flat hose attached to a handle, to fight the inferno. Sparks quickly covered his clothes and hair; breathing was a scary undertaking.

*   *   *

At 2:15 a.m. Nelda was awakened by a rustling noise. She sat up in bed and saw the motion light had come on in the back yard. Of course this didn't actually mean there was a person in the yard, because swaying branches caused it to come on too, especially with a strong wind. She hurried to the array of light switches on the wall and turned on the back porch light, nothing that she could see stirred in the back yard except oak tree limbs that needed to be trimmed.

She lay back down and turned on the bedside lamp. A woman's voice broke the silence. "Hello, Nelda, is something keeping you awake?"

Nelda froze with fear. Celeste stood at the foot of the bed dressed in black; even her hands were adorned with black leather gloves. She had a gun in one hand and a cellophane bag in the other. There was a sardonic smile on her face.

The shivering sleuth looked toward the hallway for possible help. She clutched at the covers and hoped the new deputy was on the job.

"No use you hoping to be rescued, Nelda. I've caused some diversions that'll keep the sheriff and his men too busy to worry about you."

She didn't answer right away, gaining her composure by pulling the sheet over her body. Had her expectations been wrong? She thought Celeste would try making her death appear to be a suicide, not with a bullet from a gun. While faking a coughing spell, she moved her hand under the sheet where she'd placed her cell phone, and pushed the send button. Nelda prayed she'd pressed the right button.

With as much courage as she could muster, she spoke to the coach in a near normal tone. "Celeste, is something wrong? How did you get in here?"

Celeste moved a chair next to the bed. "Nelda, oh Nelda, it was quite easy to copy that key from Winnie's purse. As to your other question, don't play innocent with me. You know exactly what I'm doing here. You should have minded your own business while you had the chance. Everybody believed those deaths were accidents, but you just had to keep prying didn't you?"

Nelda knew she had to stall for time. Maybe Joe didn't even have his cell phone near him. She needed to keep Celeste talking.

"You're very clever, Celeste. I know you tried to frighten me by pushing me down the steps in Tulum."

Celeste laughed before speaking. "Yes, that was fun, but not very effective. You don't scare easily."

"Why don't you tell me how and why you killed Justine and Doris?"

"All in good time Nelda. We have a little business to take care of first." She reached into the bag and brought out a sheet of paper and a pen. This is a little note you're leaving behind to explain why you've taken an overdose of sleeping pills."

Nelda cringed, but was relieved to know Celeste planned to use the same method she'd tried on Daniel. "What does that note say? You can't possibly force me to sign it."

Celeste bent over Nelda with the gun and pointed it at her head. "Wrong, Nelda. You will sign it and take the pills, or I'll blow your head off with Daniel's gun, and do the same with that pretty niece of yours. The Navy Seal can take the blame."

Nelda's face turned as white as the sheet. Her plan was not working as expected. The lives of two more people were involved. "Give me the note so I can read it."

Celeste thrust it in her hand. Nelda read the note with dread.

> Dear Sue and Joe, as you know I've been having a problem remembering things. I'm sure this indicates the onset of Alzheimer's. I cannot bear this horrible disease nor the pain it will cause both of you. Remember me with a good mind.

"I suppose this was written on the library computer, and you got this information about my memory from Winnie?"

"Of course, I've tried to cover all bases. I'd like to think I'm smarter than an old, worn out teacher like you. Now, I'll have three perfect murders. Hold out your hand for these pills or would you rather I cram them down your throat?"

Nelda held out her left hand that shook as Celeste placed several white pills in her palm. She closed her hand over the pills while leaning back on her pillow.

"Celeste, hand me that bottle of water sitting next to you on the table."

At first the murderess didn't move, but then keeping the gun trained on Nelda, she reached over to get the bottle. Nelda put her hands under the sheet, bringing pills up in her right hand. She grabbed the bottle extended to her with her left hand and placed all the pills in her mouth at one time, swallowing them with all the water left in the bottle.

"That's just the way Winnie told me you took pills. I'm really disappointed in you, Nelda. I thought you'd put up more of a fight. Now there is nothing left to do, but satisfy your curiosity by telling you what I've done to save my tail and ensure my life will be full of success and romance. I think we have a few minutes, before you go to never-never land."

Nelda took a deep breath before speaking, "Was Winnie involved in your plans?"

Celeste threw her head back cackling like a witch. "Do you think I'd let that spineless creature on my team? I just used her for information about you."

Nelda shifted in bed and put another pillow under her head. "You're back with Coach Sinclair aren't you?"

"Oh yes," Celeste said as she put the gun on the table and removed her black stocking cap. "You sealed your fate when you tried to talk him into staying with his wife." She leaned back in the chair and looked quite content.

Nelda didn't want to waste time on Celeste's illicit love life. She wanted to know if she was right about how and why the woman destroyed two lives and was intent to kill again.

"Perhaps you're right; you two belong together. So you were the one that brought everybody together for the cruise, and you were the one that plotted each death.

"Oh course, who else in that group would have the ability to commit two perfect murders?"

"That night after Justine's birthday party, you and Daniel brought Justine to her cabin and Daniel waited outside while you put her to bed. You then poured peanut oil in her massage oil."

"That's correct. It was a pleasure to kill that blackmailing bitch. She was so easy to get rid of. I'm just sorry I waited so long to do it. Of course Doris was another story. That took a little more finesse; after all she was my roommate."

"I thought I saw you on a sailboat the day Doris died. Did you come ashore and then swim out to that rock where she was sitting."

"Nelda, I've underestimated you. I knew Doris was taking the party boat to Playa Sol to snorkel. I really lucked out when you and Sue left her alone on a rock. I watched her through binoculars expecting Daniel to do her in, because he visited her first, but all he did was talk to her. As soon as he turned away, I jumped in the water swimming free style hoping to beat you to Doris. I did. After that, it was apiece of cake. When I pulled her off the rock, she hit her head and didn't even struggle when I held her under."

Nelda yawned. Maybe it was her imagination doing weird things to her hearing, but she thought she heard a scraping noise. Perhaps it was only wishful thinking on her part. The wind howled outside causing the old windows to rattle.

She sensed that Celeste was enjoying herself. The telling of her heinous crimes made her feel superior. Taking a deep breath she resumed her questioning. "Was your connection with Doris, drugs? You helped her hoard them in her cabinets, didn't you? I'm thinking the winning coach needed a few chemicals to have her girls play better than they would without them."

"How astute of you, of course Doris used drugs for a different purpose. I ordered them for us from Mexico, but I knew she would crack under pressure and tell all. Her guilty conscience would get us both arrested. That's why she had to go."

"And what about Daniel's close brush with death? It was you that put the sleeping pills in the chocolate milk, wasn't it? What was the reason for that?"

"Didn't you know? Daniel was more than a liaison between the teachers and administration, he is an undercover cop. Several of my students told me Daniel was grilling them about drugs. How long do you think it would take him to see the connection between my well muscled athletics and anabolic steroids? I searched his apartment trying to find the results of his snooping, but I found nothing useful except his gun. Maybe with his condition, I won't have to worry."

Nelda saw a shadow in the hall. "Get me some water, Celeste. I'm feeling faint."

"What's the point? You're fading out."

Nelda put her hand over her mouth and started gagging. She hoped the diversion would keep Celeste from looking down the hall.

"Okay, okay, I'll get the water. I don't want you barfing up any of those pills. It would ruin my plan for you. But don't try anything funny, I'm taking the gun."

When Celeste left to fill the bottle in the bathroom, Joe appeared in the doorway. Nelda hardly recognized him. He was covered with soot and barefooted. He put a finger to his lips to silence Nelda as he walked into the room. Joe stood in the middle of the room waiting for Celeste to appear. The moment she came out of the bathroom he spoke in a hoarse voice while pointing his revolver at her.

"Put the gun down on the floor slowly."

Celeste was shocked to see him standing there. She wavered for just a second and then walked to the bed, pointing the gun at Nelda's head. "I'll shoot her if you don't put your gun down," Celeste yelled looking at Joe.

Nelda swung a pillow knocking the gun out of Celeste's hand. Cursing, she scrambled to pick it up, but Joe was on her like a tiger. He sat on her while he got the handcuffs out of his pocket. Celeste had the strength of a man.

After she was handcuffed and forced into a chair, she gloated over the anticipation of Nelda's death. "You're too late to help your sweetheart, Sheriff. I'm surprised she's still with us. She swallowed enough pentobarbital to kill a horse."

Joe stared at Nelda in despair, hardly noticing his deputy run into the room with his revolver drawn. He knelt by the side of Nelda's bed, tears ran down his cheeks as he held her hand. "Is it true, Nelda? How long ago did you take those pills?"

Smiling, Nelda hugged his neck. She ran her fingers through his singed hair, and then drew back to look into his weary, red eyes. "I'm sweeter than ever after taking those sugar mints. Celeste did give me a handful of sleeping pills but I exchanged them under the sheet." She drew the covers back so he could see the sleeping pills and cell phone.

"I love you so much," he said. "Will you marry me?"

They hardly noticed as Tim Calloway led Celeste screaming and kicking to a police car parked in front.

CHAPTER TWENTY-EIGHT

Don't Look Back

Several weeks after summer school was over, Nelda was having a great time shopping for her trousseau with Sally and Sue. To Sue's disappointment, her aunt refused to buy anything from Fantasy Lingerie.

"Really, Sue," Nelda said trying to keep from laughing, "I don't have that much imagination. Perhaps for your bridal shower we'll buy you something from there."

Sue giggled like a teenage girl. "Please do, I don't want to leave anything to Walter's imagination."

After several hours of shopping, they decided to stop at a StarBucks Café. Sally slipped off her shoes with a sigh when they finally sat down. Nelda was dreading it, but she knew Sally would bring up the suicide of Celeste in her prison cell.

"Does that last case with the Witherspoon murders haunt you, Nelda? I'm having a hard time understanding why that girl committed suicide," said Sally.

Sue took a sip of her coffee and spoke up. "Well, I can understand why she did it. Celeste probably couldn't stand the thought of being confined to a cell on death row for years."

"Sue is right, Sally, but what a waste of leadership and talent. Celeste was a sick girl. Stabbing the towel rabbit and starving the mouse, led me to believe she had a mental condition. She could have done so much good in this world instead she chose to be selfish.

Every deed she did was to further her own cause, not caring who she hurt. When she was caught, there was no going back to make her mistakes right."

"Did they ever find out who slipped the sleeping pills to her in prison?" Sue asked.

"No, I don't think the prison officials will ever know."

"One other question, Nelda, how did this scandal affect the academy?"

"It was awful, Sally. Enrollment is down thirty percent for the fall semester. Phillip Witherspoon, the headmaster is devastated. He'll have to drop some of his faculty members. Winnie will stay on for now, however Daniel is moving to Houston. It will be better for him anyway. This area is a constant reminder of his fiancée."

"Enough of that dreary stuff," Sally muttered. "Let's drink our coffee and talk about your honeymoon, Nelda. Have you and Joe discussed going on a cruise?"

Nelda choked on her coffee, sending the dark fluid all over her white pant suit. They ended up laughing so hard people turned to stare.

NELDA MYSTERIES

By

Helen F. Sheffield

The first Nelda mystery, *Nelda Sees Red*, was published by Xlibris Corporation. A Texas murder mystery. Someone killed the doctor. Almost anyone who worked for him had a motive. He was a womanizer and stingy. Nelda, the protagonist, tries to crack the case. Latin warnings written in red lipstick are left behind by the killer. In a downhill bicycle chase in Aspen, Colorado, Nelda unmasks the killer.

The second Nelda mystery, *Nelda Sees Blue*, was published by Ist Books Library. A psychic's prediction of danger, romance and suffering comes true. Nelda, the protagonist, butts heads with a new sheriff in her struggle to solve the murder of her cousin and reveal the secrets in the dead woman's past. There are many suspects to track down and tragic encounters at every turn. The soothsayer's warning, "Beware the color blue," takes on a real significance when that color is sighted before crucial events. A fiery ending traps the killer in his own tangled web of deceit.

You may order these books by contacting the publishers at *www.Xlibris.com*, and *www.1stbooks.com* or other major book publishers: Amazon, Barnes & Noble, and Borders.

You may e-mail Helen at *HSheff3218@aol.com*, or write to her at 10501 Dogwood Trail, College Station TX, 77845